A Ghostly Vision

I was about to retreat when I heard a new sound—a voice that turned my blood to ice water and raised the hair, tingling, on my scalp.

"*Oh!*" it sighed in mournful, heartrending tones, barely above the sound of the sea's murmur, and yet they thrilled through me like the tone of a silver bell, "*Oh, but I don't want to die!*" And then, a second time, putting the fear of death, such as I had not felt, even through the shipwreck, into my own heart, "*Oh— but—I don't—want—to—die!*"

Petrified, I stared all around me. From where could the voice possibly come?

I had seen no other person in the grove, or near it. And yet the voice had sounded close at hand, as if it would be possible for me to stretch out my arm and touch whoever had spoken! Trembling uncontrollably, I looked upward, and now, just for a moment, it seemed to my dazed senses that I could see something—some *body*—suspended from one of the arching boughs overhead, that I could see a thin form swinging, dangling, at the end of a rope not three feet above me. . . . It faded, melted, and was gone.

BRIDLE *the* WIND

JOAN AIKEN

BRIDLE the WIND

HARCOURT, INC.

Orlando   Austin   New York   San Diego   Toronto   London

Requests for permission to make copies of any part of the work
should be submitted online at www.harcourt.com/contact or mailed
to the following address: Permissions Department, Harcourt, Inc.,
6277 Sea Harbor Drive, Orlando, Florida 32887-6777.

www.HarcourtBooks.com

First published by Delacorte Press, 1983
First Harcourt paperback edition 2007

Library of Congress Cataloging-in-Publication Data
Aiken, Joan, 1924–2004.
Bridle the wind/Joan Aiken.
p.   cm.
Sequel to: Go saddle the sea.
Sequel: The teeth of the gale.
Summary: His journey back to Spain interrupted by shipwreck, loss of
memory, and a stay in a forbidding French monastery, twelve-year-old
Felix finally continues his journey in the company of a mysterious boy
that he had rescued from hanging.
[1. Friendship—Fiction.   2. Survival—Fiction.   3. Adventure and
adventurers—Fiction.   4. Voyages and travels—Fiction.]   I. Title.
PZ7.A2695Bri   2007
[Fic]—dc22   2006022957
ISBN 978-0-15-206058-9

Text set in Adobe Garamond
Designed by Cathy Riggs

A C E G H F D B

Printed in the United States of America

To my brother John,
who asked for it

Go saddle the sea, put a bridle on the wind,
before you choose your place.

PROVERB

CONTENTS

BRIDLE *the* WIND

In which I am shipwrecked and lose my way and my memory; am privileged to witness a miraculous healing; find myself in some sort a prisoner, and resist the temptation to escape.

How wretched and grim is the sight of a seashore when a ship has been wrecked upon it! All across the flat white sand are strewn ragged portions of woodwork, wrenched and smashed by the waves, with splinters and pegs protruding like broken fingers; snapped masts and torn sails lie tossed here and there, barrels and chests bob in the rolling surf; all the careful craft and handiwork that go to build and furnish a vessel have been spoiled and destroyed with a fearful speed, perhaps even as quickly as I can write these words.

Such were my thoughts while I dragged myself, wet and shivering, up the slope of some strand—I knew not whether French or Spanish, for our hooker had been blown far to the east from its intended port of San Sebastian, which lies close to the frontier. A wild January gale, severe even for the Bay of Biscay, had swept down upon us with hail and thunder, breaking our mainmast like a daffodil stalk, and while the crew were struggling to make good this damage, wind and tides had carried the helpless vessel to an un-sheltered stretch of coast where rocky reefs, lying some half-mile from the shore, had broken up the hull, and the furious pounding waves had soon reduced our ship to fragments. The crew and passengers were lucky that the in-rolling tide had carried them, clinging to spars, casks, and pieces of wreckage, into shallow water whence they could scramble ashore, I among them. Now the sailors were attempting to rescue what they could of the ship's cargo.

For myself, I had no more than I stood up in, woolen breeches, buckled shoes, shirt, and a striped fustian jacket with steel buttons. My thick boat-cloak I had cast off when the ship struck rock and I was hurled into the waves; now I much regretted its loss, for the winter wind blew keen as a razor, and there was no shelter in the wide open bay where we had been flung. Inland lay a series of ragged sand dunes, crested with rough grass; about a mile off, at the northern end of the bay, the land rose to a low cliff and broke off abruptly, to reappear in the form of an island some quarter-mile out to sea; on this island I thought I could detect buildings, though at such a distance, and in the flying rain and spume, it was hard to be sure. Otherwise there were no houses at all to be seen in this cheerless landscape, which seemed hardly more wel-coming than the sea from which we had escaped.

"You, there—you, boy!" bawled the captain. "Come here and lend a hand hauling on the rope!"

Evidently, although I had paid good money for my passage from England to Spain, he considered that, due to my lack of years, he had a right, in the present emergency, to order me about. Indeed I was very willing to help the men with their task of salvage; hauling on the rope was a vigorous and warming activity and gave me the feeling, at least, that we were doing something to remedy our dismal state.

By and by, I supposed, some natives of the nearest town or village would arrive to claim their share of the cargo and furnish us with beds, fires, food, and information as to where we had been cast up.

So far none had appeared; glancing to and fro, between tugs on the rope, I could see that steep wooded slopes ran up at the southern end of the bay, and steeper mountains rose behind them, one great triangular peak shrouded in snow and cloud. Nowhere could I descry any dwellings, but any number of houses might be concealed behind those tree-covered ridges. They were some considerable distance away, though; indeed, as I later discovered, behind the bay stretched a wide, marshy, uninhabited region, which was why nobody had yet appeared to give us succor.

An hour's work sufficed to drag ashore a fair portion of the cargo, which consisted of woolen goods, and some of the ship's furnishings; though most of these were thrown up by the waves themselves which came surging and pounding onto the beach like white mountains of water. Among such raging seas it seemed a miracle that we had all escaped with our lives. And, this thought coming into my mind, I found within me, all of a sudden, a most powerful and irresistible wish to kneel and thank God for allowing me to escape the fury of the ocean.

At this juncture a large bale of woolen stuff had just been successfully hauled up above tide level; and, seizing a moment when the crew were taking breath and looking for some new object to salvage, I left them and walked swiftly away toward the rear of the beach, passing between two of the sand dunes which formed a rampart there. Nobody hindered my going; perhaps nobody noticed.

Behind the dunes I discovered a belt of thickety woodland, sandy underfoot, formed of some dense and twisted bushes, or rather small trees, which were covered in evergreen leaves, and grew so close and tangled together that I had much ado to force my way between them. There was no path at all. The farther in I penetrated, the thicker grew the bushes, and I was beginning to believe that I must return to the beach and find some other way, when I came forth into a kind of glade, or chamber, in the very heart of the grove. That was a most mysterious place! About the size of a large room, or small chapel, walled and roofed with close-packed leaves—for the branches met and arched overhead—it seemed like a woodland crypt or shrine, even to the dim, holy light, for all that filtered through the foliage was very faint and green in color. A more suitable spot for such a purpose as mine could not have been imagined, and my first care was to kneel down on the damp peaty sward and offer up a prayer of heartfelt gratitude to God for my deliverance from peril (also by no means the first peril from which He had delivered me, and I mentioned that I was well aware of this continuing care, and humbly obliged for it, and hoped and trusted that it would also continue to support me in future hazards).

Sheltered in such a close thicket, with the line of dunes between me and the beach, I could still hear the ocean roar, but reduced now to a deep uninterrupted moaning sigh. Clear and quiet above the sigh came, inside my head, the voice of God: Felix, if I have preserved you, it is because there are still tasks for you to perform in this world. Be of good courage always, do not forget in danger that love is a powerful weapon and laughter a strong shield. Remember, too, that you and I have had a few jokes together in the past; it may be that in the future we shall have more.

I was overjoyed to discover that God still held the same opinions as myself in this regard, and sent him a warm thought of friendship, as a son might to a father who shares and understands his feelings and pursuits.

Then I rose, brushed the sand from my knees, unbuttoned my sodden jacket, and made sure of the safety of a money belt and its golden contents which I wore beneath my salt-stained cambric shirt.

After that I began to take a careful survey of the glade, hoping to find some way out other than that through which I had made my difficult entrance. Dusk had commenced falling, the light failed fast, and, had I not snapped off two or three branches in pushing through, which hung down showing the pale inner wood, I would hardly have been able to discover even the way by which I had come. There seemed no other exit, and wondering still more whether this strange spot was made by human agency or not, I was about to retreat when I heard a new sound—a voice that turned my blood to ice water and raised the hair, tingling, on my scalp.

"*Oh!*" it sighed in mournful, heartrending tones, barely above the sound of the sea's murmur, and yet they thrilled through me like the tone of a silver bell, "*Oh, but I don't want to die!*" And then, a second time, putting the fear of death, such as I had not felt, even through the shipwreck, into my own heart, "*Oh— but—I don't—want—to—die!*"

Petrified, I stared all around me. From where could the voice possibly come?

I had seen no other person in the grove, or near it. And yet the voice had sounded close at hand, as if it would be possible for me to stretch out my arm and touch whoever had spoken! Trembling uncontrollably, I looked upward, and now, just for a moment, it seemed to my dazed senses that I could see something—some *body*—suspended from one of the arching boughs overhead, that I could see a thin form swinging, dangling, at the end of a rope not three feet above me. . . . It faded, melted, and was gone.

"*Ay! Dios mío! Ave María purísima!*" I gasped, falling back into the Spanish tongue, as I often do when startled or alarmed. And, with frantic, feverish haste, I plunged back through the dense, whipping branches, careless whether my face or hands were cut or scratched, my only wish, now, being to leave that haunted grove even faster than I had entered it.

Well did I know that shadowy form had not been real; when I first entered the glade, when the light had been brighter, I had not observed it, though I had most diligently examined all that was to be seen. The thing had not been real, it had been some specter, some phantom, not of this time or place; but why, I wondered, why, I asked myself, had it been sent to *me*? Why should *I* have been chosen to see and hear it?

Gasping, ashiver, and (I am not ashamed to confess) almost sobbing with awestruck horror, I pushed and thrust my way through the hindering branches until I was once more out in the windswept gully between the dunes. How welcome now that cold wind seemed! Then I ran, as fast as my legs would bear me, over the sliding, yielding sand, until I came out once more onto the flat white beach, and could see the stranded sailors still working to retrieve portions of their ship and cargo. More figures, in dark garments, had, I now observed, joined the crew, and in the distance I heard the faint tolling of a bell. When I drew closer, I could see that the newcomers were short, sturdy men in sandals and black robes; it seemed there must be a monastery not too far from this desolate spot and the good fathers from it had come to help us. My joy and relief at the sight of the monks could not have been greater; one of them, perhaps, I thought, might explain to me the nature of the strange vision which had just been sent to me in the thicket behind the dunes. Still chilled to the marrow and shuddering from the shock I had received, I made my hasty way toward the main center of activity, where monks and sailors were busy trundling casks and timbers over improvised rollers, while others shook lengths of net or sailcloth to rid them of water. One group continued hauling on a rope, the end of which was attached to a portion of the ship's forecastle that bobbed in the breakers. I ran to help these, hoping by means of violent exertion to shake off the chill horror which had overwhelmed me. Seizing the end of the rope, I braced myself with feet dug in the ground and arms at full stretch, adding my small portion of strength to the total of the eight or nine men already pulling.

Whether it was my final tug that did it, who can say? But next moment with a loud crack, audible even above the roar of the surf, the rope broke, and the group of men tumbled backward higgledy-piggledy over one another; I, being at the end, collapsed under a pile of falling bodies, and some hard object at the same instant striking my head a violent blow, my sight became darkened, my breathing suspended, and I lost consciousness.

AFTER that began a long, dreamlike period of darkness laced through and scattered with wandering lines and flashes of light; I am not able to reckon precisely how long it endured but it seemed forever; I felt that I was floating in eternity, a speck in the hugeness of night, a tadpole in the vastness of the ocean; I was no longer Felix, a human boy, but lost, nameless and formless, in the roots of all being. I had no thoughts, no fears; I had ceased to exist until it pleased God to gather the threads of my soul together and plait them into the shape He had once given me, or some new one.

While thus suspended in the gulf of emptiness I seemed to see great patterns, and to understand them; I heard tremendous music, and was shaken by the gales of heaven; but all this, by degrees, passed away, and I lay at length, quiet and content, like a nut in its shell.

At one point, briefly, I thought that I opened my eyes and found that I was in a small, dim, warm place, a haven of comfort and rest, deeply familiar and dear. How happy I was to find myself there! I murmured my pleasure aloud.

"Why—I am *here*!"

In those four words I was able to express all my joy and wonder at this great good fortune, all my feeling of sovereign privilege—for who, in the whole of humanity, could expect or deserve to come to this place a second time?

"I never thought to come back *here*?"

"Certainly, child," a voice with a smile in it answered me. "You are here; and in the best of care. Rest at ease, little sparrow. We shall not let you fall."

And I drowsed again, floating away with joy and trust among the mighty currents that bore me out of time and mind.

My next return came about so quietly, and by such infinite degrees of slowness, that I am at a loss how to describe it.

But, gradually traveling back out of eternity into time, I discovered myself, Felix, to be at work, with a hoe in my hand, loosening soil round the roots of thistle artichokes and vines, pulling up the weeds that threatened to smother them. A mild misty sun hung overhead and warmed me; I wiped my damp forehead. My back, I noticed, felt stiff; I must have been occupied in this work for some time, several hours perhaps. In the distance chimed a bell, its tone silvery and familiar. Soon, close at hand, I heard the click of a gate.

"Aha!" remarked a friendly voice. "Very good, boy!" The voice spoke in French, and went on: "Father Mathieu asked me to call you. I see you have finished the whole bed—and excellently well done, too. I had thought it would take more than one day. But now, lay down your hoe, wash your hands, and come to Vespers."

I straightened my back and looked at the monk who was addressing me—a thin man, with a worn, kindly face, a sprinkling of scanty gray hair round his tonsure, and two wonderfully blue eyes. Almost transparent they seemed, like the sky just before it turns green at sunset.

He nodded to me, smiling, and beckoned me to wash my hands in a stone trough of water and follow him through the gate. I saw that we were in a walled kitchen garden, a big place well stocked with herbs and vegetables and shrubs: spinach grew there and kale and other pot-herbs; parsley and thyme and garlic, bushes of lavender and rosemary and verbena such as had grown in my grandfather's garden in Spain; there were rows of onions, fruit trees trained against the stone wall, and vines twined on little pyramids of stakes. The plot sloped upward quite steeply, and as we passed through the entrance at the top, I turned to look back and could catch a view, over the wall at the foot, of waves breaking on a horseshoe-curved beach to my left, and the sea on both sides stretching away, whitecapped, into the distance.

"Are we on an island, my father?" I asked.

My tongue and jaws felt stiff and strange, as if from disuse; I found that I had to clear my throat twice before I could speak.

The blue-eyed monk turned to regard me intently.

"Why, yes, my boy, this is the island of St. Just de Seignanx, and you are here in the monastery of St. Just. I am very glad that you have found your tongue at last," he added, smiling. "It has been a long time that you were off there, in a brown study!"

"My father?" I stammered. "Pardon me. I do not understand you."

"Never mind!" he said quickly, and in a gentle tone. "We will now go in to Vespers, where you may wish to thank our Father in heaven for giving you back the power of speech. After Vespers I imagine that Father Vespasian will want to speak to you." As he pronounced this name a guarded, anxious expression came over his face, but he gestured me to go ahead of him, laying a finger on his lips for silence.

We had been walking along a grassy path between stone buildings. Now we passed through a heavy wooden doorway into a spacious warm kitchen with flagged floor, brick ovens, and herbs hanging from the rafters to dry. Then, from a door on the far side of the kitchen, into a grassy cloister with a stone-arched, cobbled walkway surrounding it on all four sides. Other black-robed monks were hastening in silence round the walk of the cloister to an arched doorway on the distant side; this, I found, led us into a high-roofed chapel, where the service of Vespers was conducted.

I stood and knelt by my friend, the blue-eyed monk, and, as he had suggested, found relief from my state of much puzzlement and confusion in thanking God very sincerely for having restored me to life and awareness, and brought me to this peaceful holy spot, though I added that I would be obliged if He would see fit to furnish me with a little more explanation as to where, exactly, I was, and how I had come here.

When Vespers had ended the monks went to supper, which they ate seated at long bare tables in a large hall next to the kitchen. I followed my friend, sat down beside him, and received a bowl of bean soup (very good) and a hunk of brown bread. While we consumed our soup in silence a white-robed novice, standing in a pulpit, read aloud a portion of the Scriptures. Nobody paid me any special attention or behaved as if my presence there were an odd thing; indeed, they seemed to treat me as if they were well used to my being among them, and took me quite for granted. I counted about thirty monks and half a dozen novices. The service and Scriptures had been read in Latin, but at the conclusion of the meal a tall monk with iron-gray hair, deep-set eyes, and a lantern-jawed, almost skull-shaped face made a number of announcements in the French language. These I was able to understand, for the tutor who taught me in my grandfather's house had obliged me to read a portion of French daily as well as instructing me in the grammar. (Indeed, many Spanish people spoke French as readily as their own language at that time, since, when I was a small child, the French armies had been in Spain for nearly seven years until we and the English at last drove them out.)

When he had finished reading his notices the skull-faced man asked if there were any questions. My friend raised his hand silently.

"Well, Father Antoine?"

"Father Abbot, I thought you would wish to be

informed that the shipwrecked boy has at last recovered the use of speech."

"Indeed? Has he so? What has he said?"

The Abbot's voice was cold, and strangely disengaged, as if, though he asked the question, he had no interest in hearing the answer. But his eyes shone very brightly. Father Antoine replied: "Just before Vespers, my father, he asked if we were on an island. That is all he said. But later I observed that, during Vespers, he made the correct responses."

"Very well. I will interrogate him. You may bring him to my lodge in ten minutes."

The Abbot's lodge, it seemed, stood at some distance from the frater, or monks' dining room, where we had eaten supper. Father Antoine led me along a narrow alley, going in the opposite direction from the cloisters and chapel. We passed between a number of ruined buildings and a derelict cloister overgrown with thistles.

"The Abbey is not so large as it was once," my guide explained in a low voice. "Two hundred years ago this was the old infirmary cloister and sickrooms. Now, alas, there are fewer monks than formerly."

"Where *is* this Abbey, my father?"

"On an island off the coast, my child, not far from St. Jean. But now, hush!" He laid his finger to his lips once more. "We are a Cistercian order, and must observe the rule of silence save when speech is absolutely necessary. Besides, here we are at the Abbot's parlor.

Now: Do not be afraid, child, but answer clearly and sensibly any question Father Vespasian may put to you." He paused, then added quickly, "If—for any reason—you are unable to answer, simply tell the Abbot that you do not know without—without hesitating, or becoming nervous. He is—he can be—somewhat hasty, if—if he thinks that people are not being reasonable. Ahem! That is all! Now, I will be waiting for you, close by."

The look on his face seemed to me anxious, though his tone was meant to be reassuring. He tapped on a door, and when the Abbot's voice called "Enter!" put his head round and said, "Here is the boy, Father Abbot. Ahem! With your permission I will wait and pull the weeds out of this path (which is becoming somewhat overgrown) and then escort the boy back to the novices' dorter, when you have finished with him."

"Very well, Father Antoine. Come in, boy. Stand there."

The Abbot's parlor was supplied with two different desks, one for sitting, one for standing; also two wooden armchairs, a prie-dieu, and many shelves of books, in many different languages. A window looked out onto the weed-grown disused cloister. On the wall opposite the window hung a picture. It was a representation of the raising of Lazarus, very skillfully painted. Lazarus was depicted as coming up out of his grave at the Divine summons: two angels were pulling him up by his arms, three devils were grasping him by the legs and waist, so as to hold him back. The sight of this picture somehow dismayed me; the details, especially of the devils, were so very vivid.

The floor of the room was of stone, covered with rush matting, which was much worn in one strip, as if the owner there walked up and down, hour after hour, day after day.

The Abbot, sitting behind his desk, gestured me where I should stand, in front of the picture. The thought of it behind my back made me uncomfortable. I cannot say why. But I tried not to think about it.

"So, boy: You have at last decided to speak?"

The question inside me, which had been rising up all through Vespers and through the meal, now burst forth from me.

"Please tell me, Father Abbot, how long have I been silent? How long have I been in this place?"

I was thinking of my poor grandfather, so many miles away in Spain, waiting to hear from me, wondering what had become of me.

"Be quiet!" snapped Father Vespasian. "It is for *me* to ask the questions, and for you to answer! Not the other way round. Just because you have now recovered the use of your tongue is no reason to employ it ill-advisedly."

This, to me, seemed most unfair. How was I to learn about my condition and my whereabouts, if I might not ask questions? And it was, after all, only by chance that I came to be in this place, I was not a member of the Order. However, making an effort, I kept silent, and gazed at him with no great humbleness or docility; I daresay my feelings were plain to read on my face, for he gave me a long and chilling look out of deep-set greenish eyes before adding coldly and gently, "You have been beaten several times before this, for obduracy in your silence; it would be well for you if you did not now incur further punishment for unbridled speech."

Beaten several times? What could he mean? I had no recollection of such beatings. But I took firm hold of my tongue and, in spite of wild curiosity, remained silent.

"Your name?" he then inquired.

"It is Felix Brooke, Father."

"*Tiens.* An English name. Are you, then, English?"

"Yes, sir, my father was English, an officer in Wellington's army under Sir John Moore. But my mother was Spanish. And I was born in Spain and have lived at my grandfather's house in Galicia, both my parents being dead."

"So. But the ship that you were in was sailing from England to Spain?"

"I was returning to Spain from England, where I had visited my father's family."

His first two questions I had answered easily enough. But this third one I found harder; I replied slowly and with some difficulty. Pulling the later episodes of the journey from my clogged and slow-moving mind seemed almost as hard as dragging those waterlogged bales of woolen goods from the pounding waves. Now, casting my memory back to England, I found myself suddenly overwhelmed with sadness, for I recalled how, hoping for friendly and welcoming cousins or other relatives in England, I had, when I arrived at my family home, found only an old, mad grandfather, who mistook me for my dead father, the son he had always detested, and who bawled insults at me.

"You had visited your English relations and were returning to Spain on the ship *Euzkadi*?"

"I presume so, my father," I answered him hesitantly. "My recollections of the journey, after embarkation, are very slight."

"If you have nothing sensible to say, remain silent!" he said sharply. "I want no untruths."

I observed that, when he was annoyed, his greenish eyes had a habit of sliding very rapidly to and fro; faster, indeed, than one would have thought it possible for human eyes to move; and he began to tap fast and irritably on his desktop with an ivory ruler.

I remained silent.

"You can recall the shipwreck?"

"Only indistinctly, sir. And then . . . after I was ashore . . . something very, very frightening happened . . ." I paused, struggling to grasp at memory, but the door was blocked, and would not open.

"Father Antoine, who had gone down to the shore with other members of the Community to help the sailors, said that you suddenly came running out of the sand dunes as if you were being pursued; looked around you wildly, then went to help pull on the rope just before it broke."

"That I do not remember at all."

"Come, now! What happened to you among the sand dunes? You have recalled the rest clearly enough. Exert your mind, boy. Make an effort, I command you!"

Why should it be of such importance to him, I wondered. His voice was low, but very intense, his brows drew together until they resembled an overhanging cliff, and in the shadowed hollows below them his eyes seemed to shine at me with a queer reddish gleam.

"Look at this paper, boy!" he commanded me, and on a paper in front of him he drew a very exact circle. Obediently I lowered my eyes to it. For a strange series of moments the circle on the flat surface of the paper seemed to become a hollow, a well, a chasm, out of which white smoke came pouring. . . . I shook my head to clear my sight, then looked up at the Abbot again. For a second or two his eyes seemed veiled by the white vapor, then they glowed at me, even brighter than before.

"What happened to you on that shore? And where have you been since then? Where has your soul been hiding since that day? In what realm? Under whose dominion?"

I was filled with dread—he seemed so strange. Obediently I exerted myself, until it felt as if my own forehead were tied into knots—but still no memory would return.

"Truly, I do not know, Father!" The words came out of me in a terrified gasp.

The Abbot stared at me, hunched forward like a bird of prey. Then, by stages, a change came over him. Several violent tremors passed through his body, his eyes blazed like lamps, he appeared to grow several inches taller, and a high, hissing voice came from him, utterly different from that in which he had at first addressed me:

"Do not try me too far, boy! It is your *duty* to remember when I order you. Remember, I say! Or I will have you beaten again, and much more severely. I *must* know where you have been! How can you stand there like a mule, saying *I do not know*? We shall have to try whether a rope's end, stiffened with tar, cannot jolt the memory out of you!"

I gazed at him struck dumb with fright, my hands clenched at my sides, my tongue locked to the roof of my mouth. There seemed something truly inhuman, infernal, about him, especially about his eyes, glimmering with that uncanny reddish glow.

Greatly to my relief, at this juncture I heard a light tap on the door, and Father Antoine thrust his head round.

"I did not summon you, Father Antoine," said the Abbot angrily. But his voice lost its shrill unearthly tone and his eyes their red glare; he appeared more human.

"Ahem! No, my father—I know—but the messengers are here from the Bishop of Bayonne; I remember you said you wished to be informed at once—"

"Oh—oh. Yes. Certainly. Take the boy away, then, for the present, Father Antoine. I will interrogate him again. He is being stupidly obstinate—he refuses to exert his memory, or to tell what he remembers. If he continues to refuse, he must be severely punished."

"Memory often returns very imperfectly at first, in such cases," put in Father Antoine quickly and diffidently. "It may well be that, in a few more days—"

The Abbot's eyes began to dart to and fro again, his hand to ply the ivory ruler with that unnatural speed. Fortunately at this moment I heard voices and footsteps outside; Father Vespasian's attention was diverted, and Father Antoine made haste to pull me away.

Holding my arm tightly he hurried me through the ruined cloister and back to the novices' frater. I had a most urgent wish to ask him questions about the Abbot—about the frightening interview which I had just undergone—but, shaking his head, placing his finger on his lips, he handed me over to a small brown-faced, brown-haired monk who was superintending the white-robed novices as they filed upstairs to bed. For the first time it struck me that I, too, wore a plain white wool habit, cut rather short and narrow, with a dark scapular over it.

"Here is your boy, Father Domitian; he's to talk no more now. I'll have him again in the morning."

"Did Father Vespasian—?"

Father Antoine merely nodded his head up and down a great many times, significantly, saying nothing at all. The other monk received this with a glance of wide-eyed comprehension, looked at me, I thought, with pity, and then gestured me to get into line with the other boys and young men. We climbed a flight of stone stairs to an upper room, made our ablutions, said our evening prayers, and lay down upon narrow wooden cots covered with straw palliasses.

The rest soon slept, but not I.

My mind was churning with questions. It seemed as if that period of time away from myself—why? how had it happened? and for how long?—had proved such a rest for my body that now sleep was not necessary for me.

I lay in the dark, listening to the others breathing, and the distant sound of surf, and surveyed what I knew of myself. I was Felix Brooke, traveling from England to Spain to rejoin my Spanish grandfather, the Conde de Cabezada, who had written me a kind and loving letter. I was aged thirteen years—or perhaps more now? My journey to Spain had been interrupted by a shipwreck. I could remember the wild howl of the wind, the fusillade of hailstones, the mast breaking with a crack like a pistol shot.

But after that all remained obscure, like a dream that, on awakening, hovers mockingly out of reach. Something dire had happened to me on the shore. . . . What had it been? How in the world had I arrived at this French monastery? How long had I been resident here? And—an even more important question—how soon would I be able to leave?

In the end, after many hours of uneasy tossing and turning, I suppose I slept. But not for long.

Shortly after two in the morning, while yet it was black dark, the monastery bell clanged to summon us from our beds, and we shuffled sleepily down the stone stairs and across the cloister to the chapel for the Night Office. This service was followed by half an hour of silent prayer (during which I prayed very heartily to God that He would soon set me back on my road to Galicia and my grandfather's house, or, if not, at least explain to me what His purpose was for me); then came the early-morning office of Lauds, which was succeeded by Mass.

Feeling by then somewhat hollow, not to say light-headed, I was glad to accompany the others to the frater, where we breakfasted frugally on brown bread and hot milk. Then back to the chapel for the service of Prime, by which time dawn was breaking; the eastern sky glowed redly through the chapel windows.

Then, for the novices, followed an hour of instruction from Father Domitian, which was succeeded by a further hour of silent study and reading. After which we returned to the chapel for Terce and High Mass. The monastery clock was chiming the hour of nine and the sun had climbed high when Father Antoine again came in search of me.

Nodding kindly and meaningfully, he said to me in a low voice, "I have leave from Prior Anselm to take you down to the seashore to gather kelp for Father Mathieu in the garden. Come, you can help me harness the asses."

Delighted to perform so simple and normal a task, and to escape awhile from the monastic timetable, which was beginning to make me feel somewhat hemmed in, I laid down the *Life of St. Dogmael* that I had been attempting to study, and eagerly followed him. We went to the stables which lay in the angle between kitchen and garden, and there harnessed two sleepy furry brown asses to a light garden cart made of plaited withies. Leading the asses (who were decidedly reluctant to budge from their quarters), we made our way past a porter, through a great arched gateway, and down a steep track from which the cliff fell away abruptly on either side.

I gasped at the keen, fresh air, and at the prospect before me. Encased inside the monastery's walls, submerged in its orderly program of worship, study, prayer, study, and worship, I had almost forgotten the close presence of the sea outside and all around. Now its blueness hit me like a blow. A wide vista of coast lay before me, stretching away in either direction: Two vast sandy bays, divided by a rocky causeway, extended below us, with white lines of surf like ermine borders dwindling into the distance, far as the eye could see.

The monastery of St. Just was perched on a high isthmus of rock, and, as we descended the causeway toward the mainland, I could see that cliffs dropped away abruptly below the very walls of the chapel itself; what a place to defend, if enemies came!

"It is a very beautiful spot, do you not think?" remarked Father Antoine placidly, leading the larger ass, Berri, while I pulled at the bridle of the smaller one, Erda. "And at high tide, as you can see, we are cut off for six hours."

"It is not, then, quite an island?"

"Near enough," he said. "We are better off than the brothers at Mont St. Michel in Brittany, where the sea, I have heard, visits only every other week or so, and the rest of the time they are high and dry. But then they have no causeway. We are fortunate to possess ours; without it we should be marooned for twenty hours a day. The tide rushes in here at great speed; never attempt, child, to cross when the water is more than ankle-deep or you will be washed away for certain."

I marveled at the construction of the causeway, which, about half a mile in length, was made from great slabs of rock bolted together with iron bolts, now weed-grown and barnacle-encrusted. At low tide the road stood six feet and more above the wet, gleaming sand, but Father Antoine told me—and indeed I could see from the high-water mark—that when the tide was full in, the way was submerged to a depth of ten to twelve feet.

"And the currents race through the channel from one bay to the other; no man could swim against them."

I observed that, once away from the monastery, Father Antoine spoke with greater freedom and more cheerfully than he had within its limits. Indeed, as soon as we had traversed the causeway (proceeding with great care, for the slabs of stone were slippery from brine and green clinging weed) and were crossing the flat, wet sand, he said, "I brought you down here, my boy, because I thought that your memory might be prompted by a sight of the beach where you were cast ashore. Also I know that it may perhaps be difficult to assemble your thoughts in the presence of Father Vespasian—"

"Father Antoine!" I burst out. "Please tell me—is the Abbot mad?"

The good monk gasped as if I had dealt him a blow on the heart, and his blue eyes went blank for a moment. He crossed himself fervently several times. But then having reflected, he answered in a mild tone, "Bless me, my dear boy! I can see very clearly that, now your wits are returned to you, they are keener and more inquiring than those of many young people your age. Have a care, though, in the monastery, how you come out with such blunt utterances!"

"No, but *is* he?" I persisted. "He seemed so strange and—and so unreasonable! You see, Father Antoine, I—I am not unacquainted with madness; my English grandfather, whom I saw not long ago, was astray in his wits, and some of his gestures were like those of Father Vespasian: that quick darting to and fro of the eyes—and—and his shrill voice—"

I stopped, hoping for an affirmation; since, in fact, what in my heart I feared was much, much worse than simple madness.

Father Antoine glanced apprehensively about the beach as if, even on this huge open space, we might still be overheard. He walked some distance before he replied; he seemed to be collecting his thoughts. Meanwhile I began, I thought, to have a dim and patchy recollection of this place. The sand dunes, the wooded hills and high snow-covered peaks in the far distance—

"Our Abbot is not—is not wholly mad, my child," said Father Antoine, clearing his throat nervously. "Indeed, judged in many ways, he is sane as you or I, and—and remarkably quick-witted and an excellent administrator. Also: He is almost a saint! He has a wonderful power of healing. Over and over again I have seen it; and so will you. Each Friday they come—the sick people; he has only to lay hands on them and, in seven cases out of ten, their affliction will quit them at once. People come here from great distances—to be healed—"

"But nonetheless," I persisted, "he is mad, is he not? Or at least, not sane. There is something very queer about him. Am I not right?"

Father Antoine frowned distressfully.

"It is hard to say it of him: in many ways such a saint; but yes; it is like this, my son: When Father Vespasian finds himself thwarted for any reason, his malady—for such I do indeed believe it to be—comes suddenly upon him. That is why I must confess that I was anxious yesterday to get you away from him—I feared that if your memory did not return to you—and he could not fetch it out . . ."

I began to catch his meaning.

"Did he, in the days before I came to myself—when I was still silent . . . Father Antoine, please tell me, how long have I been in this place?"

"Since January, my boy. It is now the end of March."

He began, methodically, to gather up the great black, brown, and green sheaves of seaweed that lay tossed hither and thither upon the sand, hoisting them into the wicker cart; and, following his example mechanically, I did likewise while my mind absorbed this shock.

Three months! I had been in this place nearly three months! My poor grandfather! He must by now believe me dead, or that I had played some foolish prank, run away to the Indies or joined the army. I must make haste, make haste, and resume my journey. Not another day must be lost—

My consternation must have shown clear in my face, for Father Antoine said kindly and reassuringly, "You are thinking, without doubt, of your friends and family, how distressed they must be not to have heard from you for so long. Do I understand that you have a grandfather residing in Spain, to whose house you were returning?"

Father Antoine must have listened outside the

Abbot's window last night, I thought, with a flicker of amusement, and then I thanked him in my heart, since plainly this had been with my welfare in mind, so that he could find some pretext to end the interview should Father Vespasian show signs of losing his temper.

I answered, "Yes, my father. Grandfather is the Conde de Cabezada, at Villaverde, in the province of Galicia."

"Ah," he said, nodding, as was his habit. "Somehow I felt sure that you came of good family. Though you do not look at all Spanish, with your round face and yellow hair!"

"No, you see I take after my father's family; he was English."

It had always been an embarrassment and annoyance to me, living in my grandfather's house in Spain, that I was so yellow-headed and different from everybody else. But now, having visited England, I felt reconciled to my looks.

"Bien," said Father Antoine with satisfaction. "We will at once write a letter to your grandfather the Conde, reassuring him as to your welfare, and letting him know that you are here, and in good care."

"But—my father—thank you for the thought of writing, and it is a kind one—but what is to stop me from leaving now, and continuing on my journey?"

His luminous blue eyes surveyed me candidly. The same thought, I could see, was in both our minds. Father Vespasian might want to stop me. But why?

"First, my boy," he said, "some legal formalities are necessary. You have no passport or papers. The French authorities will require to see those before you cross the frontier; and the Spanish ones, doubtless, on the other side."

This news threw me into consternation. It was true, I had crossed to England in a smugglers' vessel without papers of any kind; and my return on the Biscay hooker had been equally informal. Ahead of me I could see endless difficulties and time-wasting interference by French officials. How, indeed, situated as I was, would it ever be possible for me even to prove that I was Felix Brooke?

"And then Father Vespasian," continued Father Antoine, slowly and carefully hoisting a large hank of seaweed into the cart, "believes that you have been sent to us—as it were, a gift from Providence. Our Order is diminishing, sadly; as the older fathers die, fewer novices replace them . . ."

"But I do not wish to be a *monk*!" Then, quickly, for fear of giving offense, I added, "Indeed I truly love God—He has helped me more times than I can say. But I believe—I am sure—that He has other purposes for me than—than to say prayers and chant psalms all day long."

"Well, my boy, and who is to argue with you?" replied Father Antoine cheerfully. "For my part I entirely agree that you have the right to choose. Yet I think that God must have had some special purpose in mind when He tossed you onto this beach and stole your wits away for so many weeks. I was there when it happened, when you fell and hit your head upon a great stone; I saw how the rope broke, how it all came about. And I have seen many such cases. There seemed no reason why you should not recover next day; yet there you lay, week after week, in a dead swoon, with Father Pierre, the infirmarian, feeding you broth out of a ram's horn; then, when you at last sat, and stood, and walked, you were mild and biddable, ate, worked, and behaved as you ought in Chapel, but you never spoke. Your eyes were elsewhere. You seemed in a dream, still, as if you waited for the angel Gabriel to come and summon you."

"Is it true," I asked nervously, "that Father Vespasian had me beaten? For not speaking?"

"Yes, I fear that is the case," Father Antoine answered with reluctance. "When our novices commit faults, or are slow in learning, or obstinate and sullen, he has them whipped round the infirmary cloister. This happened to you, twice . . . Father Vespasian, you see, was so certain that if he laid his hands on you, the power of speech would be granted to you again. And—as I said—when he is thwarted, his malady comes upon him—"

I could not withhold a shiver. Somehow the thought of this unreasonable, mad anger—at someone who, by reason of infirmity, could not speak—and visiting upon them such a savage punishment, seemed to me most horrible. The fact that it was *I* who had suffered the punishment and that I could not remember the occasion at all, only made the whole thing worse, as if some innocent half-wit—my younger brother perhaps—had been thus unfairly dealt with.

"Do you think that he will have me beaten again? If my memory does not return?"

Father Antoine crossed himself once more and said, without answering directly, "That was why, you see—it was in order to assist your memory—that I obtained the Prior's leave to bring you down here. And indeed Father Mathieu is always glad of some seaweed for his garden."

We went on working in silence for a time, moving steadily along the shore, until the Abbey of St. Just, behind us on its pinnacle of rock, looked no larger than a sharp tooth in the distance. Inland of us lay the ragged sand dunes, crested with sea grass. Every now and then, when I took a quick look at them, something stirred faintly in the dark depths of my mind, like a carp at the bottom of a muddy millpool; but it was no more than the ripple of its movement that I caught; the thing itself was still far out of reach.

I said bluntly, "To me, Father, it seems best that I continue my way to Spain *now;* directly. I can see there would be difficulties in continuing my journey by ship; I would have to go to a port, and somehow furnish myself with a passport. But there must be many byways over the frontier from France into Spain; I have traveled alone through wild country before, and do not fear to do so again. My poor grandfather will be wearying for me; and I see no sense in returning to a life in the Abbey for which I have no vocation—or to be beaten for a fault that I cannot rectify and for which I feel no guilt."

"You speak well, child, and with spirit," he answered. "But consider! In order to reach Spain on foot you must first cross the Pyrenees. Those mountains over there"—he waved southward, to the farther end of the bay, where the noonday sun hung over the high snow-covered peaks—"those mountains conceal others, even higher. There are many dangers between here and Spain. You are wearing the habit of a novice— you have no money on you—if you quitted the Abbey without permission, Father Vespasian would have a report of you published abroad, and you would be taken up by the gendarmes and returned here—"

"But I am not a professed novice!" I was outraged. "How could they do so?"

"Hush, wait!" He held up a hand. "I am not saying that it would be right. But that is what would most probably happen. Also—a smaller consideration, but one which I hope would also have weight—I, too, would incur Father Vespasian's displeasure for having allowed you to go off without leave."

I stared at his worn, kindly face with dismay.

"Mercy, Father! I had not thought of that! It is the very last thing I would wish. But could I not quietly slip away from the Abbey, some time when the fathers are all at work, or sleeping? No blame would fall on you then. What became of my own clothes?"

And my belt full of gold money, I thought.

"Do not be anxious about them. They are in the care of the infirmarian, Father Pierre. They are safe. But he would need permission from the Abbot before he could release them to you."

Just let me find where they are kept, I thought, but did not utter this thought aloud. While I pondered the difficulties of my situation, Father Antoine eyed me mildly and kindly. Then he said, "Hearken, Felix. Do not distress yourself. Wait a little while in patience. I will write a letter today to your grandfather. I can do that, for I work in the scriptorium and have access to pens and ink. So that, I promise. Meanwhile give yourself to God's purpose. It seems to me that His causing you to remain here, unawakened as you were, for so many weeks, was, perhaps, to prepare for an event which is yet to happen in the future."

I gazed at him, deeply struck with this suggestion, which touched some response in me and moved with the current of my own thought. It seemed very familiar to me.

"Now that you have woken up, and remembered that you are Felix Brooke," he went on, "perhaps the event, whatever it is, will not be long in coming."

"Yes, I do see . . . and I believe that you are right, Father. I will try to wait in patience. I promise that I will not run off. But what about Father Vespasian? What if he questions me again?"

"Well, you had better tell him as much as you can remember, and perhaps that will satisfy him. And, to rehearse your tale for him, why do you not relate to me, now, as much as you can recall of what has happened to you in the past? I shall be only too happy to hear it," Father Antoine said with a smile. "News from the outside world is always welcome!"

Accordingly, while we continued to load the cart, I told Father Antoine about how I had decided to leave my grandfather's house at Villaverde and search for my English relatives, guided by nothing more than a letter from my dead father in which I could read only five words. I told of my many adventures along the way and how I had made several friends, kind, good friends; how one of them, an English sailor named Sam Pollard, had, through a series of accidents, accompanied me on a smugglers' ship from Santander to Plymouth in England, how the ship had been wrecked in a storm and we two the only survivors, how poor Sam had been thrown into an English jail for debt, and how I, traveling on to the town of Bath, had at length by God's guidance been enabled to find my family home, discover that my English grandfather was a duke, and that I was rich enough to be able to send money to Sam and allow him to pay his debts and return to Spain, where he was promised in marriage. I told further how, discovering that there was no friendship or affection in my English home, but only wealth and a mad old man who confused me with my dead father, I had decided to return to Spain, where my true friends were.

"And so I took passage on a Biscay ship—the *Euzkadi*—bound for San Sebastian; it was the first ship I found in Plymouth about to set sail for a Spanish port. She was an ill-found little craft and I suppose if I had been wiser I would have waited for one bound for Santander or Villaviciosa. But I was in such haste to be away . . . It seems that I am like Jonah; I have only to embark on a ship for it to founder!"

I said this half laughing, but Father Antoine replied seriously, "Beware of thinking yourself too important, my child. After all, many, many vessels are wrecked every winter in the Bay of Biscay. Here at St. Just we are always on the lookout for ships like yours driven onto Les Dents du Diable, those reefs out yonder. Dozens of poor mariners have we pulled ashore, or assisted as we did you and your companions. But tell me now, looking about the beach, does no memory of that occasion stir in your mind?"

I stared inland, at the row of curving, pointed dunes, in shape like a child's pothooks, that lay to the rear of the bay. Behind them could be seen here and there a belt of scrubby woodland from which, on the offshore breeze, drifted a faint, sweet scent.

"You came running from those dunes, just about here," said Father Antoine, "with a look on your face as if Beelzebub himself were after you."

I stared in the direction toward which he pointed and hauled at my memory as I had hauled on the rope of the *Euzkadi*. But to no avail.

"No matter!" said the monk. "Don't look so disappointed, child. God will make all plain in His own good time. Now we must return; see, the tide is rising fast. As I told you, it is dangerous to loiter, or we should find ourselves obliged to remain on this side of the causeway until midnight, and Father Vespasian would be rightly displeased."

The water was, in fact, lapping near the edge of the causeway while we hurried along it; and, looking back as we encouraged Berri and Erda up the steep zigzag ascent to the Abbey gate, I could see that the lowest part of the road was already submerged for a dozen yards, so swiftly did the ocean sweep back into the two bays.

We unloaded our seaweed onto a heap by the kitchen garden wall, then led the donkeys to the stable. Tethering and feeding them, it seemed to me that I could hear faint cries in the distance, and I noticed a troubled crease in Father Antoine's brow.

As we returned to the frater we passed by the disused infirmary cloister, where we beheld a strange and horrid spectacle: A youth, naked but for a loincloth, was being driven around and around the quadrangle by two monks who beat him alternately with tarred ropes; meanwhile another monk was chanting prayers. I recognized the boy: He was Alaric, one of the novices who had given me cautious, friendly smiles at supper and during the instruction period; he had also failed very badly in his recitation. The monks who were beating him were two unknown to me. Watching somberly, at a distance, under the cloister arch, was the tall figure of Father Vespasian. As we passed the latter his cold recessed eye fell on me and I could not forbear a shiver. But he said nothing.

Next day, the instruction period over, I was occupied in hoeing around the young bean sprouts, as ordered by aged Father Mathieu, the gardener, when I came across a dead mole. Poor thing, there it lay on its back with all four feet in the air: strange, broad feet, designed for digging, more like shovels or paddles than like pads or paws. Fascinated by its long inquiring nose, tiny eyes, and wonderfully velvetlike black fur, I picked it up to study it more closely. A black-robed monk had just entered the garden, and, believing him to be Father Mathieu, I stepped around a quince tree, holding out the mole to show him.

"See, Father—!"

But the monk was Father Vespasian, who had been quietly standing and watching me.

When he saw the mole he turned a queer, sick lemon-yellow color and began to let out little sharp cries of distress, while his green eyes, pale-rimmed, shot desperately here and there. His cries became louder, his hands clenched convulsively, and at length he turned and fled, shrieking now in spasms like somebody suffering mortal agony; I could hear his cries dying away in the distance as I stood aghast, still with the mole extended in my hand, wondering what I had done.

Father Mathieu came hurrying out of the tool-house, looking greatly alarmed.

"*Mon Dieu,* was that Father Vespasian? What occurred—?"

Then his eye lit on the mole in my hand.

"Ah, I understand. Father Vespasian has a horror of death—of any dead thing. Such a sight as that is certain to start one of his attacks."

"Heaven help me, what have I done? I had no intention of distressing him!"

"It is no matter, my boy. Do not put yourself about," Father Mathieu said kindly. "How could you be expected to know such a thing?"

"But he will be so angry with me—he will think that I did it purposely!"

"No, his fits always end in a profound sleep, which may last for many hours. Very likely when he wakes he will remember nothing of what caused his seizure, or even that it happened."

Like me, I thought. You would think that he would have more sympathy with my condition.

We did not see Father Vespasian again that day. The Prior, Father Anselm, a frail, elderly, sad-faced man, took his part at the services and in the Chapter, where the monks had their meeting. But next day the Abbot was about again, none the worse, it seemed. I thought his eye passed over me, if I happened to come in his way, with a strange blankness, as if the sight of me were repugnant to him. He did not send for me again. At intervals, working in the garden, I would catch sight of him, for he often walked for hours on end, back and forth, back and forth, over a grassy shoulder of the promontory which looked down toward the bay and the causeway. To and fro, to and fro, he walked, and I always felt that he was aware of my presence in the kitchen garden. But he never once looked my way.

Father Mathieu told me that he often spent many hours at night on that spot, pacing up and down. "The holy Abbot needs very little sleep," he told me. "One hour a night is sufficient for him. His mind is occupied with deep thought."

On the following Friday, after the service of Sext, the people suffering from maladies and afflictions were allowed to visit the Abbey, and so I had a chance to witness Father Vespasian's power of healing.

As we came out of Chapel we saw the group of sufferers and their friends patiently waiting: a boy with a badly swollen foot, who had been carried up on a litter of plaited osiers by three of his companions; a distraught-looking man whose face was splashed all over with angry red blotches; and a woman holding a shawled baby.

Father Vespasian, wearing an expression of serenity and radiance, walked slowly toward the patients, who all knelt and gazed up at him. Profound trust and hope was written clear on their faces. The rest of us formed a ring around them: monks to the front and novices in the rear. The monks began a soft chant of invocation while Father Vespasian slowly and carefully inspected the man with the blotched face, murmured a prayer over him, and gently laid his hands on the haggard particolored cheeks. Then he called for a vessel of water, blessed it, poured it over the man's face, and bade him dry himself with a napkin.

"After that, hold the napkin over your face, my brother, while you can say the Paternoster slowly twice," ordered the Abbot, and moved on to the boy with the swollen foot, whom he appeared to know.

"You wish to go fishing with the others, Tomas, is that it?"

The tousle-headed boy grinned shyly. "Yes, my lord Abbot! Papa is sick, and we need the money badly—but old Père Rotrou said the bone was broken."

"Let us see. Perhaps we can make it better, if you trust me."

"Oh, I do, I do, my lord Abbot."

As before, Father Vespasian prayed, laid his hands carefully on the swollen joint, poured holy water, and wrapped a white towel round it.

"Now say two prayers to our gracious Lady, child, while I look at this little one."

The mother holding the baby was desperately thin and sad. She appeared wretchedly weary, too, as if she had come a long way on this last hope. And a last hope it must be, I saw, by the look in the eyes she raised to Father Vespasian.

"Where are you from, my daughter? I do not know you."

"No, my father, I have traveled a long way. From Narbonne . . . My husband died of the sickness, and my two elder children. This little one is the last.

Hearing of your holy touch, I hoped—I prayed—"
With a mute gesture she held out the baby on her two
hands. Poor thing, it, too, was dwindled away to
nearly nothing; its arms and legs looked thin as the
pea-sticks in Father Mathieu's garden, its skin was pale
yellow and waxy. I heard Father Antoine, in front of
me, exhale a long anxious sigh.

At the sight of it a faint frown crossed Father Vespasian's brow; nonetheless he prayed over it long and
earnestly, sprinkled it with holy water, and bade the
mother wrap it close and repeat three Hail Marys
while she waited for the healing to take effect. She
crouched down over it with bowed head, holding the
little creature close to her breast while she prayed.

Now, suddenly, the silence was broken by a wild
shout from the boy, Tomas.

"My foot! It's better, it's better, it's really better!
Look, Pierrot, look, Garvi, look, Tonio! The swelling
has gone, it's gone!"

His friends gasped as he stood up waving the white
napkin triumphantly; and it was true, the hurt foot
was no more swollen than the other, and the dark-red
color had paled to a normal brown.

"Can you walk on it?" Father Vespasian asked,
smiling.

"Yes, Father, yes, look!"

In an ecstasy of delight he capered across the grassy
quadrangle. "I'm cured, I'm cured, now I can go fishing, oh, thank you, holy Father!" And he returned,
humbly and reverently, to kiss the Abbot's hand.

"Thank not me but a greater Father than I, my boy; and don't forget the Abbey when times are kinder for your family."

"No, my lord. No, of course I won't! Come, Pierrot, come, Tonio; just wait till I show them down at the village how well I can walk!"

As he ran out through the great gate, which stood open, his friends with the wicker litter had much ado to keep up with him.

Now the man with the skin disease removed the napkin from his face, and a sigh of mingled joy and relief went up from the surrounding monks. The man, not being able to see his own face, squinted painfully along his nose, turning his head this way and that, then demanded, "Tell me, brothers, for the love of God, am I healed? Is it for me as it was for the boy? Am I better?"

"Yes, brother, yes!" cried the joyful monks. "Praise God, your skin is as clear as new-cut oak. The disfigurement is all gone. Look in the fountain pool and see for yourself!"

The man looked and looked into the water, and was finally assured of the truth of his healing.

In deep reverence and gratitude he knelt before Father Vespasian.

"Oh, my lord Abbot, there are no words to thank you! I believed I was stricken by the plague. I felt sure that death was certain."

"No, no, you have plenty more life in you yet, friend," said Father Vespasian. "Only give thanks in your prayers, and remember the monks of the Abbey when you have money in your pocket."

"Indeed, indeed I will, my father." And off he went through the gate, beaming all over his restored face.

Now the anxious mother pulled back the shawl that she had wrapped over her baby.

Even before she did so, I felt a qualm of apprehension. For the baby itself had not been able to appeal to Father Vespasian; nor had it understood his words of hope and encouragement. Perhaps it had not even heard them. In fact, as its mother pulled aside the coverings, no change could be seen in the poor thing, and the face she lifted to the Abbot was both pleading and penitent, as if she apologized for its lack of collaboration in the ceremony, and begged humbly to be given a second chance.

Father Vespasian's face became stern and clouded. I saw his eyes flicker to and fro. With a dry mouth I recognized the pinched, indrawn look of his nostrils, the impatient compression of his lips.

Would he fly into a rage, shout at the wretched mother, order that she or the baby should be beaten? I found that my hands were clenched in suspense.

Father Pierre, the infirmarian, was quick to avert the threat.

He moved forward, bowed deeply, if hurriedly, and said, "My lord Abbot, the woman and her child must both be weary and hungry, too, if they have traveled all the way from Narbonne. Let them remain overnight in the guesthouse, and very likely by tomorrow the little one will be in better case to benefit from your healing. Come with me, my sister," he said to the poor woman, who was indeed almost ready to drop from exhaustion and disappointment, swaying as she stood. "Come, you and your babe will be the better for some hot soup," and he led her rapidly away before the threatened explosion from Father Vespasian.

Meanwhile the rest of the monks had struck up a Te Deum of thankfulness for the two wonderful acts of healing, and the careworn-looking Prior Anselm led Father Vespasian away toward his lodge, talking to him quickly, earnestly, and deferentially, doubtless congratulating him on his success in two cases out of three. But I could see that the Abbot remained displeased and unsatisfied; he glanced back sharply, two or three times, in the direction of the woman and her baby, as if he were still of a mind to try further measures on them.

What a frightening gift he has! I thought, mechanically turning to follow the others out of the cloister. How glad I am that *I* have not such a healing touch, since it seems to bring with it such cares and penalties; and I wondered very much about the woman and her baby, what would now happen to them? If I were Father Pierre, I would be much inclined to smuggle them away from the Abbey before there was a chance of another meeting with Father Vespasian, for, if he had not been able to make the poor child better today, there seemed little likelihood that matters would be any more fortunate tomorrow.

I fear that, all through the hour of dinner which followed the healing ceremony, my mind was inclined to be absent; I swallowed down my lentil soup but paid very little heed to the chapters from the Book of Proverbs that Father Roger was reading aloud to us.

Is Father Vespasian's gift really derived from God? I wondered. Or could it be a trick of the Evil One, and intended to entrap him into sinful pride? In which case, how can it be that the healing takes effect on the sick people?

Can the devil heal, as well as God? Or is it all a trick, a deception, they are not really healed? Or were they not really as sick as they thought, in the first place?

Dearly would I have liked to put these questions to Father Antoine, but feared that he might be horrified and call me a heretic.

Next morning Father Vespasian was not to be seen. And I learned from the novice Alaric, who whispered it in study hour, that the Abbot had paid a surprise visit to the visitors' dorter at dawn, and found the poor baby dead and stiff in its cot. The sight of its tiny waxen corpse had incurred in him a seizure of such terrible violence that the poor mother fainted dead away in terror; and after his fit Father Vespasian himself fell into so profound a slumber that the baby's funeral was conducted and its pitiful little body buried in the fathers' graveyard before he came to himself.

Can there be many monastic communities like this? I asked myself in wonder and fear, joining my voice in the requiem at the baby's funeral service, and then, with a lighted candle in my hand, slowly following in procession to the graveyard. This lay on a grassy seaward slope of the island, enclosed by the Abbey wall, with a distant view of blue water and rolling whitecapped waves. There the unlucky little creature was buried, in holy company, with the small tombstones of dead-and-gone fathers all around him.

"He is certain to go straight to heaven," I heard Father Pierre assuring the mother. "He will be there to welcome you." But she only wept the more.

Next moment, to my great surprise, Father Pierre approached me, giving me a friendly smile.

"My boy: You will not remember how many weeks you lay under my care, halfway between death and dream. Father Antoine tells me that you still have no recollection of that time."

"No, my father; I do not; but—but I am very very much obliged and grateful to you for all your kindness and care; I should have come to thank you before—" I stammered, thinking he must have thought me most uncivil not to have done so.

He shook his head; he was a sandy-haired, pink-faced man who looked like a simple farmer, until you noticed the shrewdness of his small twinkling gray eyes.

"Caring for the sick is my task, and you were my patient; you still are, for that matter, in the eyes of God, until you have recovered your full memory. But now it is my turn to ask a favor of you."

"Anything that I can do for you, Father, of course," I began, somewhat startled.

"This poor sister of ours"—Father Pierre indicated the bereaved mother, who was being led back to the visitors' dormitory by the guest brother, Father Ambroise—"she should leave this place, I believe, as soon as it is possible for her to do so. It—it would not be at all advisable for her to be here, still, when Father Vespasian next wakes. He"—Father Pierre gave me a flicker of a glance, then looked away again—"he becomes distressed when he has failed to cure somebody's affliction."

"Yes, I understand. Why, then, can she not leave?"

"She is tired and sick. She has not the strength to set out on her journey today. But Father Antoine could take her as far as the inn at the village of Zugarra, over the hill, where she could stay a day or two—only, she has no money. And I cannot draw from the Abbey funds without Father Vespasian's permission. But— along with your clothes, my boy, which I have in safekeeping there is a money belt—"

"Of course," I said, remembering the eleven English gold guineas and the three silver crowns that I had carried with me for my journey. "Take one of the guineas; she may have it with my goodwill, poor thing."

"Tut, tut! A crown will be sufficient," said Father Pierre. "But I will not handle your belongings in your absence; come, and you yourself shall give me the money."

He led me to the infirmary, which lay off the main cloister near the kitchen, at right angles to the chapel.

"This was once the visitors' parlor," he told me. "But when our numbers dwindled, and the old infirmary became too large for our needs, this building was thought more convenient."

There was a surgery downstairs, with wooden closets for blankets and bedding, shelves of medicines, pots of unguents, and bundles of herbs. Upstairs were the sickrooms where ailing members of the Community could be nursed.

Father Pierre opened the closet where my clothes hung, carefully put up in a linen bag with sage and comfrey leaves to keep moths at bay. It gave me a queer feeling to handle my striped jacket with the steel buttons, and remember how I had first put it on in my English grandfather's ducal mansion at Asshe, in England. What a distance from there had I now traveled; distance on land and in the mind, both! The gold English guineas seemed like fairy gold as I took them from the money belt and counted them, wondering greatly at the honesty of the people who had picked me up and brought me here, that the money should still be in the purse.

"Here, my father, this is for the poor woman; and should not I give you money, too, for the Abbey where I have been tended and sheltered for such a long period? Indeed I would not wish to be thought ungrateful or unmindful—"

"No, no, my son," he said hastily. "We require no

payment from our patients, no indeed! And one crown will be plenty for the woman. Besides, are you not rendering payment to the Order in the form of service—tending the garden, helping Father Antoine? No, keep your store for when you set out on your travels again. Here it shall stay, safely guarded with your clothes, you see, in the third closet from the stair; I carry the keys on me always, and at night sleep with them under my pillow just here—"

He replaced my clothes in the linen bag, and the bag in the cupboard; it struck me, at first idly, then with some force, that he had taken considerable pains to impress on me just where my things were kept. Was there a purpose behind his words and actions?

"You are an excellent boy," he went on, quickly blessing me with the sign of the cross. "I was certain of it. One cannot tend a person in sickness without forming a strong notion of his character. Now you had best run along to your work with Father Mathieu. And—it were better not to speak of this generous act of yours to any person here. It is our secret—between you, me, and *le bon Dieu*. Just in case Father Vespasian, waking, is displeased to find her gone."

"Of course, Father; I perfectly understand."

He gave me a quick smile; if he were not a monk I would have said he winked.

"Good boy! Run along with you, then; you can go through this side-door, which will be a shortcut to the vegetable garden."

The door opened into the monks' recreation ground, a stretch of rough turf, studded with sea pinks and nodding yellow poppies, which lay between the cloister and the walled garden.

There, on the stretch of flat land at the foot of the wall (here about thirty feet high) it was their custom to play *pelota a mano,* a very ancient game of the Basques. Most men now play this game with a *pala,* or wooden bat, with which they strike the ball against the wall, but the monks kept to the oldest form of the game, using nothing but the bare hand, for which reason their hands were all tough and callused and thick as oak roots.

The doorway through the wall from the surgery saved me a long walk round through cloister and living quarters and kitchen.

"I keep a key outside, hidden behind this stone, in case Father Mathieu has occasion to come in this way after gathering herbs for my sick ones," said Father Pierre, pulling aside a square stone to show me the hidden key. Then he returned through the door, locking it from the inside. I stood outside the door, on the flat pelota ground, thinking hard.

Father Pierre is showing me something, he is warning me, I thought. What can be his object? Is he suggesting that for me, too, it would be best to leave the Abbey before Father Vespasian wakes?

A terribly strong temptation shook me: to take the key from under the stone, unlock the door in the wall, break open the closet, remove my clothes, and depart at once. It would be impossible to leave by the main gate, because of the porter; but I knew there were many gaps in the crumbling outer wall, which enclosed a large area and many buildings, half of them ruinous, on the top of the island. A strong active boy such as myself could climb through the wall without much trouble, and over the grassy, rocky hillside beyond there were numerous goat and rabbit paths. The Abbey was not entirely surrounded by sheer cliff. While emptying barrowloads of stones from the garden, or returning with seaweed from the beach, I had noticed how it would, here and there, be possible to climb down, unobserved, onto the sands below.

Of course such an escape could only be achieved when the tide was full out. Crossing the causeway, except by night, would not be possible, for the whole length of it was visible from the Abbey gate.

How I longed to leave! I could see that the life led by the fathers in the Abbey was a noble one, devout, hardworking, every minute of every hour put to good use in prayer, work, and healing; yet something about the place both frightened and repelled me. It was because of Father Vespasian: He was so powerful, so unpredictable. And they were all bound in duty to obey him, no matter what he ordered. . . .

I wondered if he had always been as he was now.

Twice I looked back with longing at the door in the wall.

But I had given my promise to Father Antoine. And perhaps the event which would release me, as he had suggested, would not be long in coming. Perhaps quite soon now I would recapture the memory of what had happened to me among the sand dunes.

I pushed, again and again, at the closed door in my mind. But it would not open.

Not until another ten days had passed did the memory return.

2

I find a victim in the thicket. The decision to leave for Spain.
I am punished for obduracy.

It was a day of mild sun and trembling, vaporous sea-mist. Father Antoine and I had gone, as was now our twice-weekly custom, to gather seaweed in the larger of the two bays, and also collect such pieces of driftwood as Brother Guillaume could use for his kitchen fire. Larks and peewits were twittering in the marshes beyond the seashore. Once or twice I saw a pelican flap his stately way over the sand dunes.

"Why does nobody try to cultivate the marshes, Father?" I asked.

"The Marsh of Cuxaq? It is too unhealthy, child; pestilence and the lung sickness, they say, lie in wait for those who spend any length of time there. The only persons who can find their way through the boggy wilderness are brigands; for others, it is best not to venture far from the edge."

"Brigands?"

"What you in Spain call the *gente de reputación*— thieves, bandits, assassins. They, the Mala Gente, of course, cross all borders."

"Ah!"

I myself had had a little dealing with the *gente de reputación,* when, on my way to England, I was unjustly imprisoned in Oviedo. The leader of a group of *rateros,* or brigands, in Oviedo jail had believed (wrongly) that I had some knowledge of the whereabouts of General Moore's paychests for the English army—or maybe the treasure sent from Paris for the French army, chests of gold doubloons and crusadas; one treasure, it was said, had been lost in the mountains of Galicia, the other somewhere in the Pyrenees. I knew nothing of either treasure, hardly believed in their existence, and had told the chief so, roundly; but it was plain that he did not believe me. He knew that I had once met an Englishman calling himself George Smith, who claimed that he had seen where the English paychests had been left when Baird and Frazer retreated westward toward Coruna. This Englishman was now dead, and moreover he had told me nothing of his knowledge. I had spoken to him once, and he had sent me a letter about my own affairs. But I supposed that if the Spanish *rateros* had not yet found the money (if, indeed, it really existed) I would do well to keep out of their way, for they might yet believe that I would lead them to it.

However, all this had nothing to do with the present occasion, I thought, with the Marsh of Cuxaq or the French bandits. The French wars were over, the Emperor Napoleon, imprisoned in St. Helena, had died almost a year ago, and King Ferdinand the Desired had been let out of jail, where Napoleon had put him, and was once more on the throne of Spain.

Reaching this point in my thoughts, I asked Father Antoine if he could give me any news of Spain. Now that I knew who I was, I began to feel homesick for my native country. Spain, to me, would always be that.

"Ah, Spain!" said Father Antoine, pausing to brush the sand flies from his bald tonsure before hoisting up, with my help, a gray-white log of driftwood into the cart. "Who ever knows what new frenzy will afflict that country, the land of bullfights and blood feuds? But I have heard that a rebellion, under Rafael Riego, is spreading and gathering power; King Ferdinand now pretends to proclaim himself king of the people, promising to restore all the liberal measures which, previously, he had annulled. They say that the Holy Alliance (that is, Austria, Russia, and Prussia) will not permit this; they are afraid of the Spanish revolutionaries; they will send Cossack troops into Spain to put down the uprising."

This news startled and shocked me. My Spanish grandfather, I knew (though it was long since he had quit politics), felt a sympathy for the Liberals and for Colonel Riego, who had wished to bring back the Spanish liberal constitution of 1812; whereas the rule of King Ferdinand VII was already noted for its despotism, oppression of liberty, closing of universities, banning of books, and exile or persecution of any men who dared to speak against the regime.

But I thought that, while it was bad enough to have such a ruler, it would be even worse to have his rule enforced by armies from outside the kingdom. Spain, in the years when I was a small child, had been plundered and devastated, year after year, by the armies of Napoleon; was this now all to happen again, only this time with the armies of the Tsar Alexander?

I was beginning to say something about these matters, when a very strange thing happened to me. Suddenly all my thoughts, all my faculties, seemed brought within me to a numbing halt, as if a pencil of ice had touched my brain.

We were in the center of the bay, we had just levered the length of timber into the cart, and I was standing with my hand on the cart tail and my face toward the sand dunes, when I became seized by an overmastering blind urge to pass through a narrow gully between two of the silvery hillocks and see what lay beyond.

The violence of this urge hardly left me breath for speech. I knew—I felt quite certain—that something was waiting for me on the other side of the dunes.

"Father Antoine—I believe I can hear somebody calling me."

"Why, my boy!" he exclaimed. "What in the world is the matter? You have turned white as an altar cloth. Are you ill? Do you have pain?"

"No, no—I am not ill—but I believe—I believe I am beginning to *remember*. There is something that I have to do beyond those dunes; I must go, at once; it is terribly urgent—"

While I gasped out these words I had begun to run over the sand. Father Antoine, without more ado, dropped the asses' reins over their heads, to prevent them from straying, and followed me, tucking up his robe and moving swiftly on his sandaled feet.

"I will help you, my child, with whatever it is." He glanced about him, over the flat sand, and back to where the cart stood, and the donkeys with drooping heads. "I believe—yes, I am sure," he panted, following me, "that this is exactly the track through which you came running when I first saw you."

"Yes. Yes, it is! I remember now. I had wished to find a private place in which to kneel and thank God for my deliverance—"

"Very understandable, my dear boy!"

"I came through the dunes—just here—and saw that clump of trees ahead. It was twilight then—but I am certain that is the place. *Listen!*"

We were nearly at the thicket. My ears had caught something—a choking sob, a faint, pitiful cry for help.

"I heard nothing," said Father Antoine. "But you are young. Your ears are sharper."

"Quick, quick!"

Thrusting, grappling, kicking the boughs out of my way, fighting the tangled undergrowth, I forced my way into the thicket, with Father Antoine close behind me. Now I recognized again the sweet haunting fragrance of the yellow blossoms that hung overhead. I had smelled that scent before! And yet a part of my mind, cool, doubting, skeptical, said to me, "Come, now, Felix, it was the month of January when the *Euzkadi* was wrecked, and you were cast ashore. How could these blossoms have been in flower then?"

But I was certain that I remembered their fragrance.

Three or four more minutes of battling progress through the bushes, and we emerged, torn, bloodied, and panting, into a dappled, shadowed glade which also, now, I remembered. The ground here was fragrant with violets.

And overhead—

"I don't want to die," whispered a choking voice. "Help me—please help me! I don't—want—to—die—"

High overhead hung a small, thin body, suspended from one of the arching boughs. It was still in motion—kicking, struggling—

I scrambled up through the slender whippy branches, climbing as if they had been a ladder, thrusting myself upward, cursing and praying in the same words, to the same Deity. "Listen! You must, you *must* save him till I come—don't let him die, only save him till I come—"

"Have you a knife, child?" called Father Antoine in sudden agitation.

Novices were not allowed to carry knives, but I had brought one from the garden shed for cutting through the tough roots of seaweed. It was tucked under the cord which formed my belt. With clumsy trembling speed I cut the rope, and Father Antoine below received the slight body into his capable arms. Meanwhile I pushed myself out of the tree, not caring how I fell, and landed crouching beside the pair of them.

"Is—is he still alive?"

Father Antoine had already, with great care, loosed the choking cord that constricted the thin neck; then with his gnarled but gentle hands he pressed the sides of the frail chest: pressed, pressed, pressed, and released.

"Blow into his mouth, boy," he directed me. "Breathe for him! As I release my hands each time, you blow. Yes, yes, that is the way."

Kneeling on a huge patch of crushed violets I blew—waited; blew again; while Father Antoine doggedly continued to press, release, and press, forcing the emptied lungs to take up their task again. If Father Vespasian could see us battling like this! I thought, and was infinitely glad that he could not, that there were only the two of us working desperately hard without the need for speech in the quiet glade. But, oh, supposing our work was in vain?

It seemed like half an hour that we had been kneeling there, though in reality perhaps it had been three minutes, four minutes, five minutes—

At last there came the slightest, weakest sound from the body between Father Antoine's hands—a faint, choking cough.

"Ah! *Grâce à Dieu!* I think we are going to win. Do not stop blowing for a single instant, my son!"

I blew—waited—blew; and then suddenly we were rewarded. The face below mine—which was blue-white, waxy—contorted and crumpled; the chest contracted, expanded, filled with air, and expelled it again in a violent sneeze.

"*We've done it!* We have saved him! He is alive!" In my joy and relief I grabbed Father Antoine's hands; I could hardly forbear from embracing him. Perhaps I did.

"Gently, my son. We are not quite out of the wood yet."

He continued with his massage, pressing the ribs, rubbing the dreadfully bruised and discolored neck.

But his words went on echoing in my mind. Not out of the wood. No; and very likely neither were the people who had hung up this poor victim. They could not be very far away; the deed was too recent.

I sprang to the side of the glade from which we had come and began to hack at the whippy stems with my knife, to make a wider passage through. On the far side, I now noticed, there were signs that somebody had entered recently; branches were broken, grass was crushed. But that would be no way for us to take.

A few minutes, and I had cleared a path wide enough for our purposes.

"Father Antoine," I said in a low voice. "Do you not think we should carry him to the shore?"

While saying this, I opened my eyes very wide, laid my finger on my lips, and silently gestured toward the depths of the thicket—from which, indeed, I thought I had heard a slight crack, or crunch. He took my meaning instantly.

"It is well thought, my boy. Yes, let us go."

Gently and most carefully he raised the head and shoulders, I laid hold of the bare, scratched legs, and painfully, with great trouble, we proceeded back along the little passage I had cut, and so out into the fresh reviving air of the seashore. Only then did I realize that the person we had rescued was hardly taller than myself: a boy, no more; and pitifully thin. His jerkin and breeches were of old, threadbare material; his hair was long and so matted that it looked like tar; he had no hat, shoes, or stockings. He was dirty, bedraggled, and dreadfully bruised. He weighed—luckily for us who had to carry him—little more than the seaweed that we had been handling.

But why should they have hanged a boy? And who were *they*? Who in the world would do such a deed?

And why—at this thought, which came to me while carrying him over the soft, slippery sand, I almost stumbled in my astonishment—why should *I* have been given a foreknowledge of this event? For that, I now saw, was what had been sent to me. Three months ago, on that stormy evening in January, God had granted me a prevision of what was to come. Why?

Had it happened simply because, exhausted, gasping with fear and fatigue after my own narrow escape from death, I had been flung up on this very spot, where his murder was later going to take place?

Or had my destiny planned the whole happening, the whole connection, from much further back? And was that why I had been sent here?

The asses still stood with drooping heads just where we had left them; we placed the rescued boy in the cart, on a mattress of seaweed.

"Can you talk at all, my poor child?" Father Antoine asked quietly.

Two wild dark-brown eyes opened at him for a moment, enormously wide, and there came a faint, negative movement of the head.

"No matter; just lie still; we are going to take you to a place of safety."

The eyes closed again. Not, I thought, in relief at the monk's promise, but rather to keep their secrets hidden.

As we began to cross the causeway, and the cart shook violently, bumping over the uneven edges of rock, the eyes flew open again in alarm, then shut resolutely. I was leading Berri, and could not forbear, in quick glances over my shoulder, to study the boy whom I had been the means of saving from death. What a singular link now lay between us, I thought!

We had been, as it were, bound together by three months of time, three months that had been removed from my life by the mysterious hand of God.

What had become of those three months? I would never know.

And suddenly I remembered Father Vespasian. "Where has your soul been hiding since that day? Under whose dominion?" Why should he ask that? What did he expect to hear?

Another thought struck me: that I, only, in the entire human race, had knowledge of the bond between me and the hanged boy. Father Antoine might well guess at some part of the whole, but unless I chose to tell him, he would never know the complete story.

Slowly, doubtfully, I pondered this. In a way I felt that Father Antoine had a right to hear about it. He had been kind, understanding; had not pressed me; had helped me, by arranging my visits to the shore, to be in the right spot when memory caught up and became linked with reality. Yes, he had a right to know the whole. But, apart from him, I did not wish anybody else to learn about this mystery. It was my secret—mine and this boy's, whoever he was—it belonged to no one else. *Especially,* I thought, I would not wish it to come to the ears of Father Vespasian. Why not? I could hardly frame the reasons to myself, but they were there, solid as mountains in my mind. Father Vespasian would wish to know *for the wrong purpose.* He was not sane; he was not quite human; there was something wild, ungovernable, dreadful about him. He did not belong to God. His motive for doing what he did came from some other quarter. No, the less he knew about this boy, the better, I decided; and I felt a strong wish to protect the frail, bruised body curled up among the seaweed in the cart. He ought not to be exposed to the Abbot's baleful scrutiny.

Thinking this, I turned for another glance at the boy. He was little more than a skeleton covered with skin. The velveteen jerkin and canvas pantaloons he wore were so filthy and tattered that they hardly did more than decently cover him. His feet were bare; the color of legs, arms, and face was a kind of bluish brown, like the mud of a tidal river. His cheeks were so gaunt from starvation that his chin stuck up sharp as the point of a spade. Here is somebody, Felix, I thought, whose sufferings make your own seem like a fiesta. What troubles have *you* ever endured? A scolding tutor and some peevish old aunts, a few days in prison, a couple of uncomfortable sea-passages? But this poor creature has probably known terrible hardship all his life.

And following this feeling came one of downright guilt for all the luck, friendship, and unfair spoiling that had come my way; upon which I resolved to befriend the boy, since we had been so significantly flung together, and do all that lay in my power to help him.

At the foot of the steep zigzag that led up to the Abbey gate, I brought Berri to a halt and faced Father Antoine.

"My father—perhaps before we reach the entrance I ought to tell you that I have remembered fully what before I had forgotten."

He gave me a beautiful smile, filled with understanding and sympathy.

"My boy, I was sure that you had! The manner in which you hurled yourself from the beach—like an arrow from a crossbow into that thicket—showed me that some pattern had come clear in your mind, instructing you to act without wasting a moment."

"It happened in this way, Father—"

But now, to my surprise, he laid a finger on my lips.

"Hush yet awhile, child! I believe that you should wait and think carefully before imparting the story to me, or indeed to anybody. Take counsel in prayer before any action. There is without doubt some further mystery which still remains to be solved. Perhaps we shall learn it when we hear the history of this poor one. Or perhaps future happenings will reveal God's purpose. But—in the meantime—do you not think that our first care should be for our hurt lamb, who is in urgent need of Father Pierre and his salves and tisanes?"

At once I felt humbled and reproved for thoughtlessness. Here I stood, who not two minutes previously had resolved to help the victim in every possible way, proposing to waste precious time in recounting my own tale. Very self-important, Felix! Abashed, I tugged at the bridle to urge Berri on his way up the hill.

Only later did it occur to me that perhaps Father Antoine had another reason for discouraging my communication to him. I looked upward to a green shoulder of the headland, and there was Father Vespasian, in his dark cloak and hood, arms folded, head bent, walking to and fro, to and fro, in his favorite spot, like a captain on the bridge of a ship. Did he see us? I could not tell. But I realized that as a member of the Community Father Antoine was in duty bound to report anything I told him to the Abbot.

But what he did not know, he could not tell.

We bore the hurt boy directly to the infirmary, where Father Pierre drew in a deep, shocked breath at our story and the sight of the bruised neck. He set pots of broth, wine, and milk to simmer on his little fire, while Father Antoine departed, as he must, to make a report to the Abbot.

Next Father Pierre directed me to help the sufferer upstairs.

The boy, who had been huddled in a chair, protested in a faint whisper that he could manage the stairs very well if someone took his arm.

"Do not try to talk yet, my child," said Father Pierre. "Your throat has been severely strained. Only tell us your name."

"It—it is Jua—Juan."

"Good, Juan. Now say no more. Felix here, who saved your life, will help you up to bed."

The boy flashed me a queer look: surprise, inquiry, a kind of unwilling gratitude, as if he had far rather *not* have to be obliged to me. I felt sympathy at this, and gave a slight shrug, as if to say, Oh, it was nothing, what else could I do?

His feelings were plain enough to me. It is a great burden to owe one's life to a stranger. Especially when one is still not far removed from the brink of death.

His eyes, I noticed, had remarkable coppery gleams in their dark-brown depths.

Slowly and with great reluctance he put out a wrist and hand not much thicker than a chicken's claw, which I threaded round my waist and so half lifted, half supported him up the wide shallow stone stair that led to the infirmary dorter. He smelled of tar and crushed herbage and felt light as a squirrel.

Up above there was a spacious dormitory and a few little cell-like single rooms. No patients occupied the half-dozen pallets in the dormitory at present, and I would have led Juan there, but he demanded, in a peremptory whisper, to be placed in a room by himself. This, Father Pierre, who had followed us up, permitted with a nod. We lifted the boy onto a cot, then returned downstairs for water and towels.

When I carried up a basin of warm water I discovered that Juan had barricaded himself in. There were no fastenings on the doors, but he had dragged (with strength obtained from heaven knows where) a bench across the room so as to bar the door.

"No one shall come in! I do not wish anybody to come in!" he whispered urgently through a crack in the woodwork.

Father Pierre and I stood staring at one another in perplexity. He rubbed his tonsure. To break down the door would be no great problem, but who would be so cruel as to use force against the poor terrified creature? Perhaps, still half crazed by his experience, he mistook us for his enemies.

"Come, now, what foolishness is this?" called Father Pierre gently through the door. "We do not intend to hurt you, my child; we have brought hot water, to wash you and clean your wounds and untangle your hair."

"I will wash myself! I do not wish anybody—*anybody*—to come near."

Father Pierre shrugged at that, with resignation. I could see from his expression that he did not expect his new patient to make a very good job of the ablutions, but he was too experienced in caring for the sick to bring the matter to a great issue. Accordingly he replied in a matter-of-fact tone: "Very well; if that is what you wish. Your main need at present is sleep and rest. Wash yourself a little, put on clean clothes, which I will bring up, then drink a little broth, then sleep."

"Put the water outside the door," instructed the hoarse whisper. "Also a pair of scissors. I will not open the door while you stand there."

Father Pierre looked at me a little anxiously at the request for scissors.

"You do not think he intends to do himself a mischief?" he murmured.

"Why do you ask for scissors, Juan?" I called.

"To cut my hair, idiot! Can one cut one's hair without scissors?"

Father Pierre smiled a wide grin of relief and beckoned me to follow him down.

"Nothing amiss with that one that can't be mended!" he remarked, taking out of a press the formidable pair of shears used for clipping the tonsures of novices when they took their final vows. "Imagine having so much spirit only half an hour after you were cut down from the gallows tree! Perhaps, after all, he will be able to wash himself well enough. Carry these clothes up to him, Felix my boy, while I put some herbs in the broth."

From a locker next to the one where my clothes and money belt were secured, he produced a pile of clean but old garments of various sorts and sizes.

"We keep them," he explained, "for the poor, or beggars, or the sick who come to be healed by Father Vespasian; once they belonged to patients who died in the infirmary," he added matter-of-factly. So, I thought, there have been others besides that poor woman's baby whom Father Vespasian has not been able to heal, and I spoke part of my thought aloud. But Father Pierre gave me a reproving, somewhat alarmed look, gesturing with his finger to his lips and glancing at the open window. "God takes those whom He wishes to call to Paradise in His own good time," he admonished me, crossing himself; and he sorted out a canvas shirt, woolen waistcoat, and breeches, all old, patched and darned, but clean. "There! Carry those to the lad, they should fit well enough."

Up aloft I found that the basin of warm water had been removed and the door fast closed again. I tapped on it with the scissors.

"*Holà,* in there! I have brought you clothes and scissors."

"I need some soap, also."

"Soap? Who does the boy think he is, *le roi* Louis XVIII?" grumbled Father Pierre, when, grinning, I returned to him with this message. However, he turned to a great earthenware pot and scooped out of it a lump of the soap which Father Manuel made from wood-ash and lard. "Here, then, take this to him; purity of the skin is doubtless a good step toward purity of the heart."

I ascended the stairs once more with the soft, clammy handful.

"*Allo, allo,* Juan? I have brought you some soap."

"Leave it outside the door!"

"How can I? It is as soft as cream, it will trickle away and be wasted."

"Oh—! *Peste!* Wait, then, one minute."

Slowly the door opened a crack, and out came a small bony hand. I plastered the soft soap into its palm, then scraped my fingers against the thin wrist, so as not to waste any.

"*Merci, mon ami,*" whispered the small hoarse voice, and the hand withdrew.

"De rien," I replied somewhat coldly as the door began to close again. I was, I must confess, a little provoked at being used with such suspicion by a person whose life I had just saved; and, my tone of voice evidently taking effect, I heard in a moment an even fainter whisper:

"Do not be offended. I have learned to trust *nobody*!"

By this I was appeased. "Who could blame you?" I called as the door clicked shut, and I went down to report this conversation to Father Pierre. He eyed me a moment, his red wrinkled brow knotted in thought, then said, "Since this poor waif trusts none of us, and since it was you who saved him, it may be best that you continue to tend him; under my supervision of course. I will ask Father Mathieu to excuse you from your garden duties, and you may work here for the time. Wait there and stir the broth. In between stirring, chop those bundles of mint for tisane."

"Very well, Father."

In five minutes he came back, nodding with satisfaction.

"Bien, for the time you become my assistant. Go and find if that one up there is ready to receive nourishment."

It seemed that one was; for outside the door now reposed the basin of dirty water and a little pile of ragged soiled clothes. The clean clothes were gone. Feeling not unlike a servant at an inn, I took these down, emptied the water out of doors, and displayed the wretched garments to Father Pierre, who said, "Those are good for nothing but to be made into polishing rags. Tear them apart, then put them to steep in that copper there."

A great copper vat, filled with water and supported by brick pillars, hung suspended over a fire in a corner of the room. I plunged in the rags and, at Father Pierre's direction, stirred all round with a long stick.

"That is well; now you may take the broth up to Juan."

He had poured it into a horn mug.

"Should he not have a piece of bread with it, Father?" I inquired.

Father Pierre smiled at me very kindly.

"I can see that you will make a fine, thoughtful father of a family someday, Felix, *mon brave*. But no; after strangulation it is best that no solid food pass through the gullet for two days, or even three. There will be great bruising and inflammation, inside as well as outside. Soup, milk, and wine are all he should take."

I carried the mugful upstairs, tapped, called, and passed it through the crack of the door, which was opened just wide enough to receive it. How long would this last, I wondered? How long before Juan trusted us sufficiently to come out? And then I wondered how I myself would feel if, not much more than one hour before, I had been hung up by enemies and left to die.

"There is milk and wine after the soup, if you wish," I called, and went back to help Father Pierre chop his herbs. Then the bell rang for Sext, and we had to leave the infirmary.

"Suppose Juan grows frightened and tries to run away?" I asked.

"I will lock the door below, so that no one can get in. Tell him this, and that we shall return after None. But he may well be asleep already."

I went up and called the information through the door, but received no reply. Father Pierre chuckled, on hearing this.

"I put a little poppy juice into the broth; he will sleep sound as a squirrel for many hours. Sleep is his greatest need."

Sure enough, when we returned later, the patient was still in a deep slumber. Soft, even breathing could be heard, and, through the crack in the door, nothing of him showed but a tuft of dark hair on the pillow. He slept on, and this was lucky for him, as Father Vespasian sent for Father Pierre and expressed his intention to visit the boy as soon as he was awake and sensible. For, the Abbot said, the healing power in his hands would probably be more beneficial than Father Pierre's medicines.

Father Pierre promised to send word as soon as the boy awoke.

Meanwhile, after Compline, he told me that I had better make myself up a pallet outside that closed door, in case Juan should rouse in the night and be frightened.

"He has taken food and clothes from you; he trusts you so far; you had best be the one nearest to him. I will be downstairs, and you can call me at need. I excuse you from Night Office and Lauds."

This was lucky, as it proved, for Juan did wake while the monks were all in the chapel at their night orisons. I heard a most pitiful sobbing from the small room, which woke me from my shallow slumber. Trying the door, I found that it would not budge, so called, "Juan! Juan! It is Felix! What ails you? Can I fetch you a hot drink, or more covers?"

I heard a sniffing and gulping inside the door, then a hesitant whisper:

"F-Felix?"

"Yes?"

"May I have a hot drink? My throat is *so* sore."

Father Pierre had left a posset, ready to be heated, which I brought up, with some goose grease, which he had told me would be good to rub on the outside of the painful neck. I offered to come in and do this. To my great surprise, after long hesitation, my offer was accepted, and the door pulled back just enough to let me through; then closed again.

Father Pierre had left a rush candle in the room, which Juan had managed to find and light. By its dim flicker I could see that his appearance was somewhat better, in that he wore the clean clothes and his hair was shorter and less matted. But the big frightened eyes were still hollow and sunken in their sockets, the cheeks haggard and drawn.

"Get back into bed," I said, "and sip the posset, then I will rub your neck with this."

So he scrambled back under the covers before drinking the hot milk. I wondered if Father Pierre had put anything in that, but if he had, it did not have the effect of sending Juan back to sleep; instead he became wider awake and more anxious.

"I must not stay more than one night in this place!" he whispered. "They will guess that I have been taken here, and they will be after me."

"Who are they?" I asked, though it was not hard to guess.

"The Mala Gente," he said, shivering. He used the French term, Mauvais Gens, for he was speaking in French, but I understood what he meant.

"It was they hanged you up?"

"Who else?"

"But *why*? You are only a boy. What harm could you possibly do them?"

He cast me a quick, doubtful look under his lashes—they were long, thick, and bristly—then said, "I know their names, you see. I know who they are. That is the harm I could do. I could tell the gendarmes."

"Ah, yes, I see."

"They had me with them for three months," he muttered. "At first it was their plan to make me into a thief, or a beggar; they would teach me to maund and patter and feign illness. As I would not obey them, they gave me no food."

Talking made him cough, and I said, "Hush! You should not try to talk too much. Drink the milk."

He took a sip, then said, "No, but you saved me, did you not? You gave me back my life. I owe you at least to tell you why they were trying to take it." He drank a little more milk, then whispered angrily, "It was my brother who hired them to carry me off."

"Your *brother*?" I was astonished, and wondered if, perhaps, he was feverish. "How can that be? Your own brother?"

A queer, satirical expression flitted over his thin face.

"Hah! You perhaps have no brother? So you believe that all brothers love each other?" A derisive sniff. "It is not always so, believe me. Mine hates me. He is my half-brother, ten years older than I. When his mother died my father married a younger wife, my mother. She was Spanish, Esteban's mother was French. He has always been jealous, always—though indeed, Maman was always kind to him. So, after she and Papa were killed in the avalanche last winter—"

He coughed again, drank again.

"They had been on a visit to Uncle León in Spain, Maman's brother. And as they were coming back over the Pass of Ibañeta, the avalanche sent their carriage off the road, down a crevasse. Esteban became head of the house, *etcheko jaun*. He is twenty-three. He made no secret of his hatred, his wish to get rid of me. Only when he took the notion—"

Juan stopped short, biting his lip.

"There is no need for you to tell me all this," I said, deeply troubled by the thought of such hate between brothers. If I had a brother, I thought, how dearly would I have loved him! Or even a sister. I had always been so lonely. But Juan had begun to whisper again, as if he desperately needed the relief of unburdening himself.

"My Uncle León in Spain wrote then, to say he intended making me his heir, since he himself has no children now. He lives in Pamplona, you see, and his wife and children were killed nine years ago by French gunfire in the siege; he has never married again."

"And his sister married a Frenchman?" I said, in surprise.

"Oh, we are all Basques," Juan said quickly. "Papa did not consider himself French; nor does my brother Esteban."

This explained his accent, which was not like the French I had been taught by my tutor, though he spoke clearly enough.

"So then what happened?" Despite my feeling that he ought to rest, I was becoming interested in his tale.

"Then I was carried off by the Mala Gente; and Esteban wrote a letter to my Uncle León telling him that they were demanding money for my return. Many thousands of francs."

"But—how could *you* know this?"

"Because I heard the Gente talking about it. 'He has written to the rich uncle in Spain,' they said. 'The rich uncle will send money soon. He will take half and give us half.' Esteban paid them to abduct me, I am sure of that."

"How can you be?"

"They had a box of my brother's—a little brass box in which he used to keep money—and some jewels of my mother's."

"But they might have stolen those? When they seized you? Or your brother paid them as ransom?"

"Oh, you don't *want* to believe me!" angrily hissed Juan. He gave a kind of gulping sob, and I exclaimed:

"No, no, that is not true! Why should I disbelieve you? I saw you dangling like a corpse in the thicket." And not once, but twice, I thought; it would be a long, long time, however, before I told Juan that. If at all.

"Listen," he whispered more calmly. "*This* is why I know my brother Esteban is my enemy. His old nurse, Anniq—who was mine, too, but she always hated me and called me the Little Interloper—she came to the cave one night."

"They kept you in a cave? Wait, now, while I rub your neck."

Taking the empty cup, I knelt by him on the floor and began massaging his neck with my fingers, rubbing in the goose grease.

"It stinks!" said he pettishly.

"Never mind that. It will heal your skin and soothe your neck muscles, Father Pierre says."

"Yes, the thieves had a cave in the foothills, five or six hours' ride from our home, which was near Guéthary. I suppose I shall never go back home again," he whispered, half to himself.

"Your nurse came to the cave? With your ransom money?"

"No, no, no! I tell you, she always detested me. She came to tell them that Uncle León would send no money."

"He would not help you?"

"I do not believe that." But Juan sounded troubled. "Simply, I believe he did not answer the letter. Very likely he thought it some trick of Esteban's, whom he never trusted."

"You heard your nurse tell the robbers this?"

"Ha!" Juan gave a sniff of triumph. "They thought I was asleep. They smoke a stuff called kef, in little pipes. It is made from hemp leaves. They gave me some, thinking it would put me to sleep. But I only pretended to smoke, and I pretended to fall asleep. I heard Anniq's voice—and I almost called out, I thought she had come to help me. But I heard her tell them, 'The uncle does not answer. My master says you had best put an end to the business. There is no sense in keeping the child alive any longer, a danger to us all.'"

"The monster!"

"Oh, my brother Esteban is quite a villain," whispered Juan matter-of-factly. "Which is odd, because Papa, though stern, was an upright man. But Esteban thinks of nothing save money. If I had—" Juan paused, then added, "I daresay he now believes that Uncle León's fortune will come to him." Another satirical sniff.

"Your own nurse betrayed you?"

What a terrible life this poor boy has had, I thought. Surrounded by enemies! He would hardly dare set his foot on the ground, lest it prove quicksand and give way under his tread.

"Anniq's nephew, Jeannot Plumet, you see, was in the galleys at Toulon."

"The galleys?"

"The prison. He had killed a farmer in a drunken rage. He is a kind of wild idiot. Then he escaped from the *bagne*. He was one of the brigands. That was why Anniq would help them."

"I see. You had better tell all this to the gendarmes."

"*No!* The gendarmes would never catch them. They have a hundred hiding places. And they—the Gente—would certainly kill me in revenge. Even here"—he looked fearfully round the tiny shadowed room—"even here I am not safe. I must go to Spain, to my Uncle León. He will take me in, for love of my mother."

"Spain!" A light seemed to shine through my understanding. *That* was why God had seen fit to direct me into the path of this boy. I was to take him into Spain with me. For I could see that, weak, half starved, beset as he was, he would never be able to manage the journey on his own. "Where did you say your uncle lives?"

Oh, if only it were in Galicia!

But he answered, "In Pamplona, in Navarre. Uncle León is a wine merchant. As my father was, too. But how am I to get there? Tomorrow I must leave this place. Somehow I must find or steal a horse or a mule—"

"*You?* You are hardly fit to ride a donkey at present! How could you cross the mountains?"

He fired up. "How dare you say that? I can ride, and very well, too!"

"Gently, gently! I am sure you ride as well as any caballero. All I meant was that at present you are sick, and weak; only a few hours escaped from death. Listen, Juan: Be patient. I also wish to travel to Spain. I was on my way to my home in Galicia when the ship on which I took passage from England was wrecked in the bay here—"

"When?" he said sharply. "There has been no storm."

"I will tell all that another time. Only be patient for a few days, till you are stronger; and then I will accompany you into Spain and see you safe to your uncle's house."

It was with no particular enthusiasm, I must confess, that I made the offer. Pamplona, on the south slopes of the Pyrenees, would be a long way off my own intended course, and I also suspected that Juan would make a delicate, peevish, trying companion for a dangerous journey.

But I could see clearly that this was what God had in mind for me to do, and I was confirmed in this by an approving nod from Him, which I felt inside me. Good boy, Felix. That is your way. Follow along it.

Juan, however, was by no means so certain of me, or even particularly grateful. He bestowed on me a long, doubtful, wary, narrow stare, from between those thick, bristly lashes, then whispered, "*You* will accompany me into Spain? How do I know that I can trust *you*? And what use would you be in danger? You are probably younger than I. And why should you make me such an offer?"

I heard the bell ring for Prime, and saw that a faint light was beginning to creep round the edges of the windows.

"Never mind all that now! Father Pierre will scold me for letting you talk when you should be asleep, resting and mending your hurts. But remember what I said and think it over. It is a firm offer. Also—listen! This is important! The Abbot of this place—Father Vespasian—have you heard of him?"

"He can heal sickness, I have heard."

"That may be! But he is a strange man. Do not trust him!"

"Why?" The great eyes flew open again in alarm. "Is he one of *them*? The Gente?"

"No—no. Nothing like that. But worse, perhaps. He is—I think—bad. I think he has given himself to some wicked power. He will probably ask you questions. He may come and offer to heal you. Perhaps he can do so. But be very wary of him. That is all I can say. If he cannot heal you—perhaps you should try to pretend that he has done so. If disobeyed, or disregarded, he can turn savage—"

"Oh!" whispered Juan in a weeping tone, sounding, all at once, childish and piteous. "Is there *no one* I can trust save my Uncle León?"

"Of course there are trustworthy people! Father Pierre, who looks after you here, and Father Antoine, who helped me bring you in, are both good as bread. And," I said, "you can trust me. Now: Do you want to bar the door again after me?"

"Yes." After a moment Juan added reluctantly, "I thank you for rubbing my neck. It feels a little better. And for your offer. I will give it my consideration," he said with dignity.

"*Bueno.*" I picked up the cup and the little grease pot, and left the chamber. As I lay down again on my pallet I heard the patter of bare feet on the floor and the scrape of the stool pushed against the door.

To my shame I slept late the following day, waking only when I heard the bell for High Mass. I ran to the chapel with conscience-stricken haste and knelt down by the side of Father Pierre. But he greeted me with a benign smile, as if I had done nothing wrong, and after, as we walked to the infirmary, told me that the patient still slept profoundly, as could be seen through a slit in the door.

"You talked with him in the night, my son?"

"Yes, Father, I did, a little; he told me that he was afraid to stay here because—" I did not wish to speak of the Mala Gente, for that was Juan's secret, so I simply said, "because of the people who wish him harm. He feels sure they know he has been brought here."

Father Pierre frowned. "But *here* he should be safe enough. In a holy abbey!"

"He is not so confident of that, my father. He wishes to go to Spain, where his uncle will receive him."

"He has no family in France?"

"Only a brother, who—who dislikes him." Here, too, I forbore to mention Juan's assertion that his brother had been the one to arrange for his abduction and murder. Did I, then, not believe his story? No, after careful thought, I had concluded that he was very likely telling the truth. Such things did happen. But Juan had unburdened himself to me at dead of night when the tongue is free and unguarded; if, by daylight, he wished to reconsider his tale, I would not stand in his way. I went on quickly, "My father, I told him that I would be willing to accompany him into Spain, as soon as he likes, if that is what he wishes."

Father Pierre gave a gasp.

"You, my boy? But the way into Spain is long and dangerous, over a great rampart of mountains! He is little more than a child, and frail, and only just rescued from death. And you yourself in not much better case—"

"I am well enough, Father, and rested enough. And I believe that it was for this purpose that God left me here."

At this Father Pierre stopped walking—we were in the passageway between the kitchen and the infirmary, where we could not be seen—and gave me a long, intent, thoughtful scrutiny. At length he said, "My heart tells me that you are right, Felix. But, saints aid us, child, what problems lie ahead of you! I must think carefully about this—you must give me time to reflect."

"Of course, Father."

He passed a hand over his head. "In the meantime—run to Father Mathieu and ask him for chives and lettuce and chicory to make a soothing and sustaining broth for the patient. And on your way, call in on Father Antoine—you will find him at work in the scriptorium—and ask him if he will be so good as to come to me for a moment or two."

Father Antoine was at work on a beautiful illuminated manuscript, a copy of the Psalms. Each capital letter took him a day's work; they were colored in green, blue, red, and gold; he had only reached Psalm 23 and the task might last him the rest of his life. But he arose without a grumble at my message and departed in the direction of the infirmary.

Aged Father Mathieu, in the kitchen garden, was not quite so accommodating.

"Father Pierre might have considered *me* before snatching away my helper," he mumbled. "Here we are, halfway through sowing the second crop of peas, and I am left all on my own with no one to mark the rows and rake them over and hang up the bird scarers—and *he* will be the first to complain if there is no pea soup for his patients in July."

"Well, I will help you, Father, it will take only twenty minutes and I don't think Father Pierre is in a hurry for his chives and lettuce."

In fact I had a shrewd idea that Father Pierre wished me out of the way while he conferred with Father Antoine. That both wished me well, I felt certain; perhaps, left together, they might agree to my quitting the Abbey with Juan, quietly, as soon as Father Pierre thought his patient sufficiently recovered.

On my way back toward the infirmary I chanced to go near the great gate of the Abbey and became aware of three strangers, sick people, or petitioners, I supposed, who had come in and were making inquiries of the novice Alaric, who happened to be passing.

On looking at them again I thought that two of them did not seem like sick people, though they were strange enough in their appearance: one a tall gaunt fellow with a shock of white hair and a black patch over his eye, one a dwarf—or rather a midget, for he was all in proportion, not huge-headed as many dwarfs are, but not much over three foot high. The third of the group must have been the invalid: His head was entirely swathed in rags, and the rest of him covered with terrible sores, red and mustard-yellow and weeping; he hobbled on two crutches and seemed not to have the use of his legs.

As I passed I heard one of them ask Alaric: "Was a young, hurt lad brought in here yesterday, a boy called Juan Esparza?"

"No, friend, not that I heard of," said poor Alaric, who had been in trouble again and performing his penance when Juan was carried in. "Did you wish to see the Abbot?" he added, looking at the terrible sores on the cripple. "His time for seeing sick people is on Fridays, after the service of Sext. But they will give you accommodation in the guesthouse if you wish to stay here till then."

The three conferred quietly, then thanked Alaric but said they would return to the village and come back again on Friday.

I went on my way deeply troubled. It seemed that Juan had spoken no more than the truth, and that his pursuers were hard on his heels.

At the infirmary I found more cause for alarm. Father Vespasian, it seemed, had come to inspect the sick boy for himself. I found Father Antoine and Father Pierre below in the surgery, looking nervous and apprehensive.

"You cannot go up," Father Pierre told me. "Our Abbot himself is honoring the patient by a visit. Wait here quietly; you can strip the leaves of that rosemary off the stalks."

Choosing to pretend that I had not understood the first part of his order, I carried the basketful of rosemary branches upstairs to a point from which I could hear the voices beyond Juan's half-open sick-room door.

"*Naturally* you can trust me, boy," the Abbot was saying impatiently. "Lie still, let me lay my hands on your neck, and in a couple of moments you will be healed."

"I thank you, sir"—that was Juan's voice, cautious, wary, and still very faint—"but I am better already, thanks to Felix and Father Pierre. I do not require any more healing than what *le bon Dieu,* through their help, has supplied."

I was quite startled at the cool assurance with which Juan thus defied the Abbot. Not such a poor helpless ragamuffin as he had seemed! But Father Vespasian answered him sharply.

"Do not be impertinent, lad! It is not for you to accept or decline my offer! Sit up in bed, so that I can look at you properly! I insist on inspecting your hurt neck."

There followed a slight mew of sound from Juan, as if Father Vespasian had briskly tugged back the blankets; then the Abbot demanded: "Who did this to you? Who intended to kill you? Answer me!"

"Oh, how can *I* tell?" whimpered Juan. "How do *I* know who they were? They were very wicked men— that is all I can tell!"

"What is your name?" demanded the Abbot. "Where is your family? Who is your father? Where do you come from? Speak up, boy! *Answer,* when I ask you! Look me in the eye!"

Father Vespasian's voice was rising ever shriller and sharper; with terror I imagined how his eyes might be glowing red and his movements becoming more uncontrolled.

But again Juan surprised me.

"My name is Benedictus!" he whispered softly. "Benedictus, the bell ringer. Oh! how I love to ring the bells when M. le Curé gives me the order! Tin-tan, din-dan, bim-bam, bom, bo! And the voices of the bells fly away through the valleys, warning the villagers that thunder is on the way and prudent men must take cover. Tin-tan, din-dan, bim-bam, bom, bo!"

There followed a longish silence; I could not imagine what was happening; then Father Vespasian's voice, angry, but at least under control, said, "What foolishness is this? You talk like a simpleton. Come, answer my questions!"

"I *am* a simpleton," whispered Juan. "My sufferings have turned my wits. Oh, hé, hé, hé, what a poor boy am I. Tin-tan, din-dan, bim-bam. Do not come too near me; the lightning seared me and I might pass right through you like a sword."

"Be silent, boy! I am going to lay my hand on your head."

"No, no!" shouted Juan—if one can shout in a whisper, he did so. "Do not touch me! Felix! Felix! I want Felix! I will have no one near me but Felix!"

Deciding that the time had come for me to take a hand, I summoned all my courage and walked into the room, extending a bunch of rosemary in my hand.

Bowing politely to Father Vespasian, I said, "Here, Juan, Father Pierre said that you were to hold this rosemary and keep sniffing it. The fragrance will help to clear your nose and throat—"

Father Vespasian said, "How *dare* you come into this room when I am here!"

He was very pale, I noticed, and sweat ran in droplets on his skull-shaped forehead.

To my huge relief Father Pierre had pattered up the stair and at this moment followed me into the sickroom, murmuring, "I think it is time, now, for the patient to rest, Father Vespasian."

The little room seemed very crowded with the four of us in there, and Juan burst into a sudden fit of loud childish sobs and huddled himself under the covers of his bed, whining out, "Go away! Go away, every one of you! I do not want you, I want no one at all."

Father Vespasian swung on his heel and left the room, summoning me, with his glaring eye, to follow him.

And when he was downstairs: "Has that young vagabond confided in *you*?" he inquired of me fiercely.

Conscious of the frightened gaze of Father Pierre and Father Antoine, as they awaited my reply, I stammered out: "No—no, Father Abbot. Well, yes—a little. But no—n-not in any particular—"

"How did you come to know that he would be suspended in that thicket?"

"I heard his voice—"

"From halfway down the beach? Do not lie to me, boy! Father Antoine heard nothing. How could you hear him from such a distance? What did he tell you about himself? *What is the connection between you?*"

"There is no connection between us," I said. "Except that I found him and I am sorry for him. And he told me nothing that I am at liberty to pass on."

"If you will not tell me, you must be beaten!"

Father Pierre made a slight gesture of protest, but I felt quite calm.

"Beating will not make me tell what I have no right to reveal."

"We shall see!"

Father Vespasian was as good as his word. After Sext next day two of the strongest monks, Father Hilaire and Father Sigurd, disrobed me and ceremonially scourged me three times round the disused cloister, while Father Domitian read out a Penitential Psalm and Father Vespasian watched. Those brawny monks fairly laid on, too!

Father Hilaire quietly informed me, between blows, that he took no pleasure in what he did, but was obliged to obey the orders of his Abbot; Father Sigurd made no such attempt to vindicate himself, but simply thwacked away at me with a tarred rope's end, as if he thoroughly enjoyed the task.

Afterward—when I was reeling and half dizzy from pain—Father Vespasian said to me, "Have you changed your mind?"

"No!" I gasped.

"Well, you can tell your friend in the sickroom that the same treatment awaits him, as soon as he rises from his bed, unless he sees fit to mend his ways and answer my questions. Now you had best go to the chapel and ask God to cleanse your mind of rebellious thoughts." And he walked off toward his lodge.

But Father Domitian led me back to the infirmary, where Father Pierre, in silence but with a red face of indignation and tightly closed mouth, put first cold, then hot, compresses on my back until the agony was somewhat dulled, and then gave me a drink that sent me off to sleep for twelve hours.

3

The Gente; the causeway; I go to seek old Pierre; and have doubts of him; Juan and I fall out over poetry; and go to the grotto, where we are caught in a storm.

The novice Alaric woke me.

"Lie still," he ordered. "I am going to rub you with this oil of crushed wheat which Father Pierre has sent for you. Father Vespasian commanded that if you did not present yourself at Prime you were to be beaten again."

"Ugh," I croaked, shifting with difficulty on the hard pallet. "What o'clock is it? How soon is Prime?"

"Not for another ten minutes. Turn over now, while I rub your back. *I* should know how much this oil will help you; I am beaten often enough," he said cheerfully. "And Father Pierre always finds time to rub me afterward. But now he is looking after the boy you rescued."

The rubbing did indeed loosen stiff muscles and ease my sore back and thighs. I expressed my gratitude to Alaric for his rising earlier than he need have done in order to come and tend me. But he told me that he always rose early, for it was his task to ring the bell that summoned the fathers from their beds.

"Father Antoine is doing that for me today," he explained.

Then I perceived, under the orderly surface of obedience in this place, a quiet network, the purpose of which was to protect, so far as possible, the victims of Father Vespasian's injustices.

"Thank you, Alaric; I will do very well now," I told him, and rolled off the pallet. Despite my words I could not avoid letting out a hiss of agony as I came upright. But walking soon improved matters, and in Chapel I took some pains to hold myself upright and easy, as if I were in the best of health and quite untroubled. Father Vespasian's cold green eye dwelt on me several times, but he did not send for me, and after High Mass I repaired as usual to the infirmary, where Father Pierre told me that the patient was improving steadily and had swallowed warm milk thickened with a little maize meal.

"He has been asking for you. I did not tell him that you had been beaten," the infirmarian warned me. "Such tidings would only distress him, in his low state."

I could see the wisdom of this, but it was annoying to be greeted by Juan with fretful reproaches. "Where have you been for so long? I would sooner have had you than that ugly old father."

"Father Pierre is very kind, and knows far more than I do about caring for sick people," I said, beginning to rub his swollen throat with goose grease.

"I don't care! He is ugly and red-faced and smells of garlic."

Juan himself, I noticed, had either consented to Father Pierre's washing him, or had found strength to manage his own ablutions. A basin of soapy water stood on the floor by the bed, with a towel. His skin shone, and he smelled clean, like a young kitten. All the tarry tangles had been removed from his hair, by the simple expedient of cutting it very short, so that it hung over his forehead and round his head in a thick fringe, barely touching his ears and dipping to the back of his neck. Still damp from washing, it appeared now as a very dark brown color with, here and there, the same coppery tint that showed in his eyes. He had a pale pointed face, still bruised looking from fatigue and starvation; but a touch of more natural color was creeping back into his cheeks.

I carried away the basin of washing water and, when I returned, congratulated him on the manner in which he had evaded Father Vespasian's questioning by pretending to be simple and saying that he was a *benedictus.*

"What in the world put such a notion into your head?"

"Oh," he said, "there are such people in Béarn; every village has one. Only," he added, "they are mostly old women, so they are called *benedicta.* They ring the church bell to keep away devils and warn of storms. Sometimes they are thought to be witches. Good ones, of course.

"But now pay attention, Felix," he went on, in quite a brisk, peremptory manner, although he was still obliged to talk in a whisper. Father Pierre had told me that this condition might continue for a week or two, since the throat muscles had been so badly stretched and abused. "I have considered carefully your offer to accompany me into Spain," he told me, "and I accept it. Father Pierre has given me your history, and I believe that you have no connection with the ones who abducted me, and that you would have no wish to harm me. Father Pierre says that you traveled to England and back." He gave me a dubious look, as if wishing, nonetheless, that I showed a few more signs of worthiness to be his travel companion. I could not help smiling a little, inside myself, at his condescension, but replied staidly that I would do my best to justify his confidence.

"I know this country better than you," he asserted.

"That is certainly so. I do not know it at all."

"So *I* had best choose our way over the mountains. Since we have no passports, and the Gente will be on my trail, we must go secretly."

"We must, indeed."

First, I thought, we have to get ourselves out of the Abbey; but for that, my friend, we had better wait until you are in somewhat better case.

"I have been giving some thought to our route," he continued, "and I have decided that our best course will be to consult an old gardener who used, when he was younger, to work for my father. Pierre has had many dealings with the smugglers who bring sheep and wine in from Spain. He told me once there was a cave they used for their trips, with entrances in both France and Spain. It is on the mountain called La Rhune, where the witches used to congregate. When I am better we will go to see old Pierre, and he can guide us to this cave."

"Are you quite sure you can trust him?" I asked, with a grain of doubt. "After all, your own nurse, you say, betrayed you—and this man has had dealings with smugglers. Are you certain that he is reliable?"

Juan gave me a haughty look.

"If I say he is honest, you have no need to question it!"

"Very well," I replied, but inwardly resolved to ask Father Antoine if he could provide me with a map of the mountains, in case there proved to be any difficulty about Juan's plan. Old Pierre might, after all, have died, or moved away.

Then I told Juan about the three petitioners who had come to the Abbey—the midget, the tall white-headed man, and the cripple with terrible sores. Immediately all his confidence left him. He turned white as whey and began to shake.

"*Oh, mon Dieu!* They are the ones—the three leaders of the troop! They are after me already, then! The midget is Gueule, the big one Cocher, and the cripple Plumet. Of course he is not really crippled. His sores are made with mustard and saffron and spearwort and ratsbane. And he pricks his nostrils to make them bleed, and chews a bit of soap to simulate foaming at the mouth. But what shall I do, where can I hide, if they are seeking for me here?"

"They do not yet know for sure that you are here," I said, and explained about Alaric's denial. "He believed what he said, so that may throw them off the scent."

"Oh, they are certain to catch me in the end!" Juan buried his face in his hands, apparently giving way to complete despair. "While I was with them I told them that tale that I was a *benedictus*, a kind of warlock, that if they did me any harm I could put a curse on them. And they half believed it, they were a little afraid of me. They are French, you see, they are not Eskualdunak."

"Eskualdunak?"

"Basque," he said impatiently. "But now, you see, they will know that my story was not true; for they hanged me, and no harm has come to them."

"Still, you did not die," I pointed out. "So they may believe that is due to your magic powers." And there may be more truth in that than you know of, I thought but did not say.

Juan's face brightened at my words. His spirits seemed very elastic—they soared or fell at a trifle.

"I used to say a little poem in Euskar—in the Basque language," he boasted. "I told them it was a witch poem made up by my great-great-grandmother. She was a real witch, Marie Dindart, she was burned in the great witch-burning at Sare, two hundred years ago."

"Your great-great-grandmother?"

"Well, perhaps great-great-great." He dismissed that as of no importance. "She was my ancestress. At all events the troop hated the poem. They used to cross themselves when I said it and huddle at the other end of the cave."

"How does it go?"

> *Enune desiratzen*
> *Bizitze hoberic*
> *Mundian ez ahalda*
> *Ni bezain iruric.*"

"What does that mean?"

"Oh, it is nothing—a shepherds' song. 'I ask for nothing/Better in life/I don't suppose in the whole world/There's a happier man than I.' But I used to recite it in *such* a way—squinting my eyes together over my nose, and turning up the corners of my mouth to make two great dimples"—he demonstrated, looking very wild, placing his thumbs in his cheeks and waving his fingers—"that it really terrified them."

I began to see that there was more in Juan than just a scrawny, frightened boy.

AFTER Sext I managed to slip to the side of Father Antoine and asked if, anywhere in the Abbey, there might be a map of this region, and the mountains to the south. He looked at me thoughtfully, then gave a slight nod.

I told him, too, about the three beggars, and Juan's fear of them.

"They said they intended to come back today, so that the cripple might be healed. What can I do? Suppose they ask Father Vespasian about Juan? Suppose they say he is their boy?"

I felt certain that Father Vespasian was not open to advice or persuasion. It would be no use at all asking him not to reveal Juan's presence in the Abbey.

"If they are really the ones who hanged that poor boy," Father Antoine said in a troubled tone, "we ought to send for the gendarmes and have them apprehended. But since they are petitioners at the Abbey, I feel sure that Father Vespasian would not permit that."

"There they are now," I said.

The three had stationed themselves just inside the great gate of the Abbey. They huddled, with heads bowed, in positions of humble respect, but I noticed their eyes darted in every direction, watching the monks who came and went, studying the different doors and windows, to see who passed through or looked out, observing the walls themselves, as if measuring which would be the easiest to climb. That is to say, the midget and the thin white-headed fellow looked shrewdly about; the third man, as before, had his head bound up in bandages, and the sores upon his arms, and on his stumps of legs, were even more horrible in appearance than they had been on the previous day.

"Juan does not wish to tell the gendarmes about them," I muttered to Father Antoine. "He says the rest of the troop would be certain to take revenge on him if he did so."

"Well, I will have to think about what can be done." Father Antoine sighed anxiously. "Father Vespasian is looking this way. Do you go and stand by Father Pierre."

THE healing ceremony proceeded as it had on former occasions: The humpbacked cripple with the hideous sores was brought up in front of Father Vespasian, who solemnly blessed and prayed over him and sprinkled him with holy water. During which process the sick man appeared to go through a fearful paroxysm— even though Juan had told me it was all a pretense, I found myself almost taken in, so naturally did he foam at the mouth and bleed at the nostrils, while his eyes rolled horribly, right up inside his head, until only the whites showed.

There were no other patients that day, so we all sang a hymn while the healing was supposed to be taking effect.

Under the towel that Father Vespasian had flung over him, I noticed that the cripple was skillfully and surreptitiously undoing some buckle behind his back, and contriving to rub his skin with the napkin. And so, when the hymn was done, he was able to arise with loud shouts of pretended astonishment and joy; his legs and feet, which had in some cunning fashion been buckled up behind his back, dropped down to support him, the hump disappeared from between his shoulders, and a swift scrub with the napkin had removed most of the foam, blood, and mustard from his face and arms. He stood up straight: a tall and strikingly strong-featured man with long thick black curls, broad forehead, and black shaggy brows. He was dressed all in black sheepskin.

"A miracle! A miracle! By your holy power I am brought back to health and strength!" he bawled, falling on his knees and clasping the Abbot's ankles while he slobbered kisses on his feet. "Oh, my lord Abbot, is not this the most wonderful cure you have ever achieved?"

The other two beggars followed their friend's example and clustered round Father Vespasian, who looked highly gratified, and smiled on them graciously.

Oh, heavens above! I thought. Now they are certain to ask the Abbot about Juan, they will pretend that he is their lost nephew or something of the kind, and he will tell them all they want to know—

But at that moment the Abbey bell, up in the tower, began to peal a wild tocsin, or alarm call. This had not happened during my stay there—or not while I was in my right mind, at least—but I knew that such a peal was the signal for all the monks to leave what they were doing, and run down to the beach, to aid a ship in trouble.

So, on this occasion, a score of black-clad forms went scampering through the gate and down the track. Father Vespasian followed them. I noticed that he clapped his hands over his ears, and seemed distressed by the sound of the bell, which somewhat puzzled me. He seemed to go rather to get away from the sound than for any other purpose. Nobody paused to ask who had rung the alarm; the day was a dull and misty one, and in such weather shipwrecks often do occur.

I did not stop to see if the beggars had gone with the monks; my own purpose was elsewhere. I ran to the infirmary, took the stairs three at a time, and knocked on Juan's door.

"Who is it?" came his frightened voice.

"It is I, Felix. Quick, there is no time to lose; you must leave your room and follow me. The men who abducted you are in the Abbey, and they may come looking for you here."

Half lifting, half carrying him, I had him down the stairs in no more time than it takes to tell, and opened the door from the surgery that led out into the monks' pelota ground, locking it again behind us.

Juan shivered, looking about the open space in dismay.

"Here is no hiding place!"

"We do not need one," said I. "They cannot get out through the door. I have brought the key. We will sit here on the step and listen."

Sure enough, about five minutes later, we heard low voices beyond the door, in the surgery, and steps on the stair.

"The brat was here for sure," muttered a voice. "These are their sick quarters."

The voice spoke a mixture of French and thieves' cant which I could only just understand.

"That's Gueule," whispered Juan. "He says *icigo* for *here*."

"The little devil's gone now, anyway," said another voice. "The bird's flown."

Somebody rattled the door. Juan trembled and clutched me.

"That only leads to the cliff. No use, it's locked, anyway. *Maladetta,* I can hear all the fat monks coming back" (he used a very obscene word, which I omit), "we had best be away out of here."

The footsteps died away in the distance. Setting my eye to the keyhole I could just see the midget dart out through the surgery door and shut it behind him. Next moment I had Juan inside again and, picking him up bodily, ran up the stairs to place him back in his bed. There were signs that the room had been entered—the covers had been torn off the bed, and a jug of water overturned.

Juan looked ready to faint from fright, but I said cheerfully, "Don't you see, this is lucky for you. Now they will think that you have already left and gone elsewhere. They will cease to watch this place."

"I do not think they are so easily deceived," said Juan. "But," he added dejectedly, "I thank you for helping me. You were very quick." He sounded somewhat resentful, I thought, as if he wished it had not been my quickness that saved him from capture.

The members of the Community returned, greatly perplexed at the false alarm which had summoned them to the beach, and Father Vespasian in a high state of annoyance. Alaric the bell ringer would certainly have been liable for yet another beating, had not Father Domitian been able to assert that Alaric had stood by him all through the healing ceremony. Nobody was able to say by whom the bell had been rung. Only I had seen Father Antoine slip away through the cloister, and I said nothing.

After Vespers, Father Pierre called me aside. He was frowning, and looked deeply anxious.

"Father Vespasian has announced his intention of interrogating Juan publicly tomorrow," he said. "I represented to him, and also to the Prior, that the poor boy is still in no state to be questioned, but—but Father Vespasian merely replied that he was confident his touch would heal the boy and make him sensible enough to answer questions. And of course I could not argue with that."

No; not after the example of miraculous healing we had just been privileged to watch this very afternoon, I said to myself; but I kept silent.

"Father Antoine and I have consulted together about this," Father Pierre went on in a worried manner. "We both decided that the boy—that Juan—is quite unfit to be taxed with questions or—or to be punished, as he undoubtedly will be, if he displeases the Abbot again."

I thought about the beating I had received. An ordeal such as that, I was sure, would undo all the good of Father Pierre's care; might even kill the boy.

"It is not to be thought of," Father Pierre said earnestly. "We both agreed on that."

You did not say so when *I* was to be beaten, I thought, with a touch of indignation; and the voice of God sounded inside my head, clear as a hunting horn, with a kind of laughing impatience: Come, now, Felix! You are always demanding to be treated as a man, not as a boy. When you *are* accorded man's status, are you going to cry and whine, and say the usage is too hard?

I straightened up my aching shoulders and said to Father Pierre, "How do you plan to prevent this interrogation?"

"Tomorrow is the Feast of St. Gabas," he told me. "There will be a special celebratory Mass three hours after midnight, preceded by extra prayers and meditation in the chapel. The whole Community will be there. High tide this night is at three in the morning. . . ." He gave me a very straight look out of his little shrewd gray eyes. Father Sigurd passed near us at that moment, and Father Pierre, slightly raising his voice, added, "And Father Mathieu tells me that you have some experience in bricklaying and masonry. He asked me to show you a place in the garden wall which is crumbling and requires rebuilding; you are to carry stones and mortar there this afternoon, then repair it tomorrow between Mass and Sext."

"Certainly, Father."

"Come, and I will show you the place."

When we were out in the monks' pelota ground, a sudden impulse made me ask, "Father Pierre: Can *nothing* be done about the Abbot? It is so dreadful!"

"No, child; our Rule binds us. We must obey him. But never fear; *le bon Dieu* doubtless has some purpose behind it all, and will show us that, in His own good time."

"But has Father Vespasian always been—as he is?"

"Oh, no," replied Father Pierre. "He had a troubled history as a young man, before he entered; I myself knew him then. He loved a lady who would not have him—there were angers and grievances. But he was— no different from others then. Impatient, yes; but governed by reason. His—*change*—began seven years ago when a man was brought to the Abbey suffering from snoring."

"From *snoring*?"

"He snored by day as well as by night; awake as well as asleep. Oh, it was a dreadful sound! Blood streamed from his eyes, and a terrible hissing speech from his mouth. This," explained Father Pierre, "was before Father Vespasian had come to his full, present power of healing, but already he had achieved some remarkable cures. He laid his hands on the snoring man— who in that very minute lost his symptoms and rose up as normal as you or I. But, at the same instant, Father Vespasian dropped down in a dead swoon and lay so for thirty-six hours. Ever since that day . . ." His voice trailed off, his eyes looked down, absently, frowningly, over the wide bay, for we stood at the highest corner of the kitchen garden. Then he shook himself, sighed, and added, "As I said, God will certainly display His purpose when He sees fit. Now, here is the corner of the wall which needs mending. You see?"

"Yes, my father."

"You will fetch building materials immediately from the pile by the porter's lodge, and bring them here, as much as you think sufficient." And he hurried away, his black robe flapping.

I spent the next hour following his instructions.

On my way to None, later, Father Antoine intercepted me.

"Ahem! Have you managed to finish the task that Father Pierre showed you, Felix?"

"Yes, Father."

"You are a good boy. Now, come into the scriptorium a moment, I wish you to lift down some heavy volumes for me."

At his bidding I climbed up a ladder to a high shelf and fetched down several massive book-boxes, which I placed on a table for him. Close to where I had laid them I noticed a map, unrolled on the table, with weights holding it open.

Casually Father Antoine indicated it.

"See, here is our Abbey and the shoreline. There is Bayonne; here, St. Jean de Luz. These are the passes over the mountains. That village there, Hasparren, that is where I come from. My widowed sister, Madame Mauleon, still lives there; she is a good, kind woman, always ready to help those in distress . . ."

"Any sister of yours, Father, would be that, I am sure."

"Bless me, there is the bell for None! I must hurry off and have a word with the Prior. Close the door behind you, my boy, when you have taken down that last box."

"Certainly, Father Antoine."

When I quitted the scriptorium, it was with the map tightly rolled up under my belt. And, though I shut the door, I left one of the windows unlatched.

AT THE close of None I observed Father Vespasian speaking to Father Pierre; his look was stern, his gestures vigorous, and he glanced once or twice, briefly, in my direction. This caused me some concern; did the Abbot propose further punishment for me?

It was not quite so bad as that, but inconvenient enough.

"Father Vespasian forbids you to sleep any longer in the infirmary building," Father Pierre told me sadly, when the Abbot had left him, striding away to his lodge. "You are to return to the novices' dorter. It seems that Father Vespasian does not—does not wish for any further association between you and Juan."

"I see, Father," I said, thinking fast. What a good thing I had left that window open! God must have been guiding me. "Well, I—I thank you for your many kindnesses, Father Pierre. And I am sorry to work for you no longer. I will go to Father Domitian now."

"You will remember what I told you to do? About mending the wall? You can manage the task? In the time?"

"Yes, I can manage very well, thank you, Father." And I smiled at him in a cheerful and serene manner, trying to convey that this new edict, though awkward, would not put a stop to my plans.

AT EIGHT o'clock I retired to bed with the rest of the novices, and, in the dark, thumped my head with my knuckles ten times, thus instructing myself to wake at ten o'clock. Prompt on the hour of ten I woke, to hear the clock strike. All about me slept, including Father Domitian. The windows all stood wide; I rolled my blanket, passed it about the central bar of the casement, slipped out, holding both ends of the blanket, and so slid and dropped to the ground, only ten feet below. The fall jarred my cuts and weals, which had stiffened again, but did me no other harm. Winding the blanket around me like a toga, I tiptoed over the dewy grass to the scriptorium, opened the window, climbed in, and came out with the ladder, which I carried on my shoulder across the cloister and round the frater to the infirmary. This was the longest part of the business, and I felt some anxiety, I must confess, lest anybody look out and see me. But the night was dim;

an orange-red new moon, low down in mist, gave little illumination.

Planting the ladder securely, I climbed up to Juan's window, and so in. He was wakeful, and, after the first gasp of terror, not greatly surprised to see me. I think Father Pierre must have conveyed some kind of warning; for when I said, "Juan: It is time for us to leave this place," he merely nodded, and rose from his bed to accompany me. I saw that he was fully dressed, in shirt, waistcoat, and trousers. His feet were bare; no shoes had been found small enough to fit him.

We stole down the stairs. On the pallet, in the surgery where Father Pierre slept, there was a note: "If anybody should want me, I am in the chapel, keeping vigil for St. Gabas." Devout Father Pierre! I felt under his pallet, found his keys, and opened the closet where my clothes hung.

Five minutes later we were outside, and hastening to the kitchen garden, where I had left a large pile of stones conveniently stacked against the outer wall. I wondered whether Juan would be strong enough to climb over, and offered, in a whisper, to lift him, but he indignantly declined my help and scrambled up nimbly enough; then waited for me. I followed him, climbed over, dropped—again jarring my bruises; the height was somewhat greater on the far side—and stood below to receive Juan's kicking legs as he lowered himself.

While stacking the stones at that spot on the previous afternoon I had carefully studied the hillside, and now led Juan quickly down a steep grassy track which wound over the headland in the direction of the causeway. There was no time to be lost; in a whisper I encouraged Juan to follow me as fast as he could. The sickle moon, previously veiled by mist, at this moment emerged and gave us more light to pick our way.

It also illuminated a sight that almost froze the marrow in my bones: Father Vespasian, in his cloak and hood, walking, as was his nighttime habit, back and forth, back and forth, over the bare shoulder of hill that lay beyond his lodge. At the moment when I set eyes on him, his back was turned three quarters from us, and he was walking away; then he wheeled and came in our direction. But he was twenty-five feet above us on the hillside, and we were screened from him, at present, by some bushes of broom. Our path, however, led directly under where he was pacing. If he looked in our direction at that point, I did not see how he could fail to spot us, though he could not come down to us, for there was a sheer rock face between our course and where his path lay.

I clutched Juan's arm and whispered, "Crouch down!" and pointed upward. I could feel Juan's start of terror; then he huddled against me, peering through the broom fronds.

When I was a child at Villaverde, I and the servants' children used sometimes to play a game called *"coger la abuela,"* "catch the grandmother." You all steal up behind one player, and try to touch him; if he looks round and catches you moving, you must pay a penalty. Our game with Father Vespasian was like that. The stretch of ground he was pacing was about nine or ten yards; while his back was toward us we slipped stealthily as far as we could along our way, judging the distance with care so that when he turned we would be able to take shelter behind a rock, bush, or overhang of ground; then, while he walked in our direction, we must remain frozen, motionless, like two coneys on the hillside. There was an angle of hill that we must pass which was full in his view; then, once round that, we would be out of sight again until we reached the beginning of the causeway. I could only pray that soon he would retire to the chapel to begin the celebration of St. Gabas. For the tide was coming in fast; already the flat beaches were covered, and the sands on either side of the causeway. If we did not cross within the next half hour, we must wait until the water was on the ebb again, three or four hours; by which time the monks would be assembled for Night Office and our absence almost certainly discovered. I thought with despair of the ladder which I had left leaning against the infirmary wall. Idiot! Why had I not at least thrown it down, so that it would not be so conspicuous? And barefoot Juan was shivering, although the night was not cold; poor frail creature, he was by no means ready for a night vigil on a wind-swept headland. I had offered him my shoes, but they were far too big.

"Here!" I whispered. "Put this round you." I had brought the blanket, with a notion that it would prove useful when we had placed a good distance between ourselves and the Abbey. Now I wrapped it round Juan like a shawl, folded cornerways. He accepted and huddled into it with a whispered word of thanks; but then, as cursed fortune would have it, during our next dart along the track, he tripped over a trailing corner of cloth and fell headlong, dislodging a stone the size of my head, which went bounding down the hillside in ever-increasing leaps, starting off a dozen others in its progress.

Father Vespasian did not catch the sound of the stones, for the waves below us made a soft continuous roar; but out of the corner of his eye, he must have seen a movement, and he whipped round, staring down sharply in our direction. Juan had almost rolled off the track, and I was dragging him back to safety.

Father Vespasian froze, like a hunting dog, for an instant; then he started off, moving at great speed in the direction that would take him down to the causeway. He would have to go through the gate first; I judged that we had about five minutes.

Juan was whimpering with the pain of his grazed legs and hands; I pulled him somewhat roughly to his feet, grabbed back the blanket from him in a bundle, and hissed:

"Run! Follow me!"

"I c-c-can't!" he gulped.

"You *must*! Or we shall be caught, and both beaten for certain, and God only knows what else the Abbot will have done to us. Come on, now—stir yourself—be a man!" And I ran ahead, but not at my full speed or anything approaching it, looking back as often as I dared on the twisting track, sometimes extending a hand to pull Juan over a difficult stretch, for, here and there, sections of the path were no more than steep loose shale or slippery bare rock.

When we reached the hither end of the causeway we could see Father Vespasian, like some black-winged bird of night in his flapping cloak, coming swiftly down the zigzag track from the great gate.

Juan let out a little moan of fear and darted ahead of me along the causeway, where the water was already making short swirls and eddies over the road. I felt troubled for him, in his bare feet, but he seemed able to run more easily on the level, though it was rough-cut rock with shingle and mortar packed in the cracks. I followed him fast, glancing back over my shoulder now and then, at some risk of slipping, to see how much Father Vespasian had gained on us. Now he had reached the bottom of the zigzag track and was gliding out along the causeway. I felt in me a mortal terror of what he might do to Juan if he caught up with us—and fear for myself, too, though that was not quite as bad. But Juan, still weak and frail, only just risen from his sickbed . . .

Ahead of us the mainland still seemed an endless distance away, and already the waves were tugging at our ankles. I recalled Father Antoine saying, "Never attempt to cross when the water is more than ankle-deep, or you will be washed away for certain."

We were more than halfway over, I thought. But we were not going fast enough.

"Stop!" I gasped to Juan. "I am going to carry you. Get on my back"—and I knelt down. He made some demur, but I fairly shouted at him, "Do as I say! Or we shall both be washed away!" and gestured him to climb on my back.

He did so.

"Good! Now hold round my neck."

Clutching the blanket somehow across my chest, with his legs tucked through my arms, I ran stumbling, panting, gulping in cold sea-air, as fast as my obedient legs would strike the ground. They began to feel numb, as if all the blood had left them. And the footway was now wholly underwater, the waves pulled at my calves and swirled around my knees. I was in terror of turning aside from the path and plunging into deep water. Sometimes it was only with frightful difficulty that I kept my footing.

"Listen!" I called inside my head to God. "Please listen to me! I am doing what You told me. At least I think I am! So will You make haste to help us, for I need Your help as badly now as I ever have in the whole of my life!"

Just when a terrible doubt was beginning to pluck at my mind—just when it occurred to me to wonder whether God's purpose might be for Juan, the Abbot, and me all to drown together—I noticed that the pushing, sucking water was not quite so deep. Here the causeway sloped upward somewhat. Now the water was only to my shins—now to my ankles. Now we were on bare rock, and toiling up toward the high-water mark.

And then Juan let out a sharp, whispered cry.

"*Oh, mon Dieu!* On the beach—Gueule and Plumet!"

But I had turned at the same moment to look for our pursuer. Father Vespasian was now about halfway across, but I could see that he was in severe difficulties, up to his breast in water, with the waves pulling and thrusting him this way and that. I could see his face now plainly in the moonlight, and it was a truly terrible sight: His eyes were fixed upon us, and they flamed like candles. Still he came on, forging his way through the water. He is not human, I thought, the sea will not stop him. Out of the corner of my eye I could see that the two men on the beach were observing him, and us also.

At this moment I must confess that I almost fell into despair.

For whether the Abbot caught us, or they did, our fate seemed certain; we were trapped between two evils.

The men on the beach moved briskly in our direction. Evidently they had been keeping the causeway under observation; Juan was right, I thought wearily, they had not been deceived by his hiding.

I went on doggedly toward them. We had no weapons, but a pile of fence stakes lay by the track, above the high-water mark. Wearily setting Juan on his feet, I panted, "Snatch one of those cudgels and we will do the best we can," when, from behind us, I heard a long, terrible cry.

Oh, the thought of it freezes my marrow to this day.

What was it like? Like no sound I have ever heard, before or since. It was high, vibrating, not wholly human. It was at one and the same time the shriek of a wild, supernatural being driven from its habitation, and the agonized yell of a living body which had been almost torn asunder. It was in two syllables, both of which seemed to linger in the air like echoes of each other.

"Laaaaaaa—raaaaaaa!"

Heaven defend me from ever hearing such a cry again! It sounded as if a razor-sharp saw were cleaving through flesh, bone, and stone, all at the same time.

"Jesu María!" whispered Juan in consternation, crossing himself repeatedly. He was staring over my shoulder, his mouth open in horror. I spun round, regardless of the men on the beach; but there was nothing, nothing at all to see, only the swirling, white-capped waves pouring from one side of the bay to the other. No sign, none at all, of the Abbot.

And then, the following instant, away to our side we heard an equally loud, equally agonized yell. Before we had had time to do more than accept with terror and relief the fact of Father Vespasian's disappearance, we were faced with another fearful happening: The tall black-haired man on the beach, the one that Juan had said was called Plumet, who had pretended to be a cripple, was evidently taken in some form of atrocious seizure. He wailed and gibbered like a damned soul; he fell to the ground, flinging himself about, his limbs jerking with maniac violence; he frothed at the mouth, as he had earlier feigned to. But this was no pretense, it was all too real—no actor, however skillful, could simulate those wild spasms, in which his body arched back and forth, head touching heels in one direction, then toes in the other, with the snapping, whiplike speed of a wounded snake. All the time, through his anguished groans, a hissing stream of gibberish language proceeded from his wide-open mouth. And curses of a terrible violence; I had never even imagined such profanity.

Juan and I clutched one another in horror, while the little man, the midget, knelt sobbing and wailing beside his friend, calling his name over and over.

"Plumet! *Mon ami,* what is it? Answer me!"

"Oh, come away!" whispered Juan to me, his teeth chattering with dread. "Come quickly! It is too horrible."

For a moment I hesitated. Was it not our duty to try and help the wretched man, afflicted in so dire a manner?

"Should we not try to do something for him? Or summon help?"

"What could we possibly do? Besides, he is the man who hanged me," said Juan bitterly. "Should I feel compassion for him? Felix—please come! Do not wait. It is too dreadful. Besides—this is our chance."

I felt that he was right. God had seen fit to remove one of our enemies, and mysteriously strike down another. It would be no more than obedience to Him to take advantage of the occasion.

"Come, then," I said to Juan, and, breathing a silent, heartfelt prayer of thanks, snatched a stout stake and hurried on up the causeway, which mounted the headland and then swung leftward, or north, following the line of the shore. This was, I knew, heading in the wrong direction for us—we must go south—but it would be necessary to make a detour around the marshes first; any attempt to cut across them would be the purest folly.

Juan followed close behind me.

The tide was still rising; another four hours at least must pass before anybody could follow us from the Abbey. And I thought it most unlikely that anyone would. Father Anselm and Father Domitian might grieve at our loss: two possible members of the Community departed; but Father Pierre and Father Antoine would, I knew, be glad for us. I only wished it might be possible, somehow, to send back a message to those two who had been so kind and helped us as much as they dared. Then, with joy I recalled that Father Antoine had mentioned his sister. We could go through the village where she lived, perhaps, and leave word with her. Very likely she came to see her brother now and then, on Abbey visiting days.

We had reached the summit of the headland now, and the track leveled out. Looking back it was possible to see the Abbey perched on its rock against the silvery ocean, with white clouds of foam bursting up at the foot of the zigzag path.

"Did you *see* Father Vespasian's end?" I asked Juan, who had been silent since we left the shore, partly because of the steep climb, but more, I thought, from horror at what had passed.

To be made to speak of it, I thought, would be better for him. Also, for myself, I must confess I would be glad to know that the Abbot had really perished in the rising waters, and not flown away in the darkness like some great bird of ill-omen.

"Yes . . . at least I *think* so," whispered Juan. "One moment he was there, coming after us, with his arms spread wide, and that dreadful glare in his eyes; then a huge wave towered directly over him and I was obliged to look away; I could not bear to see. When I looked again, he was gone."

"Ah!"

"But Felix—my heart misgives me."

"Well?"

"Did you ever think," he whispered, crossing himself, "that Father Vespasian—seemed different, at times—as if some other power were—were in command of him?"

"Yes," I said. "I do think that. Some of his acts— the way he looked and spoke at times—seemed governed by a force that was not human."

"That was what I felt, too. Oh, he was a terribly frightening man! When he first came into my sick chamber—he began to laugh. To laugh! The strangest laugh I ever heard. And he said a queer thing: 'The scent of the yellow flowers still hangs about her—about him.' What *can* he have meant by that?"

"In the grove where we found you hanging," I said, transported back to that moment, "there were yellow flowers, very sweet-scented. But how could *he* have known *that*?"

The Abbot, I remembered, had questioned me most intently about the period when I was unconscious. What did he hope to learn from those who had recovered from death, or a state near death? Yet death—itself—was dreadful to him.

I asked Juan: "Did he question you about your hanging?"

"Oh, yes. Over and over. What did I remember? What had I felt? Had I lost consciousness, and for how long? What had happened to my soul when it left my body? How could I tell him that? I did not know myself." Juan gave an uncontrollable shiver. "He was an evil, evil man. I am glad that he is gone."

He looked forward along the path and set down his bare feet more sturdily, as if determined to shake off the horror. And I, wishing to spare him, did not utter the fear—wild, superstitious, and intense—which still held me, that somehow, one way or another, we might not yet have seen the last of Father Vespasian.

Ahead of us, presently, we perceived Zugarra, the village from which the boy Tomas had come, and we turned aside from it, going softly through damp reedy fields, so as to avoid being barked at by watchdogs or hissed at by geese; though all seemed silent, plunged in slumber, at this dead hour of night. Then we rejoined the track, which now wound southerly again, skirting inland behind the marshes. Juan was beginning to limp; I sliced strips off the blanket with a knife which I had taken from the surgery (leaving a crown in payment for knife and blanket; too much, but I had no smaller coin) and bound them round his feet.

"Thank you, Felix," he said faintly.

"Are you *very* tired? I think that we should put as much distance as we can between us and the coast before dawn breaks; then find somewhere to hide and sleep."

"Of course," he muttered in a sulky tone, as if he did not relish being told what we should do. "And, no, I am not too tired to walk. I can go on for many kilometers yet, I daresay." And he strode on doggedly.

"This old gardener of yours—Pierre—where does he live?" I asked.

"At Biriatou."

"How far is that from here, should you say?"

"Eight or nine kilometers, perhaps." Now that I had indicated a willingness to follow his plan, he sounded more cheerful. He added, "We must go on in this direction until we reach the Bidassoa River, then turn inland. The river is the boundary between France and Spain."

"Ah! Is Spain so near?" My heart lifted at the

thought. I said, "How far is it to Pamplona, where your uncle lives?"

"Oh, that is a great deal farther away, eighty kilometers perhaps. I hope my uncle is not dead," he whispered, half to himself.

"Dead?" I was startled. "Why in the world should you think that? Is he an old man? Or in poor health?"

"Oh, no; not old. But he was in agreement with the Liberals, the Constitution Party led by Colonel Riego. And we heard that the Spanish king was angry with them. I hope some harm has not overtaken him, and that is why he never answered Esteban's appeal for money."

"Well, that we cannot discover until we get to Pamplona. There's no use fretting ahead of time," I said, wondering what I could do with Juan should it turn out that his uncle had been thrown into jail by order of King Ferdinand. Take him on with me to Villaverde, another three or four hundred kilometers? What would my grandfather say to that?

"How old are you, Juan?" I asked, and was surprised when he told me thirteen years.

"You are small, then! I had thought you were younger."

"Oh, we Eskualdunak are always of small stature," he said rather peevishly. "But we have the hearts of lions. You are not such a giant yourself! How old are *you*, Felix?"

The same age as himself, I told him, and we went on for some time in silence.

I was reflecting how ill-prepared we were for such a journey as ours. Our first care, after we had slept and visited this old Pierre, must be to provide ourselves with food, a knapsack, shoes for Juan, flint and steel, and mules or ponies; for a walk of eighty kilometers over the mountains on our own feet would take ten days, if not longer, and I did not think Juan had the strength for such a march. Moreover I had heard that the Pyrenees were very steep, with high cliffs and terrible ravines, hundreds of feet deep.

By now day was beginning to break dimly; it could be seen that we were in a country of flat damp fields here and there intersected by tidal creeks, which we must cross as best we could, by wading through the mud, or by small plank bridges. But as we moved away from the shore, the land began to undulate, with green hills rising between valleys made up of small hedged fields, vineyards, maize plots, and spinneys of oak and beech trees coming into young green leaf. There were dun-colored cattle and goats in the meadows, and small hamlets here and there, but those we avoided.

"I am *very* hungry," Juan whispered forlornly when we had been walking for several hours. I looked around without much hope. It was the wrong time of year for nuts or berries. There were primroses and violets in plenty below the hedges, but nothing to eat.

"I could milk a goat, if only we had a cup." Long ago I had learned to milk from my grandfather's shepherds.

"I have a cup!" said Juan proudly, and, to my great surprise, untied from his belt a small canvas bag from which he produced several articles—a horn cup, a brass spyglass, a spoon, and a little book.

"Whence had you those?" I demanded in astonishment.

"I prigged them," he answered carelessly, using a word from the thieves' argot. "While you were putting on your clothes in the surgery I looked about and took what I thought would be most useful. And the spyglass belonged to Father Vespasian. He had it hanging in a pouch from his belt. I prigged it the other afternoon, while he was asking me all those questions."

Juan chuckled a little, in a self-congratulatory manner. But I was thunderstruck.

"You did *what*?"

"Prigged them. I just told you! The Gente were trying to make me be a robber; of course I would not learn, but I could not help watching when they showed me. It was so easy!" He chuckled again.

"But that is stealing!" I found myself truly shocked.

"Bah! What is wrong with stealing from somebody wicked—like the Abbot?"

"But the other things! Where did you get the book?"

"Father Antoine brought it in for me to read. It is poetry. It came from the scriptorium."

"But he did not intend you to take it away! And the cup and spoon that you took from Father Pierre's workroom—they were not yours! You should not have done so!"

"*Peste!*" said Juan indignantly. "What a to-do you kick up over a few odds and ends. I was not taking them from any person. I would not steal from a friend. Only from a stranger or from rich people. The Abbey can afford to lose a cup and spoon."

I did not agree with him, and argued hotly. Part of my annoyance, no doubt, arose from the fact that the blame would fall on us equally—I had taken the knife and the blanket. But at least I had paid for them. The map I felt sure Father Antoine had intended as a gift. I sighed, seeing the situation could not be mended, and said at length, "Well, I must request that you do not steal while you are with me. I have no wish to go to prison. And besides, I have sufficient money to pay for our needs. I do not like to be associated with thievery."

"I am not a thief!" whispered Juan angrily. "The Basques are a very honorable people. They are always chosen by the king of Spain as his chief equerries. '*Basques notoriamente hidalgos.*' Basques, by common knowledge, are gentlefolk."

"That may be," I said drily enough, and we went on for some time without speaking to one another.

But seeing, after a while, that he was becoming desperately pale, and could hardly drag himself along, I had pity on him as we came within sight of a large herd of milch goats. The farmer would hardly miss one cupful of milk out of such plenty. So I milked one of them (who was glad enough to have her bag eased), gave a full cupful to Juan, and took a few mouthfuls myself. Then we sat awhile on the eastward side of an oak spinney, warming ourselves in the rays of the rising sun.

"I am better now," whispered Juan presently, and we rose and trudged on, leaving the road, which followed along the crests of the hills. Instead we cut through meadows and valleys, watching out for farmers or shepherds and avoiding them, so that none could give a report of our passing.

At last we reached the Bidassoa, a swift-flowing, muddy river, and struck inland along its bank. To think that Spain was on the other side! I looked across longingly, but the water was wide at this point, and little could be seen of the far bank in the morning mist.

Presently, as we made our way farther from the coast, the banks narrowed to a gorge, with steep sandstone hills on either side. And behind them, walls of rock, thickly grown with oaks and chestnuts; here and there white houses gleamed among the trees.

Soon we were obliged to climb up, among slabs of rock and broken stones. There were shrubs and then larger trees. The footing was very insecure; at times there would be no path at all, where earth had fallen away from the side of the hill. At last we found a narrow gully at the top of which there stood a stone hut, empty and abandoned, but containing a pile of old hay which some farmer had long forgotten, for it was gray and stale.

"Here we sleep," said I, and Juan drew a long, silent breath of relief and dropped on the hay like a shot pigeon. I unslung the blanket, which I had been carrying wrapped round my shoulders and tucked under my belt, hot and troublesome enough on my tender back. Glad to shed it, I spread it carefully over Juan, then lay down gingerly myself, trying not to let the hay prick my sore weals. They had been giving me a good deal of pain as I walked. Juan was already asleep; his regular breathing told me that. But it was some little while before I could follow his example. My shoulders throbbed and stung; also the terrible eyes of Father Vespasian blazed at me like beacons the moment I closed my own. And even when, presently, I slept, they seemed to haunt and pursue me through my dreams.

I suppose we slept for two or three hours, then Juan shook me awake, saying plaintively that he was still very hungry.

"Very well. I will go out and find some food. Do you think that we are near to Biriatou?"

"Yes," he said, "for we have come along the river for several kilometers. I think we must be quite close to the village."

"Then I will go there. And, if I can, I will seek out your old Pierre."

"I had best come with you, then," said Juan. But when he tried to rise he sank back with a little moan of weakness. "Oh, my neck! And my feet! And my back!"

"You have done far more than you ought," I said in deep concern, knowing how horrified Father Pierre would be to see his patient in such a state. "Remain there under the blanket and continue to rest. Besides, it is better you do not go into the village. You might be recognized."

"Nobody knows me there, except Pierre," he protested. "Why would it matter?"

"Because the Gente might have thought of Pierre. They might expect you to go asking for his help. They might be on the lookout for you."

"Oh," he muttered. "I had not thought of that! Well, in that case, I had best give you a token, to show you came from me, or Pierre will very likely refuse to speak to you. He is a surly old man, but he has a true heart. Here." To my surprise Juan undid from round his neck a thing I had not noticed before: a medallion on a long plaited silver chain. It was a silver-and-amber locket, which opened to reveal a saint's head inside.

"It is Ste. Engrâce," he whispered, opening it to display the interior. "It was my mother's. Take great care of it! And do not be gone longer than you can help, for I shall grow anxious."

"And do not you stir outside," said I. "Cover yourself with the hay—so. Before I enter I will knock three times on the door—thus; if anybody else comes, keep quite still, and they will never know that you are there."

After which I went out and made my way eastward through the woods, eventually striking a path which led me down into the churchyard of a tiny village hanging on the edge of a steep slope. Once out of the churchyard I was in the square, which had a pelota *frontón* and Basque houses round about; that is to say, they were heavily timbered, the timbers painted in red or brown, with great eaves projecting overhead like the brim of a sombrero. One of them was an inn, where a handsome high-featured landlady asked me what I wished. At that time, early in the day, I was the only customer. I knew a little Basque, for Bernardina, my grandfather's old cook, had come from the Basque region (as many cooks do); I knew *Egg-en-noon*, for good day, *khatten*, to eat, *err-ratten*, to drink, so I was able to buy from her a couple of long red sausages (festoons of them were hanging from the rafters to dry) a cold omelette, and a long loaf of bread. I also persuaded her to sell me a *chahokoha*, or goatskin wine bottle. She offered to fill it with wine, but to her surprise I declined. Then I asked her where I could find old Pierre Unarre.

"The little house by the church," said she, and I departed with the bread under my arm, the omelette wrapped in a cabbage leaf, and the flask slung round my neck.

Old Pierre was working in his garden; indeed I had observed him as I passed before, and observed, also, that as I walked by he had given me a long, sly, squinting scrutiny. He was a villainous-looking old man, with little red rheumy eyes and a crust of unshaven stubble all over his face. He paused from digging his cabbage patch and leaned on his spade as I approached him. I, without words, drew out the little medallion and extended it on the palm of my hand.

Then I said, "Your young master (*etcheko jaun*) wishes to travel into Spain, to his uncle. I am told that you know of a cave with one entrance in France, and the other in Spain. If you can show us this way, I will give you gold."

"How much?" His little eyes glowed like rats' eyes.

"One gold piece this side; one when you have led us through."

"Give it to me now!"

"No," I said coldly. "I am not such a fool."

"Where is Etcheko?" He used the term *etcheko premu,* meaning the heir, or first son.

"That I will not say. Tell me where to come, and when."

After a long, scowling pause, he gave me directions, drawing with a twig in the loamy earth of his cabbage patch. It was not easy to follow what he said, because of his Basque dialect, and because he had not a tooth in his head and mumbled so, eyeing me sideways; also, his breath smelled most vilely of sour cider and garlic; but at last I thought I had the way clear in my head.

"How long will it take to get there from here?"

"Two hours. Perhaps three. I will meet you at the grotto entrance this evening, at the hour when one can no longer tell a black thread from a white."

"Very well."

His eyes followed the medallion yearningly as I put it away, and he stared after me very hard as I left him; for which reason I took a roundabout route, leaving the village by a road that went eastward still, striking over the shoulder of the mountain, then slowly working my way round and back toward the hut. On my way I fell in with a blue-smocked shepherd in a floppy hat, who, for a few small coins, filled my flask with milk from one of his goats. He also sold me his *makhila,* a spearheaded staff with a copper band round the base. Bernardina had told me about these *makhilas:* They are made of medlar wood, take two years to season, and can save a man from a charging wild boar, or a mountain bear. I was not afraid of boars or bears, but thought we might have other enemies closer at hand.

ALL was silent at the hut when I returned to it. I tapped on the door, waited a moment, then opened it. For a moment of dismay I thought that Juan was not there, then his dark head, garlanded with hay, poked up out of the heap. He was smiling and looked the better for his rest, with a touch of color in his pale cheeks.

"Did you find old Pierre?" he whispered urgently.

"Hush! Yes. Wait while I do this."

I crumbled some of the bread into his cup, and poured on milk to soften it.

"Now! Try a little of that, eating it slowly. Not too

much. Just a mouthful or so, and suck well before you swallow. Then take a drink of milk."

He ate all the bread and milk with great eagerness, and a little of the cold omelette. I had some, too, and some bread and sausage, which tasted like food of the gods after our night of exertion, and the monastic diet of pulse and beans and salt stockfish.

The rest of the food was put by for later in the day, since the hour was still before noon, and there were five hours or so before we need start for the grotto.

I lay down on the heap of hay and went back to sleep. Juan, too, did so for a while, but I awoke presently to see him sitting cross-legged, poring over his poetry book.

"Are you feeling rested?" I whispered, and he nodded. I gave his neck a rub with some of the goose grease, which I had brought with me in a little pot, and also rubbed his feet, which were blistered and cut from the long walk. I had hoped to buy him some alpargatas, or rope-soled sandals, in the village, but the place was too small to have a market; shoes would have to wait awhile. Meantime I rewrapped his feet more securely in the strips of blanket, binding them with shreds of cord I found among the hay. He, during this operation, was whispering out poetry from his little book.

I have always been fond of reading stories myself, and on my journey from Spain to England took much pleasure in a volume which had belonged to my father, a tale of a young lady's adventures in England. But what could be the use of poetry? That I had never wholly comprehended, and said as much to Juan.

"A tale teaches you something, or is exciting to hear, or is about people you know; but what is the purpose of poetry? Half the time it seems to have no meaning at all. It is about the moon, or love; things that have been repeated hundreds of times before in the same language. Why do poets do it? What is it for?"

Juan became quite red in the face with outrage at my stupidity.

"Oh!" he burst out in a passionate whisper, which almost made me laugh: the soft tone contrasted so oddly with his indignant expression and eyes in which copper-colored sparks were burning. "How can you be such a numbskull? Listen to this"—and he read out a poem about a lover who asks his dead lady when he may see her again. "When the autumn leaves that fall become green and spring once more," she answers him.

"Well, so does she mean that they will never meet again, because the fallen leaves will never be green again? Or does she mean that she will see him in the spring because he will die then?"

"You have to decide that for yourself," said Juan. "Each reader must find his own meaning in a poem."

I said I thought that very wasteful. "Why can they not have one meaning, and make it plain for all?"

"Oh, I have no patience with you!" muttered Juan, and closed his book.

I thought it lucky that we would soon be in Spain and he restored to his uncle. For plainly a great many of the things I did and said jarred him and made him impatient; while I, for my part, found his fretfulness and peevishness hard to bear. I knew this was unfair; he was still far from well, and half starved, and his neck swollen and painful; but one has little control over one's feelings, and mine said to me loud and clear that this boy and I were not destined to make good companions for one another.

Except, of course, by God.

WE WERE both glad to leave the stuffy hut. By midday the sun shone upon the roof and made it very hot inside, and the pile of hay smelled disagreeably of mold. I thought it would be wise to start in good time in case we encountered any difficulties along the way; also, mistrusting old Pierre, I wished to arrive at the rendezvous well before him.

Our way now led through steep sunlit forest, sometimes thick with undergrowth, sometimes among gigantic rocks, sometimes past tall, handsome beech trees, or birch, or juniper. We saw no wolves or bears, but once or twice disturbed grazing deer; izard, Juan told me they were called. He had recovered his good humor and gave me, in a whisper, much information about the witches who used, two hundred years ago,

to frequent this mountain, which was called Choldoco-
gagna; and its neighbor La Rhune, for which we were
making.

"My ancestress, Marie Dindart, could rub herself
with ointment. Then she would say, *'Here and there'* —
Juan used the Basque words—"and immediately her
body would become as thin as a hazel wand, so that
she could fly up the chimney and through the air
wherever she wished."

"Well, I wish we had her with us now," said I. "For
then she could carry us into Spain without the need of
consulting old Pierre."

"She had a herd of toads, all dressed in velvet."

"Why did she need toads?"

"I am not perfectly sure," confessed Juan seriously.
"Perhaps she milked them. And she often used to steal
children away from their homes to make them her servants; they tended the toads."

"Who told you all this?"

"Old Anniq, my nurse; she used it to frighten me
and say that if I was not a—if I did not behave myself, Marie Dindart would come down the chimney
for me. I did not wholly believe her. But still I was
proud to have such a great-grandmother."

"How old were you when your mother died?"

"It happened six months ago," he said. "I still miss
her sadly."

I looked ahead along the track, pretending not
to notice the tears in his eyes, and reflected on the sin-
gularity of his character; at one minute sharp and

shrewd, asserting his independence, dealing with Father Vespasian by a clever trick, frightening the Gente by pretending to have magical powers; and then, next minute, weak, petulant, and pitiful.

"What about you, Felix?" he presently asked. "Do you have a mother and father?"

I told him no, that my mother had died at my birth, and he exclaimed in sorrowful sympathy.

"I was brought up by my grandfather, grandmother, and great-aunts—of which there were far too many."

"And your father?"

I hesitated whether to tell Juan the story, but in the end did so, thinking it might take his mind off his own misfortunes.

"My father was an officer in the English army in Spain. My mother's Spanish family were angry at the marriage—they did not think him good enough for her. After her death he was terribly wounded in battle. And he crawled over the mountains to my grandfather's house, taking several years on the way, being nursed by peasants in their huts. When he came to Villaverde, nobody knew him. He had only one leg and a crippled hand. And his face was much scarred. I, of course, had never seen him."

"How old were you then?"

"Oh, three or four. He became a stablehand in my grandfather's establishment. He was called Bob."

"A *stablehand*? But—he was of good birth. A hidalgo!" Juan sounded horrified. After a moment or two he added, "*Why* did your father do that? What a strange thing to do!"

"I suppose he thought that it was the only thing left that he was fit for. He loved horses. And that way he could watch over me."

"Did you not know that he was your father?"

"No, I never knew. Not until afterward. He never told me. But I loved him just as much as if I had known . . . In the end he died. I think he knew that he could not live for very long. And after that I decided to go and find his family in England."

"And found them?"

"Yes; my English grandfather is a duke, and very rich. But he has gone mad. And by the time I had found him, the most disagreeable of my great-aunts in Spain had died, and my Spanish grandfather wrote very kindly, asking me to return."

"You were on your way back when your ship was wrecked at St. Just de Seignanx? When was the wreck?" said Juan. "How long ago?"

"Hush!" I whispered.

I still had not decided whether to tell Juan about my strange three-month leave-taking from my wits; and I did not intend to just at this moment. Firstly, I thought it might fill him with doubts as to my ability to help or protect him while we were together; and secondly, I did not, as yet, like him well enough to reveal this odd link between us. The knowledge was for me, not for him. So I cautioned him to silence, for we were now approaching the place that old Pierre had described to me, a cave entrance in a rock face on the side of the mountain. There was a gray cliff, all hung and fringed with ivy, and a stream gliding down over the rock face in a perpetual trickle, which ran into a shallow pool. Oak and thorn trees grew round about the pool, on the flat apron of land at the foot of the cliff.

"Now we climb," I said to Juan. For I had seen a capital lookout perch three quarters of the way up the cliff, a small natural platform where a birch tree grew and spread its roots into a fan; if we could get up there we should be able to lie in safety, unobserved, and see all who came to the cave entrance.

"*Climb?* Why?" Juan demanded in a pettish whisper. "Why not simply wait here at the grotto entrance?"

"It is too early. Strangers might come by. Come, I will help you up. Take my hand."

"No—no! I can manage very well by myself," he snapped. But he followed me with exasperating slowness, continually pausing to look round; I could have cuffed him for his sulky lack of compliance, and several times had to restrain the impulse to take his wrist and pull him along by force.

We had to take a circle round, climbing the slope farther away from the cliff, where it was easier, and then making our way along a goat or coney track which led downward across the face of the hill toward my birch tree. The last portion of this way consisted of nothing more than a few rock steps over the sheer cliff, and there Juan did permit me to aid him by holding his wrist and encouraging him from one step to the next. By the time that we were established in our natural balcony I noticed that his brow was shiny with beads of sweat.

"I do not like looking down from a steep height; it makes me queasy," he said, swallowing, and I felt impatience mixed with pity.

"What in the world is the point of coming up here?" he added irritably after a minute or two. "It appears to *me* that there is no reason for it at all, except to show off your cleverness at climbing."

"Oh, hush! If you are hungry, why do you not have another bit of bread sopped in milk?" I felt sure that Father Pierre would scold me for dragging the poor boy up here.

We had finished the cold omelette before leaving, but brought the bread and milk with us. Juan followed my advice eagerly, and then even slept a little; we were very snugly established among the roots of the birch tree, like birds in a nest, so there was no possibility of his falling. But I remained awake, lying quite still, with my chin on my arms, looking out, watching for movement among the scrub of small oak trees down below. It was still two hours, at least, before the time named by old Pierre for our rendezvous, so my expectations were not immediate.

But in the end they were rewarded.

Four men stole into the clearing by the pool. Two of them I recognized; two were strangers. And none of them was old Pierre.

Very gently I awoke Juan by touching him behind the ear. I had heard this to be a capital way of rousing somebody without startling him, and so it proved. His dark-brown eyes flew open, gazing straight into mine, and I laid a finger on his lips to ordain silence, and pointed downward without speaking. His eyes followed the direction of my finger, and he drew breath in a silent gasp of fright as he saw Cocher, the white-headed man; Plumet, the ex-cripple, apparently recovered from his seizure; and two others, all softly conferring together and looking vigilantly about them. It was not hard to guess that the third and fourth men were also members of the troop.

"Bazin and Michelet," Juan whispered. I could feel him trembling against my shoulder.

But Plumet had undergone a singular and terrifying change since the previous day and his pretended "healing" at the hands of Father Vespasian.

Overnight his face, which had (once the painted sores were rubbed away) been a healthy, ruddy, weather-beaten tan—his face was now deathly white, like the belly of a fish, and all creased and seamed, every which way, as would be a piece of crumpled muslin that had been pressed under a heavy weight. He moved jerkily, as birds do, in a series of small, sharp movements. There was something disagreeably unnatural about the motion. The distance was too great for me to see his eyes, but I noticed that the other men regarded him with a kind of awe mixed with repugnance, instantly obeying his commands but avoiding any contact with him. Cocher, I noticed, even took pains not to tread on his shadow.

Where, I wondered, was Gueule, the midget, who had been with him on the shore?

Presently old Pierre limped into view, and I heard Juan snatch his breath in a hiss of distress when the old man, without any hesitation, saluted the four brigands as he might friends or neighbors (though I noticed him give Plumet an inquisitive puzzled glance and then quickly edge away). Now they all, in lowered tones and with much and expressive gesture, evidently were laying out a plan of action.

Pierre sat himself down on a boulder in the cave mouth, measuring with a glance the setting sun's distance from the shoulder of the hill, which would shortly cut it off from our view. Plumet and Cocher withdrew among the oak trees to our left, but did not go far; sometimes I could catch the glint of the knife which Cocher wore unsheathed at his belt. The other two men concealed themselves in a great growth of ivy almost directly below where we were perched, and I could hear them conversing in confidential mutters. Not all, but some, of what they said came up to me.

First there was some reference to Gueule.

". . . terrible, that!"

"A thing from the ocean, do you think? A monster?"

". . . Who can say?"

Then I caught the name Esparza, Esteban Esparza, twice repeated, and that of the old nurse, Anniq Nay, but I could not make out what was said about these people. Some words did float up clearly: "That makes Etcheko Premu even more worth catching. Not a sardine, but a young whale!"

"Will you be quiet, you two!" called old Pierre angrily. "You will scare the birds away—stow your row!"

A long silence then followed. At my side I observed that Juan was weeping, endeavoring to do it without any noise, gulping back his sobs and licking in the tears as they rolled down his pale cheeks, furiously rubbing his eyes and nose with the back of his hand.

Catching my glance, he threw me an angry look and flushed, with shame, I suppose, at his inability to control his feelings.

As over his fear of heights, I pitied but also a little despised him. He must really be a looby, I thought, if he had expected help and good advice from old Pierre; anybody could see with half an eye that the old man was a villain; but then I tried to put myself in Juan's position. Imagine that you had nobody at all on whom to rely—that even your brother and old nurse were your enemies—that you had to trust such as old Pierre. No, that must be very dreadful, I reflected, but then recalled that I myself had been in much the same case. I at least, though, had a safe haven awaiting me now that my grandfather had written affectionately, asking me to return home. Heaven send that Juan's Uncle León was not also prepared to betray him! If I was able, I thought, once we were in Spain, I would seek out some person of integrity who knew this Uncle León, and try to acquire a just estimate of his character; not simply entrust the boy to a person of whom I knew nothing. The boy! Juan was of an age with myself, but I felt by far the older and more experienced of us two.

And Spain was still a long way off. Although, as the crow flies, it lay just over the top of the mountain, we were still perilously far from our journey's end.

No use, now, to attempt old Pierre's route. Indeed, as I was thinking this, he, by a low whistle, summoned Plumet and Cocher, evidently suggesting that they should enter the cave, perhaps to make sure that we had not arrived early and already gone inside. They disappeared under the rock beneath us, and did not reappear.

Dusk had fallen by now—an early dusk, for thick dark clouds had crept up, swallowing the sun's last rays, and a faint mutter of thunder made itself heard over the shoulder of the mountain.

After a while rain began to fall, slowly at first, in big drops the size of silver groats, then faster and faster, rattling and pattering on the ivy growth below us. I became deeply concerned over Juan, who had commenced to shiver badly. If we lay here for long in this violent rain, it might well be the death of him. We must shift; but how could we, with those men down below?

As if responding to my wish, another low whistle sounded from beneath us, and I saw the other two softly emerge from the ivy bush and slip inside the cave, evidently taking shelter from the storm. Another five minutes and I would not have been able to see them at all, it would be true dark; we must shift at once, there was not a moment to lose.

"Now is our time to leave," I breathed into Juan's ear.

"I can't!" he replied through chattering teeth. "I'm too cold to move. And too scared!"

How much I wished that our goatskin had been filled with wine, as the inn lady had suggested, or, better still, aguardiente. A little of such a stimulant might have put heart into Juan. Failing that, I took him by the shoulders and shook him fiercely.

"Don't behave like a whining baby! We have *got* to get away from here before we grow any colder, and while those men are inside the cave."

I did not mention that it was through his willfulness in the first place that we were in this situation, and that if I had not established us in this eyrie we should have been captured by now. "I am going to climb over you," I said, and did so, hoisting myself up with the aid of the birch trunk. "Now: Take my hand. Shut your eyes, if you prefer; I will tell you where to put your feet."

At that moment a blue-white glare of lightning illuminated the whole series of rock steps above and ahead of us—very conveniently, except that it was then followed by an earsplitting crack of thunder, which made Juan cry out in shock and clap his hands to his ears. I shook him again. "Come, follow me—and don't be a coward!"

"I am *not* a coward!" he retorted, setting his teeth and putting up his chin. Doggedly he began to follow me up the rock steps, I guiding his hand to such holds as there were, rock ledges and roots of trees, and instructing him in a whisper as to the footholds.

"Up and to the right with your left foot; you will find a crack which narrows—you can rest your foot in it safely. Now shift the right foot; there is a lump of rock about an inch wide which you can trust."

Once or twice he trembled, or shivered, and I thought that we were done for and would go crashing down to the ground outside the cave entrance, but somehow, by God's grace, we managed to make our way back to the sloping hill. The distance was not so very great, but our passage seemed to take several hours.

And all the while the rain was cascading down our shoulders, making the rock slippery under hands and feet; I thanked God very fervently in my mind when I at last felt soft, yielding sandy earth under my feet instead of slimy, unfriendly rock.

"Very well done, *mon brave*!" I whispered heartily in Juan's ear when we were both safely off the cliff, and I could not forbear to give him a hug, partly out of relief, partly to show that I forgave him for his poor-spiritedness. But another flash of lightning just at that moment revealed his expression of hostility, almost of hate; quite plainly he could not forgive *me*, either for dragging him across the cliff face or, more likely, for being proved right in my suspicions of old Pierre.

"What now?" said he sulkily. "Since you have put yourself in command, what now?"

"*Now* we must find shelter as soon as we can; but first let us put a distance between us and those men," said I, and led the way at a brisk pace up the leafy hillside, thanking Providence that the pelting rain and crashing thunder made it needless to exercise caution, for nobody could possibly hear our steps. The rain blew in waves and sheets, the wind buffeted us, and the thunder was almost incessant; I thought it most fortunate that Juan, among his other fears, seemed not to be too much troubled by thunder; though he occasionally started at an extra-loud peal—as indeed I did myself—he followed me steadily enough as we climbed ever up and up.

"It sounds as if your witch great-grandmother and all her friends were flying about overhead," I bawled in his ear as we struggled higher and higher, but he only set his jaw and, without looking at me, went on steadily putting one foot before the other.

At length another lightning flash showed us a huge hollow chestnut tree whose girth ten men with arms extended could not have encircled. By then we must have walked for the best part of an hour, and were warm enough, though soaked. The tree promised some kind of shelter, and, pulling Juan by the hand, I groped my way into it. The inside was dry enough, and not too uncomfortable, for a heap of leaf mold and chestnut-mast had, through the years, piled high within the hollow space.

"This will serve us," I said to Juan, and unfastened the blanket which I had carried. It was very wet, but we burrowed a kind of trough in the leaf mold, huddled in that, and pulled the blanket over us, with more leaves on top. Very soon a steamy warmth was achieved.

"What if lightning strikes the tree?" whispered Juan sullenly.

I, too, had that possibility in mind, for chestnut trees often do seem to attract the stroke of lightning, and the thunderstorms of the Pyrenees are notorious for their severity; but I answered airily that a tree in an open field is much more likely to be struck than one in the midst of a forest. "And in any case there is nothing more we can do about it. So go to sleep."

Juan gave a snort, whether of scorn or annoyance I did not know—or it might even have been laughter—and muttered some phrase in the Basque language. What it was I did not inquire. I was very near the point of swooning with fatigue myself, and next minute the arms of darkness enwrapped me.

4

We make our way to Hasparren, buy clothes, and attend a masquerade at St. Jean; receive a frightening shock; and are treated with hospitality by strange little people.

Upon awakening, the first thing that I saw was Juan's face regarding me anxiously. But this time he had not roused me complaining of hunger, as he had done on the previous day; he had waited until I awoke naturally. Sunlight shone on the forest outside our hollow tree, raindrops sparkled, and birds sang. Far away I could hear the call of a cuckoo.

"Have you eaten?" I asked Juan, but he shook his head. He said he had drunk a little of what milk was left, but waited to share the remaining bread with me.

His voice sounded hoarse, and I asked, in some concern, if the state of his swollen throat had been worsened by the exposure and soaking which we had suffered last night. But he told me no; indeed, it was better, and he proved that by managing to swallow a little bread that had not been previously soaked in milk, and a thin morsel of sausage, after he had chewed it very diligently. Then I realized that the hoarse voice in which he had addressed me was in fact his natural tone (roughened still by strain) and not the whisper he had formerly been obliged to use: thus far had he mended in health. He could not, however, speak a great many words at one time without his throat becoming fatigued; and I urged him not to tire his voice.

After we had eaten up our small supply of bread and milk I noticed that he seemed somewhat troubled and ill at ease; as we left our chestnut tree and marched off into the forest, brushing leaf mold and chestnut fibers from our clothes and hair, Juan said with difficulty, "Felix: I behaved ungenerously and childishly to you last night. I know that it was your prudence which saved me from—from those men; and it was my thoughtless, stupid trust in old Pierre which nearly plunged us into disaster. I—I am sorry. I was unfair. Forgive me."

He brought out this speech in a small, deep, hoarse voice, looking not at me but, as he walked along, at his own feet, still wound in those soiled and tattered strips of blanket. The apology thus hoarsely croaked out sounded so funny that I could not help laughing, and clapped him on the shoulder.

"You sound like a penitent bullfrog! Never trouble your head about such a trifle. I did not regard it at the time, and don't now. Come, let us take a look at the map and try to discover where we are, and what we should do next."

So saying, I unfolded the map, which, by great good fortune, I had stowed next to my skin, under shirt and jacket, so it had not been soaked by the storm. Laying it out on a fallen tree trunk I pointed with a twig and went on: "I should judge that we must be about here, would you agree?"

Looking up, I surprised an expression of baffled hurt and annoyance on Juan's face. Eh, bless me, what now? I thought. I suppose I have not received the silly fellow's amends with sufficient seriousness; if he has not a whole courtroom, judge, jury, and accused, hanging on his lightest statement, it seems that he feels hard done by.

"I am not accustomed to reading maps," he muttered stiffly and coldly. "I am unable to help you—I do not understand what you mean."

"Don't understand maps? Why, what in the world *have* you been taught, then? Did you not go to school, or have a tutor?"

"I did lessons at home," said he gruffly, "but—"

"Well, never mind! It is not too late to learn now. Look, this line of fur that resembles a fox's tail is intended to be the Pyrenees mountains. Here is the Bay of Biscay, here is Bilbao. Each of these black lines is a river—the Nive, the Nivelle, the Bidassoa. And these white patches are the summits of mountains."

"Oh!" he exclaimed, his resentment melting. "Now I begin to see! Here is Monte Perdido, Mont Perdu, the Lost Mountain. Uncle León always promised that one day he would take me there. He says there is a great glacier."

"Well, we only have to find him, and perhaps he will take you soon. See, now, we must be hereabouts, on the side of La Rhune," I said, pointing with my twig, "and on the other side is Spain. There is Pamplona."

"Well, then," said Juan, evidently beginning to comprehend the lines of the map, "why do we not just walk over here to Pamplona?"

"First, because there is a whole row of mountains in the way. We must find a pass, not climb over a peak."

"Then, let us find a pass," he said, glancing round as if expecting to see a beckoning fairy among the trees. "Let us find the nearest pass and walk through. Why not here, at Aïnhoa?"

"No, that is precisely what we must not do."

"Why?" he inquired, almost meekly.

"There will be gendarmes at all the main frontier posts. We must find a lesser path. Also, the Gente will be expecting us to take the nearest route. We will do as we did last night—make a circle round, to a point where they do not expect us."

Juan sighed, as if he found the prospect fatiguing, but said only, "Very well. Which way shall we go?"

"For a start, north. Then east."

"Which way is north?"

"We shall need to keep the sun on our right side."

It was yet early, I judged, though in this thick wood the sun's whereabouts were not too easily discovered. But we continued climbing, surmounted a ridge, and presently came out in a mountain meadow, where gentians and anemones grew, and a brook ran sweetly between rocks and banks of moss. By now, in the warm sun, our clothes had dried on us, and Juan exclaimed, "Oh, how dearly I would like to wash in that brook and bathe my sore feet."

"What's to stop you? *I* have no objection! In fact I will do the same myself."

And without more ado I flung off shirt and breeches, and splashed myself with handfuls of the icy water, which stung like vinegar on my healing cuts. It was much too cold to loiter in the stream, so I came out soon and sat barefoot in my breeches on the bank, letting the sun dry my back.

Juan, who, as I had already discovered, possessed a fierce sense of privacy and decorum, had retired out of sight round a bend in the brook, to perform his ablutions. By and by, returning barefoot, dangling the strips of blanket in his hand, he for the first time caught sight of my back, and gasped with horror.

"*Felix!* How in the world did you get those terrible cuts on your back?"

"Father Vespasian had me beaten," I replied, with as much nonchalance as possible. "Well, at least, now he is richly served. He will be ordering no more beatings, and the novices of St. Just have cause to be grateful to us."

"But why? Why did he have you beaten?"

"Oh," I said evasively, "he was forever having the novices flogged for one fault or another."

"No," said Juan, "but I believe I know when it happened. It was after he tried to question *me*—was it not? And you came into my room with a bunch of rosemary, and I heard him asking questions of you, in a fury, as he went down the stairs. Did he not question you about me? Was not that it? And you would not tell him what I had told you?"

"It was of no consequence," I said. "He had had me beaten various times before."

Juan looked at me with huge eyes.

"Oh, Felix. I am so *sorry*. And here have I been, grumbling and making a great to-do over my sore feet and throat, while all the time you must have been in much worse pain and I never even knew. What a spoiled child you must have thought me!"

"It was nothing. The cuts are almost better, as you can see."

"You must have some of that goose grease on them, that you have been putting on my neck."

With what there was left, only a smear, he insisted on anointing the worst of my cuts, doing it with the utmost delicacy, and wincing on my behalf as the stuff went onto the raw, healing skin.

"Poor, poor Felix. Father Vespasian was every bit as wicked, I do believe, as the Mala Gente. No, he was worse, because he pretended to be good and holy, whereas they do not pretend to be anything but what they are."

"Well, it is certainly a good thing he is drowned," said I, devoutly hoping this was true. "And I wish the Mala Gente were, too, or at least that they will now leave us in peace."

The sun was by this time well risen, as we could see from our alp, and, guiding ourselves by its position, we went on in a northeasterly direction, crossing grassy ridges and wooded valleys, hearing cuckoos, seeing wild columbines and gentians and many other flowers. We encountered another shepherd in blue smock and baggy beretta, leading his flock, and bought from him for a penny another flaskful of milk.

In the far distance on a mountain we could see a town of red-roofed houses among groves of chestnut trees; we asked the shepherd its name, and he said Aïnhoa; so we were able to place ourselves.

I suggested to Juan that we should make our way to Hasparren and, if she would have us, spend a night or so with Father Antoine's kindly sister.

"Why?" he demanded, but less combatively than he would have done yesterday.

"Because, if she is as kind as Father Antoine, she will give us good help and advice. We need various things before we cross the mountains—shoes for you, food, knapsacks, something to light a fire. Also, if we remain in Hasparren for a night or two—which is much farther north than the Gente would expect to find us—they may be thrown off the scent. Then we can cross the mountains farther to the east, perhaps in the Val d'Aspe, where they will not be looking for us."

"Where did you say your grandfather's house in Spain was situated?" he suddenly demanded.

"In Galicia."

"But that is hundreds of kilometers to the west."

"What of it?"

"I am taking you far out of your way," he said, as if this had not occurred to him before.

"My grandfather is not expecting me on any particular day," said I; though a pang smote me as I said it, for Grandfather was, after all, an old man, wounded from long-ago wars, crippled with rheumatism, obliged to pass his days in a basket chair. Suppose, after all, he did not survive until my coming? But I said to Juan, "A few days more or less will make no difference. And it would be stupid, having escaped them twice, to walk back into the jaws of the Mala Gente. Let us go first to Hasparren and ask the advice of Father Antoine's sister."

"Very well," said Juan, quite humbly.

And I thought, if Grandfather dies before I return to Villaverde, well, we shall doubtless meet in heaven.

We agreed not to pass through towns before we reached Hasparren, so went cannily across the foothills, avoiding the village of Cambo, on the banks of the Nive.

It was dusk before we reached our destination, for the distance we had to cover must have been close on twenty kilometers. We did not walk continuously, for I thought that Juan should have rest at frequent intervals, and so we paused at many a grove or brookside or vineyard, and lay in the sun, or bathed our tired feet. Hasparren, when we approached it in evening light, looked a pleasant, quiet village of white houses set in a shallow green valley. Juan told me that the

Basque name meant *Haitz-Barne*, or "in the heart of the oak forest," and indeed, there were many oak woods all around.

We inquired for the house of Madame Mauleon, and were directed to one on the edge of the village, a handsome timbered building, whitewashed between its beams, with a shallow sloping roof of red tiles, wide eaves, shuttered windows, and a great stone slab with a coat of arms over the door. An old Basque woman opened to our knock. At first she eyed our dusty and tattered appearance somewhat suspiciously, but the name of Père Antoine softened her, and she showed us into a brick-floored room with great pieces of carved furniture, and shuffled off to call her mistress.

Madame herself was so like Father Antoine that I should have known her for his sister at once, even if I had met her in the street; she had his luminous blue eyes and worn, kindly face. When she heard that we came from her brother, she could not do enough for us, and would have installed us each in a huge bedroom with a four-poster bed. But I said, and Juan agreed, that if the kind lady did not object, we would prefer to sleep in her barn, which was a noble brick-and-stone building across a yard from the house.

"But why, *mes enfants*? Why sleep in the barn when you could have the best linen sheets and goose-down quilts?"

I said: "Because, madame, we were obliged to escape from the Abbey of St. Just. Your brother, who has been kindness itself to me, and indeed gave me this map, will tell you, I am sure, in due course, that we did no wrong. But the Abbot has died—"

"What? Father Vespasian is no more?"

"He was drowned, crossing me causeway."

"Well, he was a strange man," she said, making the sign of the cross. "Rest his soul! But I never thought he had a genuine vocation to be a monk. I knew him when he was a young man—before the thought of joining a religious community had even entered his head. In those days he was very different." And a somewhat wintry look came over her face, as if at a disagreeable recollection.

"What was he like then?" I inquired curiously.

"Hotheaded!" was Madame Mauleon's brief reply. But then she added, "The reason why he entered the Order—so I have heard and I believe it—was due to a dispute over a female. He and a pair of brothers were all courting the same lady—she would have none of them—she came to some tragic end—so two became hermits and one a monk. Beware of the female sex, my lads! They can cause more damage than rats in a granary!" And she laughed, the old serving-woman's dry cackle joining with hers.

"What was the name of the lady who died?" asked Juan.

"I cannot call it to mind just at the moment. It began with an *L*, I believe—Louise, Loraine, something like that. It is all long ago. And indeed I knew nothing against Father Vespasian save that he was a strict disciplinarian. He has certainly achieved some wonderful cures. But my brother, I know, never felt any liking for him, and my brother is a man whose judgment I trust above all other. However, what has this to do with your preferring to sleep in my barn, rather than in a Christian bed with sheets?"

"Only that there may be inquiries after us, madame, and it may be best if you deny that you ever saw us; which you can scarcely do if it becomes known that we slept in your house."

She did not seem convinced by this argument, but said that we were headstrong children and she supposed we would do as we liked. She had sons herself, she said, but they were off in the world; one aboard a whaler, and one who had gone to make his fortune, as many did, in the western Americas. She could see that we were *good* children from our faces—here Juan blushed—any young ones that her brother befriended were certain to have hearts of gold. So she called back the old woman, Marietta, from the kitchen, and explained, first, that neither of them had ever seen us— at which Marietta looked wonderfully blank—and second, that we both seemed half starved and must be lavishly fed. At which point I intervened and said that my friend had recently hurt his throat and could not chew very well, but was obliged to live on slops. Madame Mauleon peered shortsightedly at Juan's neck, and exclaimed, "*Oh, mon Dieu, quel horreur!* What in the world has been done to you? That must be bathed and poulticed at once! Marietta, fetch hot water and towels; then make some soup and a *piperade* and anything else that you can think of that this poor boy can eat. How in the name of mercy did it happen?"

Upon which Juan, to my utter astonishment, glibly croaked forth a long and circumstantial tale of how his grandfather owned a mill—he described it in some detail, two huge wooden mallets on a timber frame, clashing alternately in a trough and operated by a waterwheel—how he, though ordered not to, had gone too close, become caught in the machinery and been dragged by a rope round his neck, which nearly killed him, only the good monks of St. Just had managed to restore him to life.

Madame Mauleon, bathing and putting hot compresses on his neck meanwhile, listened and shook her head and said that boys were willful creatures, always running into trouble, but that she, for her part, did not hold with all this modern machinery; two oxen grinding the corn had been good enough for our fathers and would still be good enough if people were not always hasting after something new. Then she wrapped a collar of white linen around Juan's throat and bade him not take it off for at least two days.

Juan then began to say something about my sore back, but I hushed him with a scowl; I did not want the old ladies to see my injuries, which were, besides, in a fair way to being healed, thanks to Juan's ministrations.

Now Marietta brought in an enormous meal: the *piperade,* which was eggs scrambled with tomatoes and green peppers; and a soup of onions and tomatoes, tripe stewed with garlic and red peppers, wine, several different cheeses, and sweet maize cakes. We both ate as much as we could; which, in Juan's case, was not a great deal, for he had eaten so little in the last few weeks that his stomach had shrunk and he was as thin as a broomstick.

We were very weary from our twenty-kilometer walk, and I said that if the ladies would excuse us, we would now retire, and thanked Madame Mauleon very heartily for her hospitality. She told us that anyone recommended by her dear Antoine received the same, and asked after him wistfully: Was he in good health? Which I was able to tell her he was, and hard at work illuminating a very beautiful text of the Psalms.

Then we went out to a couch of straw in the barn, but our hostess insisted on providing us with several sheepskins, of which we were glad enough, for straw makes a prickly mattress: it works its way inside your shirt and up your sleeves, and you wake feeling as if you had been stung by bees. But with two sheepskins apiece we fared very well.

When we were settled, each in a nest of sheepskin, I asked Juan, "What in the world made you tell Madame such a rigmarole of lies about the mill? I was never so taken aback in my life."

"Well," he said, sounding surprised in his turn, "I could hardly tell her about the Gente."

"Why not?"

"She would have been frightened. Besides, she is a stranger. I do not tell my whole history to strangers," he added haughtily.

With some irony I remarked, "I suppose I should feel myself greatly honored that you told the truth to me! And after all, at the time you told me, I was a stranger, too."

And still am, in most ways, I thought. This boy is the most singular character I have ever encountered. There is hardly one thing about him that I understand.

Juan said, "You had rescued me, after all. You had earned the truth."

"And Madame had not, with her bandage and her *piperade*?"

"Oh, I told her what I thought she would like to hear."

And he had done it so expertly that I was quite amazed. How many of the things he told me, I wondered (despite his assurance), were the truth, and how many were inventions? If I had not known that it was false, I myself would have believed his tale about the mill.

"Where did you see such a mill?"

"Oh," he answered carelessly, "somewhere on the way, when the Gente were taking me to their cave in the mountains."

I had forgotten that they carried Juan off to the mountains first. "Where was the cave?" I asked.

"How should I know? When we reached the mountains I was blindfolded; they wound bandages over my head, like Plumet pretending to be a leper. And my hands were tied behind. It was five or six hours' ride. The man Bazin rode behind me with a knife pricking my ribs; he threatened to drive it into my heart if I ever cried out."

True or false? True, perhaps, I thought.

"Then why do you think they brought you all the way back to the seashore to hang you?"

"I have been wondering about that," he said. "I believe it was so that, if my body was found, blame would not be laid at their door, for they are a mountain band. I suppose it might have been assumed that my half-brother Esteban had done the deed."

This seemed a reasonable guess. But then I began to wonder about Juan's half-brother. Could the story about him have been true? Could he really be such a monster as to plan the murder of his young half-brother? The tale about the mill had greatly shaken my faith in Juan's reliability. Still, such wickedness in families did exist, as I knew; my own great-aunt Isadora had planned my abduction, or death, so that her grandson, my cousin Manuel, might inherit the estate at Villaverde; yes, Esteban might perhaps be the villain that Juan thought him. Uncle León in Spain would doubtless have views on the matter. And I thought with what relief I would deliver Juan to his uncle, and rid myself of this perplexing responsibility.

Juan muttered something.

"What did you say, Juan?"

"It was in Euskara. I said, *gab-boon*."

Euskara is what the Basques call their own language. *Gab-boon* I knew meant good night.

"Good night, sir," I said in English, and Juan laughed.

"We will make a bargain," he said. "You teach me English, I teach you Euskara. And the most successful pupil gives a present to his teacher."

"Very well," I agreed. "We will commence tomorrow."

"I shall certainly have to give you a present," he said, "for however hard English may be, Euskara is sure to be harder. It is the most difficult language in the world. They say the devil himself failed to learn it . . ."

His voice trailed away in sleep. But I lay awake. His idle mention of the devil had brought Father Vespasian's eyes once more before me; they burned into the darkness like hot coals.

And I wondered where in the mountains the Mala Gente had their hiding place. A spot that was five or six hours' ride from St. Just need not be too far away from where we were now.

NEXT day Madame Mauleon, in the kindest possible manner, invited us to remain with her for several nights, or as long as we chose. A longer stay, so as to rest Juan, had, at first, been my intention, but various reasons caused me to feel that it would be better for us to continue on our journey. Madame, deploring our willfulness, then insisted on furnishing us with food, ointment for Juan's neck, and much useful advice concerning our route. We said a most grateful good-bye, kissing her hand; but she embraced us, and she and old Marietta stood watching us until we had turned the corner out of sight.

There was a street market in Hasparren where we were able to buy various things that we needed, flint and steel, a canvas bag, and new clothes, which we acquired so as to alter our appearance. I had a battle about this at first with Juan; he greatly disliked being obliged to depend on me for money. Indeed, at first he fell into a sulk and flatly refused to allow me to pay for his wardrobe. In the end I felt it necessary to give him a great scold, and tell him that his pride was standing in the way of our safety, that it was both selfish and thoughtless of him to raise such trifling objections.

"You are behaving like a child!" I hissed, standing in the dust at the side of the wide road under a plane tree while the marketing crowds thronged and jostled past us. "When we find your uncle, if it is so important to you, he can supply you with the money to pay me back. In the meantime it is only common sense that we should alter our appearance from that of the two boys who left the Abbey, so that if any descriptions of us are issued, people will not be able to recognize us. For all we know, Father Vespasian's death may be laid at our door, we may be accused of murder."

At that Juan turned pale, staring at me with that queer copper spark in his dark eyes. Two tears for a moment glimmered on his lashes. At last he swallowed, visibly took a grip on his pride, and said, "Very well. I suppose there is reason in what you say," and allowed me to pay for his things.

For myself I bought a wide-brimmed black hat, to hide my conspicuous yellow hair, a *zamorra,* or black sheepskin vest, tight-fitting leather breeches, and a canvas shirt; for Juan we purchased a dark-blue beretta, a woolen knitted vest of dark brown with a fret of crimson, a wool jacket, sheepskin breeches, and gaiters; and we each had a pair of rope-soled shoes. I was sorry to part from my good English buckled shoes, but no other in these parts wore such footgear, and they made me too noticeable. I had wanted to buy Juan a blue knitted vest with an embroidered border, and a crimson *faja,* or sash, such as many boys seemed to wear in this region; but he protested that would make him look like a girl, it was too gaudy, and he himself selected less brightly-colored garments—in which I was bound to admit he showed prudence and discretion.

While we were choosing alpargatas he gave a sudden start, looking sharply across the wide street.

"What is it, Juan?"

"I thought I saw—but I may have been mistaken."

"Whom did you see?"

"It looked like the one they called Jorobado—the hunchback; he went behind that group of farm wives."

By the time the women, with their trays of eggs, chickens, and cabbages, had moved on, the man was not to be seen, and Juan was not certain that it was the same man—after all, there are many hunchbacks—

or, even if it had been a member of the band, that he had set eyes on Juan or recognized him. But still it seemed unwise to linger in Hasparren. Madame Mauleon had told us that in the town of St. Jean Pied de Port, south and eastward of us by some twenty kilometers, there would be a horse fair all this week, at which we should be able to purchase ponies or mules to take us through the mountains. So we set off at a round pace.

In the first oak wood we changed into our new garments, Juan retiring behind a massive tree for the purpose. In ten minutes he reappeared, his expression rather shy, as if he expected me to laugh at him. But I clapped him on the shoulder and told him that he looked a fine caballero, no one would recognize him as the waif that Father Antoine and I had fetched out of the thicket.

We rolled our discarded garments into a bundle, and I was about to thrust them into a bramble thicket when Juan said, "No, wait. I have a better plan; for someone might find them there, and that would be a clue to start them on our trail." And he drew out Father Vespasian's brass spyglass, unscrewed the lens-piece, and, using it as a burning glass, focused the rays of the sun on my striped jacket and soon had it, first smoldering, then aflame. He piled the other things on top, and in a short time they all, including the shoes, had burned down to a heap of ash, which we quenched with water from a brook and trod down, to make it appear old and much rained-on.

"That was very well thought of, Juan," I said, as we recommenced our journey.

I suppose I must inadvertently have employed a somewhat patronizing tone—or he chose to think so at all events—for he answered angrily, "*You* think that nobody but you ever uses their wits. Felix the great! As for me, it is perfectly plain that you consider me nothing but a thieving, lying, storytelling baby!"

I was somewhat confounded. I had, I must confess, been in much anxiety, both in the house of Madame Mauleon and in the Hasparren market, lest Juan be tempted to exercise his newly acquired skill in pocket picking. Naturally I could not stomach the idea that our kind hostess might be so used. While we were in the house I had narrowly watched Juan to make sure he did not purloin any of her treasures. And the thought had made me anxious that if he were caught stealing articles from the market stalls, we would both have been flung into jail. Knowing Juan's prickly nature, I had not liked to issue any warnings, but I now realized that he had correctly read my fears, even though they had not been spoken aloud. His thin pale face was full of resentment.

I replied to him, however, peaceably enough, that if I had misjudged him I begged his pardon, and also that I had no intention to condescend to him.

"Indeed I think you are a very clever boy; I am sure you know many things that I do not. Come! Do not let us begin the day by dispute! Help me now to study the map and find the path to St. Jean that Madame recommended."

By degrees he allowed himself to be placated, and after we had discovered our path, he kept his promise of attempting to teach me the Basque language. But I could soon see that he was right, and that he would be speaking fluent English long before I had mastered more than the rudiments of Euskara.

"Aski dakik bizitzen badakik," he would say, and I would carefully repeat what I thought he had said, and he would almost fall down on the grass laughing at my accent, which, he said, sounded more like a duck quacking than an Eskualdunak.

"No doubt! But what does the sentence mean?"

"To know how to live is to know enough."

Then he recited some little poems in Euskara, and set me to learn them. "Tell me some English poems!" he demanded. "I would greatly wish to hear English poetry. For it is my intention to travel to that land before—to travel to that land when I am older, and read the plays of Esshak-sip-pere, and the poems of Poppe, and Dreeden."

Now it was my turn to fall about laughing, as I instructed him in the correct pronunciation of those names. But I am bound to relate that he was a gifted scholar. By the end of the day he was able, with a good accent, to recite many stanzas of a poem entitled "The Castaway," by William Cowper, which I had taken a fancy to and committed to memory when in my English grandfather's house; while my progress in the Basque language was still not much advanced beyond *ya-ya,* almost; *aita,* father; *ahizpa,* sister; and *anaie,* brother. So complicated a language I could never have imagined. Latin, French, Spanish, English, which I spoke with tolerable ease, were all child's play in comparison.

The scenery as we approached St. Jean Pied de Port became wilder and more mountainous. A steep road carried us upward, winding between high peaks, and for many kilometers there was not a dwelling to be seen. The thick oak copses, the substantial-looking farms and hedged fields, gave way to a land of heath and moor; the hills, becoming ever higher, were no longer green and grassy, but craggy with rock or gray and glittering with slopes of shale. The air grew cooler, and we were glad of our warm and thick new clothing. Juan skipped along delightedly in his rope-soled alpargatas; he said that after so many days barefoot it was like walking on velvet.

St. Jean Pied de Port is set on the River Nive, and stands encircled by high green mountains, with a castle-crowned hill behind the town, which is old and handsome. There are high walls, and you enter by a majestic arched gateway beyond the river bridge. The mansions inside the town are surprisingly large, for such a remote mountain spot; but Juan told me that it was once the capital of King García of Navarra, and two hundred years ago belonged to Spain. At one time the town was a stopping place for thousands of pilgrims on their way to Santiago de Compostela.

We found the marketplace without difficulty, but, as dusk had fallen before we reached the town, trading had ceased for the day, and the stall holders were packing up their wares, pushing wooden trestles to one side, and sweeping cabbage stalks and rotten oranges into the gutters. The beasts for sale had been driven away.

"We shall have to wait till tomorrow to buy our ponies," I said. "We had best find a place to spend the night."

Madame Mauleon, kind to the last, had furnished us with the address of a distant cousin who lived on the edge of the city, and had written a few words for him on a scrap of paper.

Discovering by inquiry that the house we sought was on the opposite side of the town, we were making our way along a tree-bordered path on the outskirts when a loud noise of barking and screaming attracted our attention.

"It is one of those English dogs!" said Juan, peering ahead into the dusk. And he added indignantly, "Savage brutes of animals they are!"

"English dogs? What can you mean?"

"When the English were in this region before the siege of Bayonne, the Duq de Vailanton"—by which I assumed that Juan meant the Duke of Wellington— "kept a pack of his English *chiens de chasse*—"

"Foxhounds—"

"Foxhounds," Juan repeated carefully, "and they have run wild, and their descendants have plagued the farmers and wild animals ever since."

It was true that the black, brown, and white animal barking and leaping at the foot of a lime tree did bear a strong resemblance to the pack of foxhounds kept on my English grandfather's estate—except that it was smaller and thinner and a great deal wilder and more vociferous.

"There is a poor terrified cat that it has chased up the tree," said Juan. "Be off, you detestable brute!" and he aimed a kick at the frenzied hound.

"*Malepeste*, Juan!" I exclaimed. "Do not involve yourself in more trouble than you need. Come away, for heaven's sake!"

But Juan, snatching up a dead bough, thwacked the dog with it, and reached up to rescue the cat, which, hurt and bleeding, had scrambled six or seven feet up the trunk of the tree, but seemed unable to climb any farther, and was hanging by all her claws, looking over her shoulder at the dog, in imminent danger, it seemed, of slipping backward into its jaws.

Juan took hold of the cat, and was rewarded by being sharply bitten.

"Ah!" he cried out, but kept his grip of the animal, and commanded, "Felix, beat that brute of a dog with your *makhila*."

"It is probably somebody's faithful house-dog and I shall be seized by the town watch." But I did as he suggested and gave the beast a poke with the point, which sent it howling off down the street. Next moment Juan was almost knocked flying by a tiny girl who rushed at him crying, "Minou, Minou!" and tried to grab the cat.

"Gently, *petite*," said Juan. "Is she your cat? She is hurt, poor thing, see, and must be treated with care." The child stared at him uncomprehendingly, and he switched from French to Basque. At this juncture a very small, wizened man arrived, apparently the child's father, who in a torrent of incomprehensible language evidently scolded his daughter for permitting her pet to stray, ordered her to return home, and thanked us for our intervention. Then he took the cat from Juan, handling it more delicately than, from his rough appearance, I would have expected, touched his beretta to us, and vanished with his child into the dusk.

"Now perhaps we can attend to practical matters," I said to Juan, who, sucking his lacerated hand, merely shrugged and followed me without replying.

However we were due for disappointment. When we reached the cousin's house, up a steep, narrow street, we found that the big handsome mansion was closed, dark and silent; evidently the cousin was away from home.

"We had best find some barn or straw stack on the edge of town," I was beginning, "and return to the horse fair early tomorrow"—when we heard a loud, gay sound of music: flute, drum, bagpipes, and stringed instruments.

"Oh, listen!" cried Juan joyfully, "I believe it must be a masquerade! Do let us go and see!" And without pausing for reflection, or to see if I agreed, he bounded off down the street at a run.

I, perforce, followed him, thinking that to be in charge of Juan, since his health had begun to mend, was hardly easier than looking after an unbroken colt or a wild hedge bird.

Back at the main square, which was now illuminated by flaring lamps, we saw that what seemed the entire population of the city had assembled round the sides of the place, while in the center a series of amazingly costumed characters pranced and capered, receiving enthusiastic applause.

Juan, whose arm I had managed to grab before he disappeared in the throng, pulled me along to where we had a good view and excitedly told me the names of the dancing characters as they performed.

"See: Those are the Reds; they always come first. Look, that big one with the bells on his sash, waving a horsetail—he is Tcherrero; and that one behind him is the Standard-bearer; then the one in black, prowling and pouncing—is he not wonderful!—he is Gathuzain, the cat-man; those two holding tongs, they are the Marichalak, the blacksmiths; the gorgeously dressed couple are Jauna *eta* Anderea, the Earl and his wife; those ones in scarlet jackets with bells and flat hats, they are the Satans, that is, Satan and Bulgifer; and the one with the wicker horse's head and draped body, he is Zamalzain."

"But what does it all mean?" I asked, watching the dancers, who were, indeed, amazingly skillful and spirited. "Who are these characters? What do they represent?"

"Oh, how should I know?" Juan replied impatiently. "They are themselves, that is all. Why should you ask for a meaning? Listen to the music! Does it not make your feet itch to dance?"

The music was strange to my ears, but full of a wild energy; it was performed on two drums, flute, trumpet, a small three-holed instrument which Juan told me was a *tchurula,* and a six-stringed guitar called a *soinua.* The players sweated with the vigor of their performance, while the first group of dancers gave way to a second, of comedians and clowns, dressed as gypsies and tinkers, who hopped about performing all manner of antics, evidently making fun of local worthies, for there would be roars of laughter from the crowd at references we did not understand. Then the first group returned to perform a series of intricate and formal dances.

"These dances are called the *bralia,*" whispered Juan. "Are they not superb? Oh, how I wish I could put that motion into words."

Some of the dances were performed with swords, or with staves, which the performers handled with wonderful dexterity. Then they placed a large goblet, full of wine, in the middle of the cleared space, and proceeded to do a most remarkable ballet over and around it.

"This is called the *godalet danza*!" Juan instructed me.

Time and again each of the dancers leaped over the glass, they spun round it, passed by it, skimmed on either side of it, and finally the big one called Zamalzain, who greatly excelled all the rest in the agility and elasticity of his bounds, twiddles, bounces, and pirouettes, was left to dance by himself. At times he seemed to hang in the air over the goblet, remaining suspended apparently in defiance of gravity—and all this was done without spilling one drop of the wine!

Juan, clutching my arm, seemed wholly taken out of himself in delight at the spectacle; he had almost ceased to breathe in his absorption and admiration. When Zamalzain finally concluded his dance with a sweeping bow, Juan joined frenziedly in the applause, then drew a long, long sigh of contentment.

"Oh, how I love to watch the dancing! How I have always wished to take part in it. But, of course, my father would never allow such a thing."

"Why not—?" I was beginning, when he gripped my arm again in an entirely different way. This was a grip of shock and terror. He had gone deathly pale.

"*Oh, mon Dieu! Felix!* Do you see—over there—under the big lime tree—standing under the light—there are *Cocher and Father Vespasian*!"

"No, no, Juan, you must be mistaken—surely"— But while one of his hands was still frantically gripping my wrist, the other pointed, and following the direction of his shaking finger, I saw two figures, one of which was indubitably the man called Cocher, readily recognizable by his tallness, shock of white hair, and the black patch over one eye; while the other . . .

"Quick! Come away!" I hissed to Juan, and dragged him back into the crowd, glancing over my shoulder for an instant as I did so. It seemed to me that the two men, after a word had passed between them, were moving in our direction.

The crowd had broken up, now that the formal dancing was over, and many smaller parties of dancers were capering about the streets, to the music of fifes, tabors, tambourines, and *zambombas*. On the edge of the main square I noticed a pile of costumes, cast off by the group called the Reds while they refreshed themselves with wine. Struck by a lightning notion I clapped the wicker framework of the character called Zamalzain over my head, and Juan, instantly divining my plan, thrust his beretta and jacket into his bag, and pulled on the scarlet bell-embroidered jacket, scarlet silk scarf, and three-cornered hat hung with ribbons of a Satan. He also snatched up the Satan's wand, a stick adorned with red ribbons ending in fishhooks.

"Dance!" I shouted in his ear, and myself broke into a series of gambols, capers, twirls, and prances, which I hoped would sufficiently resemble the steps of Zamalzain to deceive the onlookers; I had occasionally (unknown to my grandfather) danced at the peasants' celebrations in Villaverde, and learned some flamenco steps which were not too unlike these Basque dances;

while Juan, with admirable spirit, considering the fright we had just been given and the distance we had traveled that day, followed my example, striding with a springing gait, leaping into the air, spinning round, and flinging out the hooked ribbons of his staff as if to snatch members of the audience into his power.

"I am Satan!" he cried. "Beware, beware, ye sinners!"

I could not help but admire his courage, since the moment before he had seemed almost paralytic with terror.

And I myself, indeed, had felt a most singular clutch of dread at my heart when I set eyes on that figure under the lime tree. Surely it was *not* Father Vespasian? Surely it *was* Plumet? The two men had been much of a height; I thought I must have been mistaken. Father Vespasian was drowned, he had sunk below the waters of St. Just bay; or, by this time, his drowned corpse would have been retrieved by the monks of the Abbey and would be lying at rest in the graveyard on the headland. What could the Abbot possibly be doing in the *place du marché* of St. Jean Pied de Port? I *must* have been mistaken, I thought, as I swung and capered and gesticulated, making my way all the time, erratically but steadily, toward the edge of town, while Juan followed close behind me.

Then, rounding a corner, we saw the two men again; this time they had with them a shorter one, hunchbacked, his small pointed head sunk between his shoulders. They stood at an intersection of ways, talking urgently, looking in all directions, evidently uncertain which road to take. The one who might or might not be Plumet had his head turned away; I could not see his face.

There was no choice but to dance past them, for our example had been followed by a dozen others and we were now at the head of quite a procession, while the spectators laughed and cheered us on. I felt confident enough in my concealing horse's head, but what of Juan? Spinning around, I saw that he had pulled the Satan's red silk scarf up to cover his face, so that only his eyes showed above it; thus disguised, he boldly danced up to the three men, casting out his hooked ribbons as if to tweak them; then, as the third man turned round, he bounded after me, taking a huge leap, which looked as if it were done in exuberance but which I thought was really prompted by sheer terror; for, seen thus close to, there could be no question but that the third man was the Abbot of St. Just de Seignanx, white-faced, flame-eyed, unmistakable. What could he be doing here, with members of the Mala Gente? One could not even begin to guess. My heart felt like an icy stone inside me as we quitted the flare-lit streets of the town and plunged into the darkness beyond.

The other dancers had left us and turned back into the town; we were suddenly alone.

"Are they after us?" gasped Juan.

"No, we have lost them—I think. Let us hide here and wait."

A beech grove bordered the highway; we plunged into its shadow, put twelve yards or so between us and the road, then stopped, hidden behind trees, and waited to see if we were pursued. A long time passed and nobody came; all we could hear was the distant music of the masquerade, and the beating of our own hearts.

At last I drew a long breath and said, "I think we have managed to lose them. But we had better not go back into the town."

"Oh, no, no!" breathed Juan. "Let us not lose a minute but put as much distance between us and them as possible. What shall we do with these?"

He was pulling off his Satan's hat and jacket.

"Hang them on a tree," said I, doing so with my horse's head. "Somebody will be sure to find them." And I laid a few coins at the foot of the tree to pay the owner for their use.

Despite his terror and chattering teeth, Juan could not refrain from a chuckle.

"Even you, virtuous Felix, sometimes steal!"

"That was not theft but borrowing," I replied coldly.

I felt his thin, cold hand steal into mine.

"I know it! I was only teasing. And I think you showed wonderful *présence d'esprit* in clapping on that horse's head and beginning to dance. *I* felt so paralyzed with fear that I was like a rabbit hypnotized by a serpent; I was on the point of walking up and offering myself back to them! But how well you dance, Felix! I had no idea that an English boy could foot it so nimbly."

"You did not do so badly yourself! And I am not English, but Spanish."

Then we saved our breath for walking through the wood, which was very dark, for the moon had not yet risen. On the far side, beyond the trees, we almost tripped over a village; I say almost tripped, for the houses, or hovels, were so low that they seemed more like pigsties or dog kennels than dwellings meant for humans. But human they were, lit by small gleams of light, enlivened by low human voices, and made welcoming by smells of food and cookery.

In fact a shrill astonished babble of voices greeted us as we stumbled into the dim circle of illumination; voices of wonder and alarm, then of welcome and goodwill. For a moment or two I was filled with fearful uneasiness, remembering a strange heathen hamlet of mountain folk I had wandered upon in Spain, where the inhabitants seemed prepared to make me into a human sacrifice; but I soon saw that these little people were of a very different kind.

Little they certainly were; none of them was higher than myself or Juan, and many were far shorter; they were blunt-featured, with strangely shaped ears, but not otherwise peculiar or ill-looking; the garments they wore were similar to all others in the region, but each had, embroidered upon the shoulder, a three-toed crow's-foot emblem. They clustered around us, smiling and pointing, but speaking among themselves such a rustic form of the Basque language that, so far as I was concerned, they might well have been a flock of crows cawing.

Juan seemed in no way disconcerted by their appearance, and they were plainly prepared to be friendly and hospitable to us; I soon saw why, for among them was the small man with the wizened face and the tiny girl whose cat Juan had saved from the foxhound; the latter went up to Juan and wound her threadlike arms round his knees—she could reach no higher—while he, looking somewhat embarrassed, patted her head.

Then we were ushered into a hut—for their thatched houses were little more; the thatch came down to the ground, and a hole let out the smoke from the fire in the middle. We were given something in wooden bowls that seemed to be a mess of biscuit, onions, liver, and beans, all boiled together, washed down with rough red wine; it was tasty enough, and we were in no mood to be critical. We then made signs indicating a great need for sleep, and were respectfully led to a smaller hut on the edge of the settlement, which contained a heap of bracken and straw piled high.

"Felix?" whispered Juan through the silence when at last we had been left alone.

"Yes?"

"Was that *indeed* Father Vespasian? It looked like him—yet it also looked like Plumet. *Which of them was it?*"

His cold hand stole once more into mine.

I took a long time trying to decide what to answer him, and before I made up my mind, he whispered, "Do you think it could be *both* of them?"

"Yes. I do. That is what I do think."

"S-so do I," he said, shivering. "And the thought makes my heart die of terror within me."

"Come, now," said I, though I knew exactly how he felt, for I felt the same, "pluck up your spirits. Think! God has seen fit to help and preserve us so far. Why, we do not know. But He must have some purpose in leading us along. I do not believe that He will desert us now. So we must not let ourselves be too afraid. It would be ungrateful."

"Y-yes," Juan agreed, but he sounded unconvinced.

"Ask me some questions in Euskara."

After a moment Juan said, "What is a man?"

"Gizon."

"Men?"

"Gizonek."

"What is 'I have seen the house'?"

"Ikusi dut etxea."

"Very good, Felix. You are coming along."

Then he repeated a couple of lines of Basque verse which I could not understand.

"What does that mean, Juan?"

"I will wait until I can translate it into English to tell you," he said, and chuckled. *"Gab-boon,* Felix."

"Gab-boon, Juan."

And so we slept.

5

We encounter gypsies and buy pottoka; *are entertained by a hermit and obliged to visit a smith; the* bertsulari *contest; fleeing the Gente, we enter the mountains.*

I was awakened by a sharp cry and sprang confusedly from my pile of bracken, fearing I do not know what—devils, brigands, wild beasts. I had been roused from some black and fiery dream, in which Father Vespasian, with a white crumpled face and eyes like beacons flaring, pursued us, wielding a pronged trident, over an oozy marsh in which we sank at every step, while he rapidly overtook us.

"What is it, what is it?" I mumbled in fright, looking all about me.

But the cause of Juan's alarm was merely a large rat which had sniffed inquisitively at his nose and now, startled at our noise, scampered away and out through a hole in the thatch.

"Only a rat!" I exclaimed in disgust. "I thought at least we were surrounded by the Gente! What a child you are!"

"I hate rats." Juan gave me an angry look. "If it had sniffed at *your* nose, I daresay you would have jumped and cried out. You need not be so superior!"

"I'm sorry—it was just a joke," I said hastily, not wishing to begin the day with bad feeling between us. We had enough to lower our spirits, remembering last night, not to let ourselves be disputing over trifles. "Let us get out of this frowsty little hut."

So we crawled through the door hole into fresh air and looked at the place we had come to overnight. A queer small village it was, of stone-and-thatch hovels, each surrounded by a vegetable patch. The men were all gone; doubtless to work. A rocky brook ran nearby in which some of the women were washing their linen. Others came smiling to us, their brown creased faces full of goodwill, and soon offered us a bowl of coffee—rather rank and rusty, with blobs of greasy goats' milk floating on top—and some lumps of stale bread. This unpalatable breakfast I choked down as politely as I could, but Juan drank the coffee only, indicating by signs and whispered Basque phrases that he had trouble in swallowing.

Several of the women conferred together, and fetched another, who, from her small hunched shape and deeply wrinkled face the color of a brown walnut husk, looked to be the grandmother of them all. She carefully and frowningly inspected Juan's throat, removing the bandage that Madame Mauleon had placed on it, then fetched a small clay pot full of strong-smelling thick dark-green ointment, and spread this over Juan's skin, rubbing the neck strongly for a long time with aged fingers as dark and knotted as tree roots. Rolling his eyes at me in one expressive glance,

Juan patiently submitted to this treatment; afterward she replaced the bandage and uttered some long admonition, to which he appeared to listen with great attention, nodding his head obediently from time to time.

She then questioned him; as to our direction, I thought, for I heard the name Pamplona in his reply, and Orria; also the words *zamariz, zamaria* several times repeated. At last she appeared to bless us, making an odd crow's-foot shape in the air with her gnarled hand; the other women and children seriously saluted us, and the little one whose cat Juan had saved once more hugged his knees. Then we were permitted to go on our way; and I did so, I must confess, with no little relief, for in spite of their friendly behavior I had felt a sense of discomfort in the queer little place; also it did smell most vilely of rancid fat and other things not proper to mention.

"Who *were* those strange little people?" I demanded of Juan when we had put a fair distance between ourselves and the village, walking southward toward Spain and the high mountains.

"They are Cagots," Juan replied, as if the name should mean something to me. But it meant nothing at all.

"What in the world are Cagots? They are not brownies? Fairy people?"

He burst out laughing.

"*Nom d'un nom, non!* Ai! Laughing makes my neck hurt. But to think that I should hear the practical, sensible Felix ask such a question!"

"Well," I said, somewhat nettled, "only a day or so ago you told me that your great-great-grandmother was a witch. And besides—" Besides, I might have said, you and I last night saw something the strangeness of which far outruns the oddity of a tribe of dirty little pixies or leprechauns: we saw a man apparently risen from the dead and inhabiting the body of another.

But I held my tongue. The day was too young for such dire and haunting topics. Practical and sensible, Juan had called me; practical and sensible I must endeavor to be.

"Well, I have never heard of Cagots. Who or what are they?"

"Why, they are Cagots," he said. "That is all I can tell you. They have always lived in the Basque country, for many hundreds of years. They have their own little villages, mostly on the outskirts of larger towns, and by law they must wear the crow's-foot mark to distinguish them, for they are not allowed to marry folk other than Cagots, or to sell things in the market. So they are mostly carpenters, or roadworkers, or masons."

"Are they Christians?"

"Of course! And they have their own little entrances and windows in the churches, so that they may hear the service without troubling the rest of the congregation. I do not know *what* my father would have said," Juan remarked cheerfully, "if he had known that I spent the night in a Cagot village. Some people think that they are lepers."

My flesh crawled at the notion, but he added reassuringly, "That is not true at all. Well, you could see so for yourself. Others say that they must be descended from the Saracens, or the Moors, who lived in this land long ago, and became converted to Christianity."

"Well, they were certainly very hospitable," said I, "and it was lucky for us that we encountered them, for we could not have gone back to the town. What was all that rigmarole the old dame was telling you?"

"Oh, first she told me to leave the green paste on my neck for three days, and to say a prayer to St. Benedict before I wash it off. Also she asked where we were going, and when I said that we wished to buy ponies to cross the mountains, she told me that if we go eastward we may very likely meet a train of gypsies coming to the horse fair from Jaca."

This was useful information, and we sat down to study the map.

It would plainly be folly to travel anywhere near the Pass of Roncesvalles, or Orria, as the Basques call it, for the Gente would be most likely to expect us there; so this advice chimed well with my own inclination, which was to continue eastward along the flanks of the mountains and cross into Spain by some small pass. Accordingly we set off walking with the sun in our faces and presently came to the highway which led up from St. Jean to the Pass of Roncesvalles, where Roland, with his great sword Durendal, defended France against all the might of the Saracen army. Looking warily all around us for signs of the Gente, we paused here, but seeing none, crossed the highway and struck into the woods again. Our way now was over a series of tree-covered ridges with high peaks on our right and yet higher ones beyond; every now and then, through the neck of a valley or from some high point, we would catch a heart-stopping glimpse of huge snowy crests glittering in the early light. We crossed brook after brook tumbling down from the mountains into France, and the woods about us were of larch and spruce and beech.

To steer my mind away from anxious thoughts, I recommenced teaching English to Juan and found that he was a lightning-quick pupil, able to remember all that he had learned yesterday and eager to acquire more. I taught him many of the ballads which I had heard, as a tiny boy, from my father, when I believed him to be a stableman; and various others that I had learned from the English sailor, Sam, who accompanied me from Llanes to Plymouth.

Juan speedily caught the English words and pronunciation; he seemed to have a wonderful facility for remembering such things.

"You have a great gift for learning, Juan," I told him with truth.

"Well," he said seriously, "I wish to be able to write poems in many languages. That is my intention."

"Poetry? You wish to write *poetry*?" I was somewhat confounded at the ambition of putting his talent to such a use.

"I already do write poetry in French and Euskar."

His tone was a trifle haughty. "I am a poet! And when I am grown, that is what I hope to do most in the world. That is—" He stopped abruptly.

"But—!" Poetry is not proper work for a practical person, for a grown man, is what I first intended to say. Looking at Juan's resolute eyes and tight-pressed lips, however, I amended my remark to "How could you ever make a living by writing poetry? I am sure poets are not well paid. Cervantes was a great writer. But he did not make a living from writing *Don Quixote*!"

"People will wish to buy *my* poems," said Juan stoutly.

"But suppose that you should marry? How could you ever support a family?"

"I shall never marry," he said quickly. "I have other intentions. And perhaps my Uncle León may leave me a sum of money so that I may be independent."

I thought of the wide uplands of Villaverde which would one day be mine, and the care and trouble of looking after such an estate.

"A mighty easy life, yours will be! Doing nothing but write poems all day, and living just as you please."

"Writing poetry is not at all easy!" retorted Juan, firing up. "Sometimes you can fret and sweat and frown, and feel as if you were pushing your whole soul out of your body, and yet hardly one line comes as it ought."

Well, then, I thought, why not find some other occupation, something more useful in the world, be a merchant or a lawyer? But I knew what trouble would follow if I uttered such a sentiment aloud, so instead I asked, "Can you recite a poem that you have made up? I should indeed like to hear one."

"They are mostly in Euskara," he replied. "Basque is a wonderful language for poetry. But I will try to translate one into English as we go along, and then I will say it to you."

Now, faintly, ahead of us we began to hear the jingling of bells, and after a while half a dozen lean wolfish dogs loped up and sniffed around us with lowered heads until I flourished my *makhila* at them, whereupon they slunk farther off but continued to eye us hungrily.

Presently their owners came in sight: a long gypsy caravan, trains of horses, mules, and asses, some led, some driven, by a dozen men and women—dark, swarthy, and somewhat Moorish in their appearance, with gold rings in their ears and black tangled ringlets. The old *zingaro*, or leader of the tribe, had a massive gray beard, and his bushy grizzled hair was confined in a netted bag. The men wore red canvas breeches, deerskin jackets, and sandals that laced up to the knee. Some had wolfskins over their shoulders, which gave them a fierce appearance. The women wore striped skirts and petticoats, and carried musical instruments, tambours and mandolins. They had brilliantly colored shawls knotted over heads and shoulders. Two of the younger ones displayed golden arrows passed through their knotted black locks as a sign that they were unmarried.

"*Egg-en-noon*," we greeted them in Euskara, but the old *zingaro* replied in excellent French: "Bonjour, messieurs! How can I serve the young gentlemen?" And he looked very sharply at us, especially at Juan, with his twinkling black eyes.

We said that we wished to buy a couple of ponies. The *zingaro* nodded to a pair of the younger men, and they led forward six or seven tiny beasts.

"Why! They are hardly bigger than dogs!" said I.

"They are *pottoka*—mountain ponies," Juan informed me. "My Uncle León had several. They will be quite suitable for our purpose, as they can find their way over any kind of country. They are strong as oxen, sagacious, and obedient."

This, to me, seemed just as well; nobody would select the *pottoka* for their looks: they have huge heads, pot bellies, short knobby legs, not particularly straight, and coats so thick and rough that they resemble sheep or bears rather than ponies. Compared to my Spanish grandfather's Andalusian steeds, or the magnificent hunters of Arab descent that I had seen in England, these were like dwarfs or gnomes rather than ponies— mounts more suitable for Cagots than for ordinary people.

I daresay I regarded them somewhat superciliously, for Juan nipped my arm and whispered, "Do not curl your lip so, or the old *capo* will take offense and clap half as much again on the price."

After long consideration, we selected a pair: one, a bay, the most handsome of the string, with something of spirit in his eye; he flung up his head and lashed out at the boy who led him; the other, a piebald with particolored hooves, a white face, and a black forelock. Juan took a mighty fancy to this one and urged me in a whisper to make an offer for him.

I had chaffered for horses before, on my grandfather's estate and during my journey to England; so I commenced by telling the *zingaro* that these two appeared to be the best of a very poor string, but that, nonetheless, they seemed wretched, slow-paced, knock-kneed, broken-winded beasts, hardly appropriate for such noble riders as we, and we would feel it a condescension to offer him ten shillings for the pair. At this his eyes and hands flew up to heaven; he exclaimed that it must be our intention to ruin him, either that or we were joking, and named a sum six times as much, which I then divided by three. We continued dickering in this manner for about forty minutes, carefully examining the two ponies point by point, breaking off sometimes to converse about the weather, the country, the condition of the mountain passes, then beginning again. At last our bargaining was concluded by my offering a gold guinea for the two beasts, with their harness (a sum about double what I had first named, and a third of what had been asked). I thought it was a little more than they were worth, but felt that we had made not too bad a bargain. The *zingaro* gripped my hand in his, and the sale was concluded.

Meanwhile a couple of girls had lit a fire, pounded chocolate, heated water, brought out flat cakes of unleavened bread and earthenware cups; presently they offered us a dish of *miga*—breadcrumbs steeped in water, sprinkled first with salt, then with hot oil in which garlic has been scattered—as well as cups of hot chocolate. Of which we were glad to partake, for our breakfast had been scanty, and the walk long.

While we sipped our chocolate one of the gypsy girls began to play on her mandolin and sing, a barbaric chant not unlike the flamenco singing of Spain. After that the *capo* invited us to contribute a song, so I obliged with an English ballad about a faithful farmer's son that I had been used to singing with my friend Sam. This was received with friendly applause. Then Juan explained with signs that he could not sing for them since he had hurt his throat, but he then, after some hesitation, proceeded to recite a Basque ballad about a poor girl who was sent away from her home to marry the king of Hungary and there died of grief for her Basque sweetheart. I could not understand it all, but caught a word here and a word there. Juan recited the poem in a kind of whisper, softly, but very affectingly, and the gypsies listened to it in most concentrated silence, with deep frowns and sighs of appreciation. At the conclusion Juan received quite an ovation, one of the girls kissed him, and the old *capo*, taking one of the younger men on one side, gave him some instructions, which ended in our bay pony being led away and replaced by a black one.

"Better for you—this one!" explained the chief with a grin. By which, a little abashed, I gathered that the bay must suffer from some defect which we would only have discovered later, when the vendors were far away.

"So we have your poetry to thank for saving us from a bad bargain," I said to Juan, after the money had been handed over, farewells cordially exchanged, and the gypsies had continued on their journey toward St. Jean, while we, in high spirits, astride our new mounts, rode on eastward. Juan had taken the piebald, I mounted the shaggy black, who proved to have more energy in him than had shown at first appearance.

Juan looked a little smug, smiling over his pony's parti-colored mane, but he said only, "That was a fine song about the farmer's son, Felix. You must teach me the words."

Thinking of the gypsies on their way to St. Jean, I said in sudden anxiety, "You do not suppose that the gypsies will tell the Gente about us?"

"No. The Gente have nothing to do with gypsies. Neither trusts the other. The gypsies do not mingle with other people. They move about the country on their own concerns. When I was with the Gente I heard them speaking of gypsies with dislike and suspicion."

"Tell me your ballad about the king of Hungary," I invited him. "For I caught only one word in three of the Euskara."

"It is not my ballad," he explained carefully. "It is an old one from Tardets. I heard it from our cook, Barbe." Then, to my utter astonishment, after a fairly long pause for thought, he gave a rendering of it in English, as follows:

"Two gold lemons grow in our town
The king of Hungary has asked for one
They are not ripe, the king has been told
But soon he'll be given a lemon of gold.

Father, you sold me as if I were a cow
If Mother were living, you'd not have done so
To faraway Hungary I'd not have gone
I'd have married my love in Tardets town.

By my father I was sold
My elder brother received the gold
My next brother sat me on my steed
My youngest brother rode by my side.

Sister, from Sala's house look forth
Feel if the wind blows south or north
If north, send word to my love, and say
Soon my soul will have flown away.

The bells are tolling in Tardets town
And every lass wears a funeral gown
Since out of the gate our sister rode
The horse she sat wore a saddle of gold."

"But that is wonderful!" I cried. "Juan, you really are a clever boy! I could no more turn a French poem into a Spanish one than I could take wing and fly over those mountains."

To my surprise Juan did not seem particularly impressed or gratified by my words of praise. He took them quite as a matter of course. Indeed he rather put my congratulations to one side, and treated me, instead, to a lecture on the wretched lot of girls, especially in the Basque country.

"I know the happenings of that ballad took place long ago—if they are real at all—but girls, even of good family, are still bought and sold like cattle at a fair."

"I do not know any girls," said I, "save a miller's daughter in Galicia and a blacksmith's daughter in Llanes. And *she* was able to suit herself about marrying the man she loved. But it is true," I added, "that her father liked the man, too. If he had not, I suppose it might have been otherwise."

"If I had had a sister," said Juan, "she would have been given in marriage without her wishes being consulted at all. And she would never have been free, as we are, to ride about the world and see strange places."

"Unless she was married off to the king of Hungary," I pointed out.

He laughed. "Yes, that is true! But I daresay the king of Hungary was old and hideous, with breath that stank of rotten onions. And once married to him, she would have been a prisoner. I had a cousin," he went on, "who wished to become a nun. She had vowed it. But her family intended her to marry, despite her wish to enter a convent."

"Why should she wish such a thing?" The question came from me half idly. *I* would never wish to enter a monastery, part of my mind was thinking. How glad I was to get away from St. Just! And another part of my attention was concerned with my new pony, who, though so small, was amazingly strong, and not at all prepared to agree that, in our relationship, I was to be the master.

"Why? To pray for the soul of her aunt, who had died tragically. And because—because the life she had was not to her liking."

"How strange! When there is so much to do—so many things to see!"

I guided the steps of my pony through a shallow, rocky brook—*gaves,* the Basques call them.

Juan said, "For boys, yes. Girls are not so lucky. If I had a sister, she must stay at home, and mind her sewing, and marry some person she had never met, chosen by her family because of his wealth."

"True," said I. "Well, I am glad that I am not a girl. Come up, son of Satan!" and I dragged at the enormous head of my tiny mount, who was trying to take a late breakfast from the ferny riverbank.

We rode on, slowly enough, getting accustomed to our new mounts, and trying to decide what names to give them. Juan finally decided that his must be called Harlequin, because of the black and white patches, while I, after some experience of my pony's temper, gave him the name of el Demonio; he was strong and full of spring, had a far better action than might have been expected from his uncouth appearance, had great sagacity, and also a wide range of vicious tricks, doing his best to break my leg against tree trunks, or taking a sudden bolt under low branches in the hope of dashing out my brains, so that I had continual battles with him, and must belabor him briskly on various occasions with my *makhila* before he learned to obey me. Harlequin was more docile; his faults were sulkiness and cowardice. He slouched along as slowly as possible unless continually kicked and urged on his way; and when the *gaves* that we crossed appeared to be more than knee-deep, his eyes had to be blindfolded by wrapping the blanket over his head before he would consent to cross. Despite these drawbacks, Juan's delight in his new belonging was like that of a child with a new toy: At our rest stops he carefully led Harlequin to the best forage, found him handfuls of tender grass, brushed the pony's coat with a wisp of bracken until it shone like a magpie, and, as we rode, would be continually patting and encouraging him with a flow of nonsense talk.

"You treat that animal as if he were your brother," I said, laughing.

"My brother! I would not give a cup of *water* to my *brother*!" retorted Juan, solicitously escorting Harlequin to a convenient pool in a brook by the side of which we had paused to eat a *merienda*, or noon meal.

When saddling up to resume our journey, Juan discovered with dismay a small running sore on his pony's shoulder, evidently caused by the clumsy, over-large straw-stuffed saddle.

"*Miséricorde!* What can we do about this?" he demanded.

"Best bathe it and protect it by a pad," said I. We washed the sore with river water, and contrived a pad from sheep's wool (which, at that spot, hung in plenty from the brambles). But I could see that if Harlequin continued wearing that saddle, plainly not one suited to his size, the sore would become worse, and might, in the end, render him unfit to carry a rider. There was nothing to do, therefore, but repair to a town with a saddler's shop. We accordingly consulted our map again and turned our course northeasterly, through wooded valleys, until we sighted the small town of Tardets, situated between a forest and a river, with mountains to the south. Here, fortunately, we found an excellent saddler's, filled with piles of new leather mule collars, and wooden ox-yokes ornamented with bells, heaps of saddles, and whole groves of leather harness dangling from the rafters. We were able to sell the straw-stuffed saddle and purchase a smaller one, stuffed with wool, and we also bought some *alforjas,* saddlebags, to carry our food and the blanket. Also, at a feed store close by, we bought a sack of grain mixed with chaff for the ponies and a small quantity of caustic ointment with which to anoint the Harlequin's sore shoulder. Juan accepted my word in all these affairs, for it was plain he had no experience in stable matters, whereas I had acquired considerable lore from Bob, my father.

Feeling better equipped, we left the town again, for since our alarming experience at St. Jean we felt that towns were best avoided. While we were in Tardets, Juan continually glanced about in apprehension of seeing somebody from the Gente. I, too, was glad to be away from houses once more, and our horses' heads turned toward the mountains. We soon forsook the highway and followed a bridle track that ran in the direction we wanted. From a hill not far from the town we were able to obtain a huge panoramic view of the land ahead: over the lower hills to the high Pyrenees, with a great peak to the right, another to the left, and a whole line of crests filling the horizon, along which lay the boundary line between France and Spain.

"Now we have our ponies we shall make nothing of the journey!" said Juan joyfully, patting Harlequin's parti-colored crest. "Oh, Felix! I am so *very* obliged to you for buying the *pottoka*. I have never had something of my own before. And, with all his faults, I love the Harlequin dearly."

But then he fell into deep thought, and added in a troubled manner, "I fear, though, that this day's purchases must have made a great hole in your money."

"It is of no consequence," said I. "Money is there to be spent. And we made a little by selling the other saddle. Besides, no doubt your Uncle León will reimburse me," I continued, smiling, a little, to myself, as it occurred to me how much more willingly Juan had accepted the pony than the suit of clothes, which cost only a few reales.

But Juan rode along plunged in concentrated reflection for several miles, and at length said, "If we could chance on a *bertsulari* contest, I could earn money by reciting."

"What are *bertsulari*?"

"They are poets and musicians. At this time of year they hold spring festivals."

"And the contests?"

"Oh, people in the audience call out a theme, and then the *bertsulari* make up a poem about it, or sing a song."

"Well," said I, humoring him, "if we come across such a contest, when your voice is mended, you must certainly enter it. You will very likely win, and then our fortunes will be made."

"Now you are teasing," said he, quite good-humoredly.

So we went on in friendship, and continued to teach one another portions of our languages. But I am bound to admit that Juan made much better progress than I.

Running southward, our path continued by the side of a river into wild scenery—deep, steep valleys, some of them gloomy with pine trees, others bare and rocky with heather and low shrubs. Steeper and steeper yet the valley sides rose about us. Sometimes cave mouths showed black among the overhanging rocks.

"Do you think bears live in those caves?" Juan said, shivering.

"Oh, if they do, I daresay they are no more anxious to be disturbed than we to disturb them."

It was not yet quite dusk, but the air was thickening, and after a while I began to wonder if we should consider passing the night in one of those same caves, for no village or farm or human habitation had come into sight for a long time.

"Oh, Felix, look!" whispered Juan suddenly, reining in his pony, and pointing ahead with a hand that trembled. "There *is* a bear, I do believe!"

The mountains were shrouding themselves in mist for the night, and the light was now very poor. The valley along which we rode was filled with the sound of tumbling water, from the river below us among its rocks, and numerous small cascades that leaped down the hillsides to join it.

And ahead of us, in a larch grove, we could see something perhaps the size of a bear, black in color, moving about. Yet the ponies, strangely enough, showed no fear.

"These fellows would shy and scamper off fast enough if it were a bear," said I, and urged el Demonio on with a kick.

The figure in the larch grove then turned and straightened, and we were able to see that it was a man. For a moment my heart thumped uncontrollably, because the man wore a black monk's robe; could this, *yet again,* be Father Vespasian come back to haunt us?

But as we drew nearer, I saw that he appeared wholly different from the Abbot—a small, somewhat puzzled-looking man, with scanty soft gray hair and a nut-brown complexion.

"I did not expect riders to come along this path so late," he murmured, gazing at us as if we were members of some strange species. Yet he did not appear unwelcoming; only a little confused, as if, perhaps, he were not quite right in his wits.

"God must have sent you," he added after a moment.

"Certainly, my father," I said, dismounting and saluting him. "We travel in the hand of God."

"Well you had better come . . . to my . . . to my . . . house," he told us slowly; I thought that perhaps he had not used human speech for some weeks, or even months; it seemed to come away so rustily from his tongue.

His "house" proved to be an old barn, built perhaps for storing mountain hay. It was strongly constructed of round boulders mortised together, with a massive roof and deep overhanging eaves, and stood snugly at the foot of a hillock in a turn of the valley, protected from wind and weather by a clump of great chestnut trees.

Inside he had established his dwelling quarters at one end, and a kind of chapel at the other, with a shrine and statue of Ste. Engrâce, and a burning lamp.

We hobbled the legs of our ponies and let them

stray outside, for the grass was sweet and plentiful and the air not cold.

A round pit, dug in the center of the barn, showed where the hermit sometimes permitted himself the luxury of a fire, and I took the liberty of gathering sticks and lighting one, for we were somewhat stiff from the unaccustomed exercise of riding, and the warmth was welcome. Juan pulled out some of our provisions: ham of the mountains (said to be cured in snow) and bread, and milk, and ewes'-milk cheese, which we had procured in Tardets. The hermit provided a thin soup on which, he said, he mainly lived; from its bright green and bitter flavor it might, perhaps, have been made from wild sorrel and such herbs. He accepted a little of our cheese and a mouthful of milk, but would not touch the ham.

Slowly, through the course of the evening, we heard his story, which was a sad one: He and his brother, twin sons of a landowner at Bidarray, had both loved the same girl.

"Ah, she had a wonderful beauty!" he murmured reminiscently. "Like that of a waterfall, or the evening star! You could not take your eyes away from her. If I close mine, I can see her still. Indeed, all the young men from the whole region were after her—not only I and Laurent. There was another, also, a wild fellow—but we two were her favorites . . ."

"What was her name, my father?" I asked gently, seeing him so lost in the past.

"Her name? Her name was Laura."

I felt Juan beside me make a slight movement. Then he was still again.

"And what happened?"

In the end, the hermit said, he and his brother had made the poor girl so unhappy, with their quarrels and demands and protestations, that at length she killed herself, by jumping off a crag, rather than be put to the pain, both to herself and them, of choosing between them.

This story made me very indignant. What a piece of folly! I thought. Surely any course would be better than that, which ruined three lives, and perhaps more. But of course I did not state my feeling aloud.

"What did you do then, my father?" quietly inquired Juan.

Then, the hermit said, in bitterness and grief, he and his brother had both abandoned the world and become priests, and, after some years in devotional houses, deciding that this was not sufficient penance, they had resolved to be hermits, and lived thus, each of them alone in the wilderness.

"And I am glad you have come here," he told us, as if now beginning to see us a little more clearly. "For lately I have been certain that my brother—his name is Laurent, mine is Bertrand—I believe he is now very near to dying. Something tells me so. You say that you are traveling over the mountains to Spain?"

"Yes, my father; that is our intention."

"You will go, perhaps, by the Pass of Larraun?"

We said we had as yet made no plan; the most direct route would be the best for us.

"I think," said he, "that you will pass by my brother's abode. He is in an ancient chapel—a ruined Roman tomb—on the slopes of Orhy. What great, great happiness it would give me if you were able to see him, and take my parting message to him."

"Of course we will, if we can, my father," I said, though feeling it highly improbable that, in all that great wilderness of peaks and valleys ahead, we should chance on the ruin where his brother lived. Juan made some affirmative murmur, and I asked, "What is the message?"

"The message is that I love him as a brother. All anger and bitterness have long passed away, and I look to see him soon in a better place, where perhaps *she* will be waiting for us."

We said of course we would do this if it lay within our power, and he then kindly inquired after our own fortunes; by now he seemed more easily attuned to human conversation. At first, I thought, he had hardly been able to catch or understand the words that came from our mouths, and took some time puzzling over them as if they had been in a foreign tongue.

On a sudden impulse I told him the strange tale of Father Vespasian. I told it from the beginning: the unusual power of healing that he possessed, how it had come to him; his fear of death, or the sight of any dead thing; his unnatural, feverish curiosity in Juan and myself, particularly as related to our periods of unconsciousness; our escape from the Abbey and his pursuit of us over the causeway; then his apparent drowning and later reappearance in St. Jean with the Gente, wearing the clothes, and some of the outward look, of Plumet the brigand.

Brother Bertrand listened to all this with silent attention, questioning me now and then.

"You were out of your wits, my child, for how long?"

"Seven or eight weeks, my father. They told me that I was walking about, working, eating, and going to Chapel normally during that time; but I was not conscious that I, Felix, was doing those things."

"And shortly after you recovered you were able to rescue your friend, who had been hanged by those evil men?"

"Yes, my father."

I saw Juan's great eyes turn to stare at me wonderingly in the firelight. I had not told him, before, about the period of my unconsciousness, and I could tell that he was profoundly struck by the tale. I added, "And it was the very man who hanged my friend—Plumet—who has now—who seems to have—to have become Father Vespasian."

I stammered slightly as I said these words. Who would not have? They sounded so strange, so mad.

But Brother Bertrand remarked, placidly enough, "Ah, it will not truly be Father Vespasian. Only part of his external semblance. An unclean spirit from outer darkness has unquestionably been making use of his body. Do you know, my child, what was Father Vespasian's name before he entered that Order?"

"No, my father. I never heard it."

Vaguely I remembered Madame Mauleon saying, "He was a strange man. I never thought he had a genuine vocation." Had she mentioned a name? None that I could remember.

"Ah, well," said Brother Bertrand vaguely, "I merely wondered . . . But it is no matter." He resumed: "I have encountered such cases of possession before. Then, when he was drowned, the spirit will have been driven forth, with great wrenchings and rackings, to take up some other habitation where best it could. And its first choice would be the one nearest to hand, the one waiting on the shore, ready and prepared for any kind of wicked deed."

To hear him say these things, to have my wild guess confirmed, should have been a kind of comfort. But it was not. I felt even more afraid; the blackness and silence of the huge night outside, the great expanses of unseen mountains and empty country seemed pulsing with danger, which we could do nothing to avert. Juan and I huddled together, as close to the fire as we could draw, sensing the strength of the darkness even in this homely, holy place, with the shrine, and lighted lamp, and Ste. Engrâce at one end, the crackle of the fire beside us.

"What can we do, Father? We are very afraid of this man. And he seems able to pursue us wherever we go."

Juan cast a glance at the door and I could not forbear to do likewise; neither of us would have been at all surprised if the scarecrow figure had appeared there at that moment. But, by God's mercy, it did not.

"I feel certain that you are in God's keeping and will, without doubt, escape in the end," slowly answered the hermit. "Yet it is indeed strange how he has such power to follow you. I must devote thought to that. You seem good children . . . What does he want of you? And why should this evil yearning have been awakened because you have both been so close to death, your souls, as it were, separated for a period from your bodies? Damned spirits, of course, are always drawn to children," he went on, more to himself than to us.

"Why is that, my father?" asked Juan, in a low, trembling tone.

Brother Bertrand lifted his eyes from the glowing embers.

"Every being is divided between good and evil; God has willed it so, that each of us resembles a coin, with a white side and a black side. Both sides are required; take either away, and what you have left is not a complete soul."

"I think I understand that," said I.

"Doubtless in the next life it will be otherwise; or, perhaps, endlessly on up through every stage of heavenly excellence, there will always be two sides, but of a different nature. But here, in children especially, the difference between the bright side and the shadow can be very complete; for children are born innocent, straight from the hand of God, and yet the shadow they cast is a long one, long and black, like that of a man at the rising of the sun."

I heard Juan draw a long, deep breath, and then he asked, "What does the evil spirit want, then?"

"He wants that black shadow, for his nourishment, for his sustenance."

"But how can he take one thing without the other?"

"We must pray that he will not be able to," said Brother Bertrand, and he stood up, laid a gentle hand on each of our heads in turn, and added, "Come; let us do so now," walking to the shrine, where he knelt in prayer. We were glad to follow his example.

His prayers must have continued all night. Next morning when I awoke he was still there. But at some point Juan and I must have fallen asleep, for when daylight roused us we found ourselves sprawled on a heap of dead leaves and pine needles at the side of the barn.

After we had washed in the brook, and groomed the ponies, and breakfasted frugally, Brother Bertrand showed us a strange little garden that he had planted in a patch of mountain meadow sheltered by the larch grove where we had first set eyes on him.

His garden contained many different flowers: rock-roses, gentians, wild pea, and hundreds of others that I did not know, all set out neatly in rows, with space to walk between. Very different from Père Mathieu's garden at the Abbey! But the queerest thing of all was that beside each plant was set a little cross, made from two slips of wood pegged together and painted white. And on many of the crosses names were written. It was like a miniature graveyard—the plants, with their crosses, stretched a considerable distance across the meadow.

"What are all these, my father?" I inquired.

"Why, they are all the people in France, my son; or at least, all the ones I know about. And the people in Spain, too. See, here is King Louis XVIII; here is *le roi* Ferdinand of Spain; here is *le duc* d'Angoulême . . ." and so he went on, naming many famous persons, and many more of whom I had never heard. "Here is my brother Laurent; here is old Mère Marmottan, who kept the auberge in our village, and the blacksmith, whose name for the moment escapes me. Here is another man, who also loved my beloved Laura. But," he remarked, eyeing the brown and wizened plant that drooped beside the little cross, "I think Victor must have died; I must remember to say a prayer for his fierce, tormented soul." Casually he pulled up the dead plant, throwing it to one side. "Now, my young friends, I shall put in a plant for each of you. I think, my child, for you," he said, eyeing Juan, "an orange rockrose; and for you, my son"—to me—"a yellow lily of the woods, a tiger lily."

How strange, I thought. For in Spain my nickname bad always been "Little Tiger."

"But—my father—"

"Yes, child?"

"These people are still alive. They are not dead? King Louis is on his throne, and King Ferdinand?"

"Certainly they are; it is when they die that I pull out the plant and burn the cross. And I shall know when that moment comes, never fear! See my poor brother's plant—" It was a clump of violets, which had evidently at one time been large and flourishing, but now drooped, with yellow leaves, plainly near its end. "When he dies," Brother Bertrand said, "I shall know, and then I shall take up his plant and replace it with another. These shall be your places"—and he took two small crosses from a pile and set them in the ground. "After you have gone I shall walk up the hillside and find a plant for each of you. And they will remind me of your visit, which has done me good."

Before we departed, Brother Bertrand inspected the Harlequin's sore shoulder and gave us excellent advice about how to foment it before putting on the caustic. He also pointed out a small wound on the fetlock of el Demonio, where he had cut himself with the heel of his off-shoe. To remedy this we made a kind of wet bandage, or gaiter, with some bits of cloth that the hermit provided, lashing it in place with cords. I began to see that we were insufficiently provided with such articles as cloth, string, and sewing materials, and that we must once again visit a town; also Brother Bertrand recommended that we find a blacksmith and have him file down the shoe that was doing the damage. We thanked the hermit for his good counsel, and he told us that he and his brother had been wealthy, and had bred many horses and cattle when they lived at Bidarray. He asked where we came from, and I said Spain; I noticed that Juan did not reply, but busied himself adjusting the Harlequin's girth strap.

Then, rather timidly, I inquired whether Brother Bertrand had given any more thought to our singular and frightening tie with Father Vespasian, or the Something that had taken possession, first of him and then of Plumet. How could we escape him? Or how could we combat him? (Though even to suggest such a notion filled me with an icy horror all up and down my spine.)

"I have been thinking deeply all night about your situation," said the hermit. "I laid the matter before God. And He told me that you must seek out my brother, who is wiser than I. Laurent will give you better advice than I can; or perhaps he will be able to defend you from your assailant. You must certainly visit him, and that without delay, for the invisible tendril that joins us is tightening daily, and this warns me that his end is now very close."

On hearing this reply I gazed with a certain blankness at Brother Bertrand, wondering if God had *really* told him to advise our visiting his brother, or did the suggestion merely come from his own wish to be reconciled before it was too late? And how in the world would we be able to discover a ruined chapel somewhere on the slopes of the Pic d'Orhy, a large mountain covering many kilometers of country? And supposing the brother had died already by the time we got there?

"I can see that the Demiurge is putting other thoughts into your mind," said Brother Bertrand calmly. At which I blushed. "But I hope, and not only for my own sake, that you will do as I recommend."

Then he went back into his barn and came out again with a tiny silver bell, about the size of a crab apple.

"Unclean spirits hate the sound of a bell," he said, smiling, handing the little bright object to Juan, who exclaimed, "Why, of course! Of course they do! Why did I not think of that? I used to help the old *benedicta* in—" he stopped short, then added, "She said the power of bells would keep away any number of devils. Thank you, my father! But what will you do without it, here in this lonely place?"

"I must rely on the power of prayer, my child, which has never failed me yet."

So, leaving him our supply of milk and bread (he would not take cheese or ham) we rode off and left him looking after us somewhat wistfully, his hand upraised in blessing for as long as he could see us, before the track turned round an angle of the valley.

After that we rode for many kilometers in silence.

I WAS feeling not a little sad, and heavy; Brother Bertrand's talk, his account of having been, as it were, in conversation with God all through the night, had reminded me of my own trouble, which was that for the past few days, ever since we had left the Abbey, God had remained silent and had not spoken to me, either to communicate His wishes, or to scold me, or to let me know if I was following the right course. Each night I had duly said my prayer, and sometimes during the day as well, when danger threatened; but I had no intimation that my petition was acknowledged, or even heard. I was reminded of how one drops leaves and twigs into a brook: they are swept away to an unknown destination. Nothing ever comes back. I had never felt myself so disjoined from my Adviser before, even at times of dire danger; and I could not help wondering miserably if, somehow, I had gone astray from the direction that I was meant to follow, and thereby cut myself off from God's discourse. Or was He testing me, to see how well I could manage when left unguided? The only thing that cheered me at all (and that not greatly) was to believe this; I had to battle, at times, against a most forlorn sense of dragging discouragement, loneliness, and abandonment. Yet, Felix! I said to myself, you should be accustomed to that. You managed without help from earthly parents; you cannot expect your Heavenly one to be keeping an eye on you every minute of the day; fie, for shame! And you have Juan to care for now; so show a brighter face and come out of the dismals.

Juan, also, seemed unusually silent and preoccupied as he rode along, despite the cheerful tinkle of Brother Bertrand's bell, which he had fastened to the

Harlequin's browband. Sometimes he sent a frowning, pondering glance in my direction; sometimes he rode deep in thought, with his chin sunk forward and his eyes on his pony's shoulders.

After perhaps a couple of hours he suddenly exclaimed, "Felix?"

"Well?"

"Was that *true*? That tale you told the hermit? That you had been astray in your wits—out of your senses—unconscious for so many weeks, before you and Father Antoine found me in the thicket?"

"Yes, it was true," I answered him rather drily. "I do not tell untrue tales."

He flushed up, but went on: "Do you not think that is exceedingly strange? It seems almost as if you were *waiting* for me in that Abbey; as if you had been sent there to await my arrival." He ended in rather a diffident tone, but I answered,

"Yes, that is how I felt about it."

"That we were meant to travel together? But why? What is the purpose behind it, do you think?"

"How can I tell?" I began to say, rather impatiently, but then added, the notion suddenly coming into my head, "Perhaps it is because of—of Father Vespasian. Singly we would not be a match for him. But together—with the help of God—"

"Ah, yes!" he agreed, his face lighting up. "Perhaps that might be the reason." But then he shivered. "I wish, though, that it were *not* so."

"Do you wish that we were not traveling together?"

"Why, no," he said slowly. "I—I am growing accustomed to you, Felix. You are teaching me a great deal that I did not know before."

This in some degree warmed my troubled heart, and I said, more cheerfully, "Well, let me continue to teach you English, for I begin to fear that there is no hope of my ever mastering Euskara. You are right, it is a language of the devil! Have you made a translation of your poem yet?"

"Yes, I have done so," he replied. "I did it last night while you and Brother Bertrand were at your prayers."

"You did not pray?" I was a little shocked.

But Juan said, "Oh, I can only pray to God in one sentence. He understands that. I greet Him, then it is done. I hope to live some day entirely in His honor, but I am sure He does not want me to be continually dinning my petitions into His ears, or repeating meaningless words by rote. Besides," he added thoughtfully, "I believe that poetry *is* a form of prayer. Whom should it be addressed to, if not to God?"

This made me look on poetry in a new light, and while I was thinking about it, Juan recited his little verse, first in Euskara, then in English:

> "Bortian artzana eta
> Ez jeisten ardirie;
> Ontza jan edan eta
> Equin lo zabalie

Enune desiratzen
Bizitze hoberic
Mundian ez ahalda
Ni bezan iruric!

Shepherd on the green hill
Guarding my sheep
I eat and drink at will,
Peacefully sleep;
Why should I ask
More than my share?
Who could be happier
Anywhere?"

After he had spoken the words I, in my turn, was
silent for a considerable time. Then I asked him, "You
think that poetry is a kind of thanks? For the things
we see, the things we have?"

"Why not?" said Juan. "If a friend gives you a gift—
as you gave me the Harlequin, as the hermit gave us his
silver bell—you say, do you not, 'I thank you, friend,
for this beautiful black-and-white *pottoka,* for this bell
which cheers me with its sound and keeps away unclean
spirits.' You say, 'My heart is filled with thankfulness
at sight of the wooded hills and the rivers pouncing
down like white arrows.' What is that but a poem?"

"Yes. I think I begin to understand a little of what
it is all about."

"Very good!" said Juan, laughing. "For indeed, I
was beginning to fear that you never would!"

And so we rode on feeling comfortable with one another.

Yet, that very evening, we were quarreling again.

We had agreed that, since Brother Bertrand advised finding a blacksmith to file el Demonio's shoe, that had best be done without delay, and we therefore made our way to the banks of the Gave de Mauleon, which, according to our map, farther up its course passed by a little village named Licq-Athérey. By late afternoon we had reached this place, which contained several houses and two large inns; for, as we learned, the waters that spring from the ground hereabouts possess a healing virtue, and sick people come from both France and Spain to be purged from stiffness of the joints or afflictions of the kidney and stomach. The village is not large, but thriving, and there were a number of wealthy-looking people strolling about. We found a forge without difficulty, but the smith was busy replacing a metal hoop on the wheel of a lady's coach, and we were obliged to wait our turn. I suggested to Juan that I should remain with the ponies outside the smithy, in case some other customer should push in ahead of us; for I wanted to be away from there as soon as might be. The atmosphere of the village made me uneasy, though, to be sure, it seemed a clean, pleasant enough little place.

Juan therefore volunteered to go and buy provisions, cloth for more bandages, tape, and thread. I gave him a couple of francs from my store and urged him not to let himself be cheated by crafty stallkeepers.

It had struck me several times that Juan must have led a vastly protected life; he seemed quite unaccustomed to such practical matters as buying, selling, and bargaining. Perhaps, I thought, his father had been an extremely rich merchant and Juan had been reared like a young prince, secluded from the common people. He seldom said more than a couple of words about his homelife.

At my admonitions he flushed a little pink, but grinned and said that he would do his best.

Time drifted slowly by, the blacksmith eventually completed his work on the coach wheel, and then I led in el Demonio, who lived up to his name, snorted, lashed out, whinnied, and behaved as if all his legs were to be chopped off, instead of having his shoes rendered more comfortable. While he was about it, the smith tightened several nails in them, and then performed the same service for the Harlequin, so that we need not risk a cast shoe in the mountains. He inquired whither we were bound, and I replied, to visit my aunt at Lescun on the Pic d'Anie, and then reddened at the lie, thinking how Juan would mock me if he were there. But the blaze of the smith's fire concealed my blush and he did not observe it.

After that a pair of oxen were brought in for shoeing. This was carried out in a singular manner, which I was interested to watch, for we do it differently in Galicia: The forge contained a stout framework of timber on which each ox in turn was hoisted up by a broad belt passed under his belly, and his legs were lashed together so that the smith could work at leisure without fear of being gored or kicked. The bellowing of those uplifted beasts was amazing to hear; I daresay the poor things thought their last hour had come. I wished that Juan would return, so that he, too, might enjoy the spectacle, but he did not; and then I thought that this was just as well, for it might have reminded him of his own narrow escape from death.

Both oxen having been shod, they were yoked up and led away, and the smith proceeded to quench his fire and shut up his forge for the night. Juan still had not returned, twilight was falling, and I was by now growing decidedly anxious. What in the world could have happened to him? Surely he could not have taken all this long time in the purchase of bread, milk, sausage, tape, and cloth? My fears were heightened because, earlier, while I had been holding el Demonio's bridle in the smithy, I had beheld a little hunchbacked fellow somewhat closely scrutinizing first me and then the Harlequin in the road outside. I had not set eyes on the member of the Gente called Jorobado, and had no means of knowing whether this could be the same hunchback as Juan had seen in Hasparren, but his curiosity in me and our humble mounts seemed excessive; which was one of the reasons why I had told the smith that lie about our destination.

"My friend is a long time about buying bread," said I to him now as he closed his door. "May I tie up our *pottoka* behind your forge while I go to look for him?"

And welcome, he said—there was a dusty patch of ground under a walnut tree where his fat wife was washing linen in a tub and hanging it over currant bushes to dry; so I thought the belongings in our saddlebags would be safe enough—and I walked off along the village street, looking sharply this way and that, with my mind deeply misgiving me. There were hardly any people about now; I saw neither Juan nor the hunchback.

Arrived in the main square—which was no more than a tree-bordered widening of the street—I realized where the population had got to; they were all here; some kind of performance appeared to be taking place.

A platform had been erected in the center of the place; it was supported on upended wine barrels, and adorned with swags of white muslin and bunches of flowers. Music had been playing gently on fifes, drums, and bagpipes, but ceased as I arrived in the square. After a moment or two—as if all had been awaiting my arrival—three people climbed up onto the stage: an old man with sheepskin vest, white beard, and crimson beretta; a younger man, dark, thickset, and beak nosed; and—to my cold horror—Juan, looking quite composed, but a little excited, his eyes very bright. The three of them sat down side by side on stools, while a master of ceremonies introduced them. Their names were fanciful. The old man styled himself something like the Lord of the Hillside. Juan's name was given as Ongriako Erregek. I forget the other. Then the *bertsulari* contest (for such I soon guessed it to be) began.

A member of the crowd would shout some phrase, or question, and then each of the three on the platform proceeded, in his own way, to give an answer. The old white-beard would bawl out some brief, earthy piece of wisdom, which drew gasps, and laughs, and groans of horrified agreement from the audience. The stocky dark fellow was much more long-winded, and declaimed for nine or ten minutes every time, which evidently tried the patience of some of his hearers, who doubtless were eagerly waiting with questions of their own, so that some began to shout *"Ya-ya-ya-ya!"* though others appeared to like what he said well enough. When it came to Juan's turn, I could see that he had a degree of difficulty in making himself heard, for his voice was not yet strong and clear. He gave his replies in a kind of rusty croak, and I devoutly hoped that he was not doing the cords of his neck dreadful damage. But whatever it was that he recited (as it was in the Basque tongue, I of course missed a great deal) seemed to charm and amuse the audience greatly, for they listened to him in complete silence while he spoke; and then, almost always, afterward, there would follow a ripple of affectionate laughter and some handclapping.

While these proceedings went forward I, for my part, grew steadily more and more uneasy. For quite soon I had spotted the little hunchback once more, weaving his way among the crowd; also another man who, I thought, might have been one of the four seen waiting for us at the grotto entrance. Again and again I attempted to catch Juan's eye but without the least success. I was on the outskirts of the crowd, and the audience were closely packed, but by slow degrees I contrived to work my way forward, edging and wriggling between large and thickset bodies, a process for which at least my small stature was an advantage, until I reached the last row but one below the platform, and was almost within touching distance of Juan.

A large fat woman stood in front of me twirling a distaff and loudly shouting, "Bravo, bravo!" at each recitation; the wool, as she spun it, went into a pouch at her side. The man beside her, evidently her husband, looked like a sailor; his black hair was twined into a tarry pigtail and he wore gold rings in his ears.

He called out a question in Euskara, which, to me, sounded like "How do you make a pie for a sailor?"

And the old man, first clearing his throat, answered something that sounded like:

"Don't make him a cake, he won't need it,
He'll be drowned before he can eat it!"

which made the audience laugh and hoot. Then the stocky poet produced some long piece of philosophical reflection which seemed to be about the lot of sailors, and how they traveled the wide world over in pursuit of whales and knowledge. On and on it went, and soon had a great many people fidgeting and whistling; the stout woman with the distaff sighed with irritation and trod on my foot.

Then Juan, who had been frowning in extreme concentration all through this oration, stood up and, quite softly, recited no more than half a dozen lines, which had the crowd so delighted that they began to stamp and cheer and shout *"Holà, holà!"* as if we were at a bullfight.

In the midst of which commotion I, very quickly and quietly, slipped past the fat woman, seized hold of Juan's ankle, and sharply tugged him off the platform. This had the unlucky effect of unbalancing the whole structure, the platform tipped over, the other two poets were catapulted into the crowd, and the wine barrels rolled in every direction.

"Come with me! We have to get away from here!" I hissed into Juan's ear, hoisting him to his feet; and keeping a tight hold of his wrist, I dragged him after me through the pressing, shifting people, endeavoring, as I did so, to look sharply about me so as to avoid the hunchback and the other man.

"Keep your head down!" I muttered to Juan. *"They* are here!"

I am not sure that he heard me.

As soon as we were away from the square I obliged him to run fast, ducking in and out of the shadows of trees that grew beside the road, making as little sound as possible—though, indeed, the shouts and clamor from behind us would have drowned a cavalry charge.

"I have left the things behind!" Juan cried angrily.

"Hush! Keep your voice down! What things?"

"The food—and bandages."

"Then we will have to go hungry. Come on—*faster*!"

Behind us the noise of the crowd swelled louder; laughter, and shouts, and indignant outcry suggested that the collapsed platform had started a fight. Or perhaps the people of Licq-Athérey were searching for their mislaid poets.

Juan was still resisting me strongly, which made heavy weather of the run; he tugged furiously at my hand; also he seemed to be panting violently. When we arrived at the quiet, dusty patch behind the forge, which was illuminated by a beam of lamplight from the smith's window, I saw that Juan was not panting, but sobbing with rage; tears sparkled on his cheeks. He burst out at me in a torrent of mingled French and Basque:

"Infamous *tyrant*! Why does everything always have to be as *you* order? Just because you saved my life once, you believe I must always obey you and do as you say, but it is not so—it is not so—it *shall* not be so—I will go back there—"

"Indeed you shall *not*!" said I. "Don't be such a hotheaded fool! Will you *listen* to me—just for one minute—"

But he would not listen. He called me all the bad names he could think of in his two languages. "I wish to heaven you had never saved me, if I must always be subject to you!" and finally even recollected an English insult. "You *pig*!" he burst out, made at me as if to hit me, and aimed a blow at my chest, which I easily parried, holding his two wrists tightly together.

"*Will you pay attention?* A small hunchbacked man is in the village—he was looking hard at your pony and saw me in the forge. Also another man—I think the one you called Bazin who was at the cave entrance—I am fairly certain that I saw him, too, in the street, listening, following, watching you."

There followed a short silence, then—"*Oh, mon Dieu,*" whispered Juan. All the fury drained out of him, his shoulders slumped, his hands fell away out of mine. "What shall we do?" he muttered wretchedly. "Where shall we go?"

"Back the way we came. And fast. We must be away at once. Come, I have already fed and saddled the horses; they are all ready."

Without another word he mounted his pony; I did likewise, and as softly as possible, we left the village at a walking pace, darkness and silence encouraging us to believe that we were unobserved.

Behind us we could still hear shouts and sounds of riot. "Good," said I, trying to sound as brisk and cheerful as possible, "in all that disturbance it will be impossible for the men to make sure we are not still there."

Juan made no answer.

As soon as we were well away we broke into a trot and, after half a kilometer or so, swung around to our right and made our way through oak forest, always continuing to circle to the right until, at length, I reckoned that we were headed once more in our original direction. Even in the dark it was possible to be fairly sure of this, for we could see the great pointed shapes of mountains, like dragons' teeth, standing ahead of us against the paler sky to the south.

Juan spoke never a word.

Hour after hour we rode on through the darkness, with stars bright and cold above, our ponies cleverly picking a path, which we ourselves could never have found, among forest and rock, scree and coppice, ascending knolls, threading their way through narrow defiles, all the while climbing, climbing. They were tired now, the fight had gone even out of el Demonio; he plodded soberly along, minding his footing. And still Juan never spoke. His silence was as deep as a well; perhaps, I thought, it was a well that had no bottom. I felt within me an aching, sorrowful heaviness, and began to inquire of myself whether I had indeed behaved unreasonably in snatching him away from a performance that meant so much to him and promised to be his triumph.

The Gente seemed able to follow us no matter how we dodged to elude them; had I saved him, or were they still on our track? In which case I might as well have left him to enjoy his contest.

Now it occurred to me that, since their apparent ambush at the grotto on La Rhune, they had made no attempt to close in or seize us; they merely followed.

What was their purpose in this? Did they, I wondered, perhaps intend to dog our heels until we had found the rich Uncle León, and then abduct Juan when they could be certain of reaping a reward for their trouble? Was that it? And was Plumet—the terribly changed Plumet—still with them, guiding them on our trail like some grisly bloodhound of hell?

And, if he was with them, how could they endure his company?

Occupying myself in these comfortless reflections, I rode almost unconscious of my own weary body until the Demon stumbled badly, reminding me of his equal weariness. Meanwhile the stars had vanished, and a fine rain had begun to fall. It would, I knew, be folly to continue any farther.

Under a thick stand of larches we found a tilted black shape, which on closer inspection proved to be an abandoned oxcart with a broken wheel.

"This will have to be our habitation for the night," said I, "since no other presents itself."

Juan still made no reply. In silence he slowly and stiffly slid from his pony and I did likewise. The ground was thick and soft with larch-mast, and taking handfuls of this, having unsaddled our poor wet beasts, we endeavored to rub them down, and then hobbled them. This was no country in which to lose them, though I thought that in any case they were probably too tired to stray far.

I drew out the blanket from one of my *alforjas* and climbed into the cart.

"Come," I said to Juan, "it is not the best bed we have slept in, but it is better than none."

Slowly and with reluctance he followed me. The cart, like the ground, was lined with soft needles; plainly it had stood there for many months.

Pushing a good half of the blanket toward Juan I lay down and said, "*Gab-boon*, Juan. *Buenas noches.*" He did not reply, but remained sitting up, hunched, with his arms round his knees, staring out at the larch branches which drooped around us like a tent. I reached to pat his shoulder, but he flinched away, so I withdrew my hand.

That was a miserable night.

Juan must, at length, have lain down to sleep, for in the course of the night, since the cart was tilted at an angle, we kept rolling down into the lowest corner, one on top of the other, and having to pull ourselves straight and rearrange ourselves and the blanket.

When dawn came and I awoke, stiff, cold, and unrested, it was to discover that torrential rain was falling. Our larch grove gave us some slight protection from the downpour, but even the thickest trees had begun to drip, so that we were far from dry. Juan had awakened before me and was sitting in the same position as he had last night, arms round knees, staring, pale-faced and impassive, into the gray and misty wilderness which lay all around our grove. The higher slopes of the mountains about us were all veiled in raincloud, and nothing could be heard but the rain, the hurrying water of a brook somewhere close by, the cries of a few dispirited birds, and the occasional distant call of a cuckoo.

"Well," said I, endeavoring to make a jest of it, "if the Gente can find us *here,* they are indeed guided by Satan, for I doubt if even God knows where we are . . ." and then wondered if this might be the case. I have seldom felt so unhappy, deserted, and forlorn as I did in that far corner of the mountains.

"Come, Juan," I said, when he did not answer. "Do not punish me forever! Indeed I am sorry that I had to whisk you away in the middle of your performance. I did it only for your safety and my own. I meant well, not badly, I promise you."

He turned and looked at me, for the first time since the occurrence. I was much struck by his pallor and the grieved, bruised, hollow look of his eyes; their copper-brown sparkle was quite extinguished; they were like dark, peaty pools on a mountaintop.

I had, I must confess, last night thought his behavior rather sulky and babyish; like that of a child, happily performing some conceited antics before company, who is reproved by his parents and sent to stand in the corner. But now I saw that the case was otherwise. His distress was of a different order, and went much deeper.

"You can't quite understand," he said slowly and hoarsely. "It was not vanity or vainglory that made me do it. To begin with . . . I wished to earn some money, to pay you a portion of what you have expended on me."

"But that is of no consequence!"

"If I had won," he went on, ignoring my interruption, "if I had won that contest—and I believe I had the chance—"

"Indeed, I believe so, too. It seemed very probable." I could not help breaking in, doing my best to comfort him. "The crowd liked you best. That was very plain! And you spoke very well, Juan."

As on other occasions he seemed to find my praise irrelevant.

"If I had won," he said, "there would have been a prize of two gold louis."

"Twenty francs? As much as that? Indeed, that would certainly have been useful," said I heartily. "But remember—after the contest there would certainly have been great rejoicings, and a feast, and you would probably have been expected to spend some of the money on buying wine for your defeated competitors."

He turned his eyes on me in surprise. "Yes—perhaps. That may be true," he acknowledged, after thinking about it; and then, broodingly: "The old man was good. Very, very good. He was so quick-witted—and he had a sharp, shrewd turn of speech—like a spade slicing through turf. I could not have given my answer so quickly, or bettered his lines. But the other"—he shook his head and made a dismissive gesture with his hand—"worse than weak soup! And too much of it, all the same. Flat and dull. It was a piece of luck for me, though. Gave me time to think. But, oh, Felix—what a joy it was!" At the memory, he kindled, his remaining anger and stiffness falling from him. His eyes shone once more. "To stand up there, like a runner, waiting to start, poised ready to leap at the sound of the bell—one's mind alert, set to spring in any direction—"

"And I had to come and spoil it!" I said, remorseful, beginning now to realize more of what he had felt. It was like the sight of some rare beauty of a plant, which one has heedlessly trodden down, lying there in the path, bruised and broken. "But surely there will be other contests, Juan—many, many of them! I can see now that your ambition is right for you; you must become one of the *bertsulari*."

He gave me a very strange deep look, eyes wide and grave, then slowly shook his head.

"No, never again. But I am glad that I had the one chance. And I think that I would have won. I do believe so."

"For sure, you would have! What was the last question that man shouted out?"

"The sailor? He called, 'How do you make a sailor's pie?'"

"What kind of a question is *that*? How can one answer it? How did *you* answer it?"

Without replying he stood up, shook himself to throw off the pine needles, and dropped out of the cart.

"*Maladetta!* I am stiff as a plank. Have we any food left?"

"Only a few mouthfuls of bread."

"And I had bought all kinds of good things!" said he crossly. "Sausage, and cheese—and cakes. I had them hidden under the platform."

"Well; we shall just have to manage without. Perhaps we may come across a shepherd. Just at present, though, I think we should be foolish to move; the mist is too thick. While he was shoeing el Demonio the smith warned me that higher up in these mountains there are many terribly deep gorges. We had better remain in what shelter we have until the clouds rise."

He yawned, stretching. "Oh, well, in that case, if we are not going anywhere, I shall bathe in the brook."

"In all this rain?"

"Why not? I prefer to be clean."

He went off upstream out of sight, as was his habit, and presently came back, clothed once more and shivering, but with a better color, to announce, "*Quel bonheur,* Felix, the brook is full of fish! If we can only get a couple out, there is breakfast provided. But how to do that?"

"Oh, there is no difficulty," said I. Pablo, one of my grandfather's shepherds, had, when I was eight or nine, taught me how to catch trout with my hands. So I went and lay on my stomach in a wet patch of bracken by a rocky pool, and in twenty minutes or so had the satisfaction of catching three fish. Juan, meanwhile, had collected kindling for a fire, picking out dry sticks from under rocks and tree roots. This I lit with flint and steel (no chance to use Father Vespasian's lens today) and, in due course, we had a fire hot and glowing enough to toast our fish on larch prongs, which gave them a very choice aroma. While Juan tended the fish, I managed to tip the cart onto its side by tethering the ponies to it and making them pull it over, so that it formed a kind of sloping shelter, and we were able to sit under it, on the dry patch that it had protected. There we retired to eat our breakfast.

"This is not so bad!" said Juan, whose spirits appeared to have risen a little. "In fact it is a better breakfast than those poor little Cagots were able to give us."

"You were going to tell me about your poem," I reminded him, licking my fingers.

"I had not forgotten. I was trying to turn the Euskara into English. Well," he said, "it went something like this:

"Tell me, pray, if you may, how to make a sailor's pie?
First, then, you must take a teacup full of sky!
A strand of hemp, a silent star
And the wind's lullaby,
A flake of foam, a scent of night
And a gull's cry;
A taste of salt, a touch of tar
And a sorrowful good-bye:
Mix all these together, to make a sailor's pie."

"A teacup full of sky!" I said. "Where *do* you find such notions, Juan?"

"Teacup is not quite right," he muttered. "Wineglass? Salt bowl? No, that is not it. Such notions? Oh, inside my head. There are plenty more; if only I can find a way to make use of them."

"Well, I feel certain that you will be able to do so. I wish that *I* had such a talent! All I am good for is to light fires and catch fish."

"And to keep me alive," said Juan with a sigh, and a wry grin.

So we became friends again, and since the weather continued our enemy, we spent all of that day squatting under the cart; Juan told me tales and recited many more of his poems, I taught him a great quantity of English, and he endeavored to teach me more Euskara, kindly not laughing too hard at my many mistakes. By the end of the day I had learned *"Atharratz jauregian bi zitroia doratii,* In Tardets Castle there are two golden lemons"; that seemed as much as my thick head would accommodate.

"They do say," Juan told me comfortingly, "that it took the devil seven years to learn 'yes' and 'no' in Euskara. Then he forgot the words again, and so threw himself into the river Nive."

We fed and watered our tired ponies, groomed them, washed the Harlequin's shoulder and anointed the Demon's fetlock, and in general made much of them; they, as much as we, seemed glad of the rest. And we talked, a little, of the Gente and Father Vespasian, puzzling over what it could be that made them consider it worthwhile to keep so pertinaciously on our trail.

"Do you believe that it was what Brother Bertrand said—about the shadows?" demanded Juan. He cast a somewhat fearful glance at the gloomy sky and cloud-wrapped peaks. Any kind of demon, dwarf, or specter might, it seemed, come out of those high and misty regions; if we had heard a Satanic cackle or hobgoblin howl we would not have been much surprised. Yet we heard nothing but the scream of eagles and the lonely call of the cuckoo.

"How can I tell? I do not understand, though, why the Gente should follow us—unless they are too frightened of—of that Being—to break away."

"Perhaps they think that we shall lead them to a hidden treasure," said Juan fancifully; and then, with a shiver: "Do not let us talk about them anymore. I will tell you, instead, about the *laminak*."

"What is the *laminak*?"

"Are, not is. They are little people. They live in the forest over the mountains to the south—the Iraty Forest." He waved an arm to where the pale sun, momentarily, was trying to peer through wreaths of mist. "They are little old ghosts, very, *very* old, they have been in the world since long before human people came here. Once they had the whole globe to themselves. But then the people came and built houses and towns, so the *laminak*, who hate noise, went away to live in the forest. But they are not enemies of men—*good* men; in fact they would dearly like to be friends with us, and help us. During daytime they hide in dark corners, under yew trees' roots, or behind carts in barns, watching, watching, watching the way that people do things; then, at night, when the farmer is in bed, out will come the *laminak* to try to help him, churning his milk or turning his cheese or leading the horses out to plow or collecting the eggs in the hen-houses. But they are so clumsy! They drop the eggs, they spill the milk, they break the plowshare. They have no proper fingers, only ugly small stumps. And they are stupid, poor things; however often they try, they can never learn human ways of doing tasks."

"Like me trying to learn Euskara."

"Never mind, Felix!" said Juan kindly. "You are good at many other things. Whereas the poor *laminak* are good for nothing at all. And this makes them sad, so sad that sometimes you can hear them crying, crying, in the forest or farmyard, as if their hearts were ready to break; as if they could not endure their existence one moment longer. Poor little outcasts! It must be dreadful to feel that you have no place in the world, that nobody values you or can use what you offer."

He spoke with such feeling that I looked at him in surprise.

"Keep your heart up, lad! *You* are not one of the *laminak*! Think how happy your Uncle León will be to have you with him, if he has lost all his own family."

But Juan merely sighed, and made no answer.

Toward evening, as the rain and fog still did not abate, I caught four more fish—indeed, they were so fat and fearless that it was plain no human beings ever troubled those waters—and we cooked two for our supper, leaving the other two in the hollow of a rock for breakfast, wrapped in fern.

When night came, as it did early, we retired to bed under the tilted cart and huddled together, beneath our blanket, on a pile of damp larch needles.

"*Gab-boon,* Juan."

"Good night, Felix." Then he added a short phrase in Euskara that I had heard him say on several previous nights.

"What does that mean, Juan?"

"It is something our old cook Barbe used to say when she bade me good-night." He thought for a moment, and then, with a chuckle, translated:

> "If I die before I wake,
> You can have the birthday cake!"

And so we went laughing to sleep.

But I still felt, in a corner of my mind, that by obliging Juan to leave the poetry contest, I had accidentally dealt him some wound from which he would not recover.

6

A venomous neighbor; we recommence our travels; enter a gorge; yet another encounter with the Gente; succeed in eluding them for the time; discover the hermitage of Brother Laurent; are visited by the Demon; and see our refuge destroyed.

I awoke with a start, feeling something heavy and clammy that tightly constricted my arm. Leaping up, letting out a yell as I did so, I flung out my arm to cast off whatever it was, and suffered, as I moved, a keen stabbing pain in my right wrist. A tangle of coils flew through the air; they resolved into a thickish black-and-yellow snake which straightened out with lightning speed as it struck the ground and flashed away, vanishing into a clump of fern before I could stamp on it or find a stone to dash out its brains.

"Oh—what is it—what *is* it?" gasped Juan, rousing from deep sleep and jumping up in terror.

"A snake bit me, a viper—cursed thing! It must have crept under the blanket for the warmth, and twined round my arm."

"*Ugh!*" shuddered Juan. "If I had known! I cannot *endure* snakes! But—oh, poor Felix! What can we do? Is it a bad bite, do you think?"

"How can I tell?"

I sucked at my wrist and spat; sucked and spat again. There were two neat little punctures.

"You had best wash it in the brook," suggested Juan, and I did so, holding my arm in the icy water until it was numb and blue. Meanwhile Juan rekindled the fire from last night's still-warm embers, and contrived a grid of green saplings to toast our two remaining fish.

"How does your arm feel now—is it very sore?" he inquired anxiously, as we breakfasted. "Should we burn the wound with a hot ember, do you think? Or—I remember hearing it said that a good thing to do is to slash over a snakebite, slash a crisscross; that lets out the poison, they say, and protects the wound."

I, too, had heard this, and said resignedly, "Well, if that is best, that is what I had better do."

I sharpened our knife on a stone, rinsed it in the brook—all this while using my left hand, for the right one was commencing to swell and throb—and then studied the bite, which was on the inside of my wrist, about an inch from the base of the thumb. I had no wish to cut through the great blood vessel which runs close by there.

"Is it very hard to do it with your left hand? Would you prefer that I do it?" asked Juan in a voice that faltered a little.

I was about to say yes—then glancing up at him observed that he was white as death, although his eyes were resolute; noticing also that his hands trembled uncontrollably, I shook my head, grinned at him wryly and, with two quick slashes, drew the blade of the knife twice over the snakebite, this way, that way, then again held my arm in the brook until the blood stopped flowing.

Juan meanwhile had torn some strips off the bit of cloth that the hermit had given us, and when my arm ceased to bleed he dabbed on some of the caustic we had purchased for the Harlequin's sore shoulder.

"What is good for a *pottoka* cannot do you any harm," he said gruffly. Then he neatly bandaged the small wound.

"Thanks, Juan; I daresay I shall do very well now. What devilish bad luck, though! Who would ever have expected to come across a viper so early in the year?"

"Remember how very warm it was two days ago; that hot sun must have waked him from his winter sleep," said Juan. "Oh, Felix, I am so very sorry for you. I would not have had such a thing happen for the world."

"It was not your fault, lad! It was pure misfortune. Come, we had better leave this forsaken spot and find a track as soon as we can, while the weather favors us."

The day was indeed glorious—as a kind of atonement, it seemed, for the wretchedness of the previous twenty-four hours. A hot sun beamed over the ridge to our left, the raindrops sparkled on the larches, and hundreds of thrushes were singing joyfully. We saddled our ponies—Juan solicitous to help me when I had trouble tightening my girth—stamped out the embers of the fire, mounted, and rode on our way, following the course of the brook in an upward direction and singing, *"Halte-là, halte-là, halte-là! Les montagnards sont là!"* which is a song they sing in the Pyrenees.

In spite of my misfortune with the snake, our spirits were high. We were friends again, nobody appeared to have tracked our course from Licq-Athérey to this neighborhood, the day was young, and the weather good. Our ponies, well rested, tossed their heads and champed on their bits; they seemed as eager as we to explore new ground.

For three hours or so we proceeded uphill at a walking pace; the going was rough, rocky, and set about with trees and smaller bushes; after a while the glen gradually grew narrower until there was hardly more than a footway by the waterside, sometimes not even that; once or twice we were obliged to turn back; for, though we ourselves might have scrambled through on foot, the valley sides were too steep and broken for the ponies, and we were obliged to find a detour over thickly forested hillside. But we always rejoined the stream (now a young torrent dashing between close rocky banks) and presently our glen joined another, wider and shallower, opening in a southeasterly direction, which we decided to follow, for it seemed to go toward the Pic d'Orhy.

There were mountain pastures up here, spangled with flowers, so many and of such different kinds and colors that Juan was continually crying out with rapture; every now and then he must dismount in order to study some especially beautiful or unfamiliar bloom; indeed, I could not help becoming a little impatient with him and was tempted to say something sharp, but held my peace, remembering the grief I had caused him by obliging him to quit the poets' contest. So I let him gaze, and exclaim, and pick the blossoms, which he then carefully inserted, to flatten them, in the little poetry book which he had brought away from the Abbey of St. Just.

I myself endured increasing discomfort from my bitten arm, which burned and throbbed in a dull, continuous nagging torment, so that I found myself reluctant to speak, except in short sentences, or move in the saddle; I was glad that the track here appeared reasonably well marked and smooth, promising to lead on steadily, perhaps to some pass over the mountains into Spain.

There were flocks here and there in the pastures, sheep, goats, and cattle, where the snow had melted off the upland meadows; the sound of their bells echoed sweetly among the hills, and Juan remarked, "If bells can disperse evil spirits, as they say, there must be very few devils in the mountains."

"In these mountains at least," I amended.

We found a shepherds' encampment, and were able to purchase milk and bread from them, and some cheesecloth to replace the bundle that we had lost at Licq-Athérey. We asked our way, too, and were able to confirm our hope that the snowy peak ahead and slightly to our right was the Pic d'Orhy. But the men, itinerant herders, knew nothing of any hermit's refuge and shrugged at our questions; the mountain slopes, they said, were studded with old ruins, huts, barns, and shelters; the one we sought might be in any of thirty different valleys.

On we went, climbing steadily, our ponies' hooves sometimes breaking the crusts of old snow which the sun had not yet melted. Now and then, looking back, we were able to see a wonderful panorama of peaks, ridges, and ravines, and, farther away, plains, forests, and cities; at one time I thought we had a glimpse of the blue Atlantic Ocean, many kilometers to the west of us. But by late afternoon I was hardly able to appreciate these vistas, for my arm was giving me such pain that I felt sick and feverish; a clanging hammer seemed to be beating inside my temples, my tongue was clogged, my vision dulled, and, going aside from the track, I was obliged to dismount and vomit up the milk that I had drunk for the noonday meal. Climbing back onto the fidgety, willful Demon was an almost impossible task; and when he flung his head up, dragging on the reins which I held in my right hand, it required all my control not to cry out with the sudden pain. After that experience I rode on without attempting to dismount again. Although I longed with all my being to drink from the icy, plentiful mountain brooks and miniature waterfalls which zigzagged down the sides of our valley to join the main *gave,* the prospect of the exertion needed for alighting and remounting again was too grim, so I remained in the saddle, kilometer after painful kilometer.

That Juan eyed me anxiously at frequent intervals I was vaguely aware, but riding on at a steady, plodding pace was now the extent of what I could manage; I had no strength to look about me and could not waste energy on idle speech or pay much heed to our route; I held all my attention on my pony's black shaggy mane, allowed him to pick his own way, and, sometimes, thought of Father Vespasian's eyes; they seemed to float ahead of me in the air, like two ruby-red coals.

Once or twice I heard Juan inquire, with diffidence, "Do you think that we are heading in the right direction, Felix?" and I nodded, or made some mumbled reply, but in truth we could have been riding along the highway to Gehenna for all the attention I really gave to the matter.

Toward twilight I noticed, through my fog of pain and sickness, that the steep track we had taken threaded a gorge which was becoming so exceedingly narrow and dank that it seemed as if we were riding along in the bottom of a sewer. The rock walls, here only ten or twelve feet apart, rose up sheer on either side to a towering height above us; they must have been at least six to eight hundred feet high. The sky overhead was no more than a thin strip of light, and our ponies could only just see to pick their way along by the side of the mountain torrent, which must, at one time, have carved this tremendous gash in the face of the rock. It was an eerie, unchancy place, dusky, and damp from the spray of the stream and many other trickles down the rock walls; the ponies liked it no better than we, they shivered and snorted, and tried to break into a trot, but the ground was too slippery and strewn with fallen shale for this to be safe. I shivered, too, feeling dizzy, feverish at one moment, ice-cold the next.

"What an evil spot this is!" said Juan. "It is like a tunnel through the mountain. I hope that it leads to Spain!"

The gorge did, after a while, widen out, and ahead of us we beheld two cascades, white and gleaming in the dusk.

"Oh, Felix, how beautiful!" exclaimed Juan. His tone was full of wonder. Painfully I lifted my head and saw that one of the falls described a great arch of water, an unbroken white bow falling from cliff to ground. It must have done so for many hundreds of years. At another time I, too, would have exclaimed and gazed at this sight in admiration; now I felt too ill to give it more than a brief, incurious glance.

Beyond the cascades could be seen the dark arch of a cave entrance in the cliff, and beyond that the track came to an abrupt stop, save for a faint zigzag up a steep rock slope, suitable for izard or wild mountain hare, but quite impossible for our ponies, surefooted and agile though they were.

"*Miséricorde!*" exclaimed Juan in consternation.

"The path goes no farther! It is a cul-de-sac. We shall have to turn back, Felix."

He gazed at me in great distress. I tried to rouse myself to reply, "Well, if we must, we must . . ." but the words would hardly leave my tongue.

"Oh, why, why did this have to happen?" he lamented. "Of all the times! When you are so ill—I can see that you suffer atrociously, your face is very flushed and you keep twitching your brows. Should we, do you think, stop here and pass the night in that cave? Perhaps you will feel better by tomorrow morning—?"

But I croaked, "No—no!" Why, I could not say, but I had a most unreasoning dread and horror of the cave mouth that showed black beyond the cascades. Once we set foot inside there, I felt sure that we should never emerge again. The ponies shuddered their coats and whinnied nervously; if I had been able to express my thoughts, I would have said they agreed with me.

Juan made no argument, but reined the Harlequin round in a circle and started back down the slippery path. El Demonio followed him unbidden, and I sat slumped in the saddle, with my head hanging forward, my chin resting on my chest, regardless of our surroundings, heedless of my horse's movement, or the sound of the waterfalls and river beside us; mindful of nothing save the blazing pain in my arm and the urge, which had been growing in me for the past half hour, to tumble myself off my pony and into that foamy torrent; to plunge deep, deep into that cool water and be at rest.

Ahead of us the walls of rock drew together.

"Perhaps it is the cleft in the rock that Roland made with his sword Durendal!" Juan called back, trying to sound cheerful.

To me the narrow cleft seemed like a crack in the side of a house, which we must enter.

"As if we were ants," I muttered, but to myself, not aloud.

And then, out of the cleft, came filing a group of men, leisurely, taking their time, neither hurrying nor threatening, but quiet with satisfaction, like farmers who have concluded a bargain, seeing the new flock of sheep brought into the fold. There was a tall white-haired man with a black patch over one eye; a hunch-back astride an ass; one man grossly fat, with a tiny pea-head sunk between his shoulders; two of them carried muskets, others had clubs; I lost count of them, I could not hold up my head long enough to take a lengthy survey. In any case, what difference did it make? They had us now, there was no question of that.

"*Grand Dieu,*" I heard Juan whisper.

The white-headed man said politely, "*Bon soir, mes amis!* So we meet again! How pleasant that now we shall be able to invite you to dine and pass the night with us—on other occasions you have seemed so shy! You have not appeared anxious for our company. And yet we love you so dearly! We have such esteem for you. We have been so eager to entertain you."

"Cut the cackle, Cocher," grumbled the fat man.

"Let us by, Cocher," said Juan. "We do not choose to remain here with you."

His voice was as cold and thin as winter rain.

"Ah, but it is we who do the choosing now, my little bird of paradise! So grand you are now, in your fine new clothes—hardly the poor ragged sparrow that you were when you stayed with us. No, no, I can see that your new acquaintances have been feeding you up until you are as fat as a gamecock, and the result is charming. Plumet will be so happy to see you."

"Where is—Plumet?" breathed Juan. Though he did his best to disguise it, I could hear the fear in his voice.

"Why, waiting for you in the cave, just up there, where else?"

At the thought of that black cave mouth, where, hidden inside the ancient cold and dark of the mountain, Father Vespasian, clad in Plumet's body, was hidden, *waiting for us,* I began to feel so dizzy that for a moment my spirit slipped away, entirely out of reach. I clung blindly to the saddle pommel, with sweat starting on my forehead. All my surroundings were a black buzz and crackle. Then, coming back, as it seemed, from immense distances of pain and shadow, I felt words on my tongue and heard myself speak. In a voice that I did not recognize as mine, so parched and hoarse was it, I croaked to Juan, "The *laminak* are waiting to help us . . ."

Why those words should have come into my head, God only knew. Doubtless He put them there.

"Ay, that is so," agreed Juan, sounding astonished. "The *laminak*." His voice, too, was different: higher, hoarser; it resembled the voice that he had used while taking part in the poetry contest. "You had forgotten, I think," he said to the group of men, "that the *laminak* are my friends? Mine, but not yours—oh, no, they are not yours!" And with an eerie change of pitch to a high, shrill, keening wail he suddenly lifted up his head and called, *"Ohé! Ohé! Ohé! Laminak, laminak, laminak!"*

The sound he let out was so piercing and so unexpected that our startled ponies let out high, terrified whinnies; and the notes of his cry and theirs flew upward, echoing and resounding between the steep black rock walls of the gorge. The two results of this were wholly unforeseen: From somewhere high up above us a huge swarm of black bats abruptly wheeled out, keening, squealing, and dashing themselves blindly from one rock face to the other, whirling about our heads, causing the men to shout with fright and fling themselves back to avoid the cloud of flapping, fluttering leather wings and whizzing furry bodies.

But also—and much more awe-inspiring—either the echoes of Juan's first shout, or the bats in their sudden emergence, dislodged a great boulder and a series of smaller ones, which came volleying down from the heights of rock above, landing among us in a thunder of sound and a cloud of dust. And when the dust cleared, we could see that one man—the gross, pea-headed fellow—had been struck down by the biggest rock and lay lifeless with his head in the river.

"*Sacré nom de Dieu!*" gibbered Jorobado the hunchback. "The *laminak*! The *laminak* are angry—are angry with us!" and he clapped heels to his ass and scampered off up the gorge, while the rest of the troop followed him helter-skelter. All but the white-haired man with the black patch, who bawled after them angrily not to be a set of puling children but to come back.

"Dolts! Cowards! Imbeciles! Come back, there is nothing to fear but a couple of children. Come back, I say, or when I catch you I'll slit your tripes and drag the skin off your tongues!"

But they paid no heed.

Ignoring these shouts, Juan kicked the Harlequin into a walk, and made for the narrow gorge entrance. Cocher strode furiously to intercept him, standing in the middle of the way with arms wide.

"You don't deceive me, you little rat, with your talk of ghosts and *laminak*. That rock—" He looked at his fallen comrade, crossed himself, and said hastily, "That rock falling was nothing but a queer accident."

"Eh, Cocher, is that what you think?" Juan answered, sweet as quince. "Then it will just be another lucky accident if it happens again?"

And he raised his voice again in that eerie ascending wail, "Ooooooooh! Ooooooooh!" until the cloud of bats flew round once more.

The combination of the sound and the bats proved too much for Cocher. Almost despite himself, it seemed, he drew back and let Juan ride past him. Shrouded in my fog of pain as I was, yet I had presence of mind enough to give the Demon a kick, and obediently he broke into an uneasy trot—which, jolting me, almost made me shriek with agony—and made haste to follow his companion.

Sometimes still, in dreams, or if ever I am feverish, I find myself back there, in that hideous dark, slimy gully, with the horses slipping and trembling, the last light of the sky paling from blue to apple-green above, and the thought of those men behind us, hesitant, eager to seize us, angry at the death of their companion, yet cowed and indecisive, not able to pluck up courage to come after us. And behind *them*, in the dark cave, the Being that inhabited the body of Plumet.

What would he do now? Would he follow us, angry at their failure?

That ride through the gorge seemed to last for several lifetimes. I was too ill to measure time sensibly; inside my head I could hear a booming, and the light came and went as if veils were being waved before my eyes. I clung with my left hand to the pommel of the Demon's saddle; my knees felt as if they had melted away, my back was aching and stiff, and my right arm seemed the size of my whole body. The dank twilight of the place enwrapped me like a suffocating net.

Dimly, at last, I was aware that we had come out

into clearer light and better air; then, later, that Juan had dismounted and was walking, leading my pony, while the Harlequin followed behind, on a long halter.

When had Juan done this? I did not know. Where were we? I did not know.

Sometimes I heard Juan murmuring words; I had no strength to follow the meaning, but the sound of them filtered slowly into my throbbing head like flakes of snow:

> "The wind is rising
> While I am falling
> While I am listening
> The wind is calling . . ."

Then he would break off and say, "Felix? Can you hear me? Are you strong enough to keep on—to go a little farther?"

I would mumble some reply, and he would say, "Keep your heart up. I know, I know the pain is terrible. I do not understand how you can bear it. But I see that you can. I am trying to find a way out of this wilderness that we are in."

Then we would plod on, kilometer after kilometer, league after league, up over ridges, down through valleys, and after a while I would hear his voice again, murmuring about the wind:

> "While I am laughing
> The wind is weeping

The wind is sighing
While I am sleeping . . ."

The lilt of these words, of Juan's voice, somehow
formed a band of curving smoothness, like a path over
gently rounded hills, which my spirit could follow
while my wretched body obediently, doggedly continued to sit on the pony and submit to endless pain.
Could it have been like this for Juan, I wondered,
when he was dangling by his neck from the branch of
the tree? Did he suffer so? Why did I never think of
that before?

And on we went, scrambling over uneven ground.
And his voice came, gentle but insistent:

"While I am silent
The wind is raging
The wind is ageless
While I am aging . . ."

Vaguely, through all my pain, I understood that
what he said about the wind was *true;* all the time,
since we had left the hateful gorge, it had been rising,
and now moaned and battered around us like a live
thing, pushing, fluttering, urging us forward; it held
us in its cold arms; it led us, dragged us, pulled us, and
thrust us. Great swags and wads of black cloud came
hurrying over the sky, piling into thunderlofts; and
then, with a loud hiss, a whole world of rain fell on us,
plastering the hair flat against our heads, even under

our hats, drenching our jackets, sleeking down the ponies' rough coats until they looked like satin.

And still we rode on, on.

> "The wind is rising
> While I am sinking
> The wind is speaking
> While I am thinking . . ."

Now a bright saber of lightning cleft the sky, and not long after there came a giant crack, as if the whole nut of heaven had been split open, and the rain fell even faster.

"The storm is our friend," remarked Juan with satisfaction, "for the Gente won't be able to follow our tracks."

Indeed, the path we followed was like a running brook. Even the water-shy Harlequin seemed not to heed it, but patiently followed while Juan trudged up to his shins in mire and water.

"Ah!" I heard him exclaim some while later. "Now I truly do believe that God must have been guiding us."

I pulled up my head and stared about. For some time I had been aware that we were descending, not climbing; I saw that we were coming down a narrow col, or mountain pass; around us lay a jumble of woods and rocky peaks, illuminated from time to time by the lightning flashes. To the side of our track, ahead, stood a crude stone cross, and beyond that was a small stone building, square, with a domed roof, and a door supported by two solid stone columns. The building was almost grown over with creepers and vines; ivy and wallflowers sprouted between the cracks of the masonry, which was plainly very old. Behind the building rose a rock wall; there was a lean-to at one side, and, close by, a spring trickled into a stone trough.

There were some words carved over the lintel.

Juan led my pony up to this building and knocked on the heavy wooden door with my *makhila,* which he was carrying.

A faint voice called from inside: "Come in! Whoever you are! And heaven bless you!"

Now, with the most solicitous and tender care, Juan helped me dismount. I rolled off the saddle like a sack, supported by my left hand on his shoulder, and somehow landed on my feet. He pushed open the door of the cabin and helped me inside.

A tiny lamp, placed in a niche in front of a crucifix, faintly glimmered and illuminated the place.

On a bed of leaves and straw in a corner lay a desperately pale, emaciated man dressed in a canvas robe. His long shaggy white hair had not been cut, by the look of it, for years; his eyes were sunk back in his head, he held a rosary in his sticklike hands. He looked like a corpse; yet he still had strength to turn his head and gaze at us.

"Are you Brother Laurent?" said Juan.

The answer was a faint nod.

"Then we come to you with fraternal greetings

from Brother Bertrand. But my companion here is sick—as you can see—he was bitten by a snake. May I take some of these things to make him a bed?"

Taking the faint croak of assent as permission, Juan found a pile of dirty sacks and a bundle of hay; my legs were on the point of collapsing under me, but just before they did so he carefully assisted me to lie down. Oh, the blessed relief of reposing full length on that unsavory couch!

Then Juan went outside to see to the ponies and bring in our saddlebags.

While he did so I gazed up at a crucifix above me on the wall; the life-size figure upon it was made of black, polished bones.

"*Cordial*—" faintly articulated the hermit when Juan returned. "In the chest—by the holy book."

Juan knelt at a chest under the crucified skeleton. Its skull stared down at him as he pulled out a little flask. Matter-of-factly he administered a few drops to the sick man, and then a mouthful to me. At once a wonderful tingling warmth ran through me from head to toe, and I began to realize that, in fact, my state of sickness had turned, at some point on that agonizing ride, and that I had commenced the process of recovery. Perhaps the storm and the rain had done me good, washed the poison out of my arm, and now this cordial helped knit my faculties together. I felt more like Felix; understood that before too long, next day if God willed it, I should be restored to normal health.

Thanking God in my heart, I was able to smile at Juan, thank him, too, and whisper, "Take a sip of cordial yourself! You must be worn to the bone."

His look lighted up at my smile. He said, "Well, I will just have a taste!" and did so.

Then he busied himself kindling a fire in the crude hearth (fortunately there were dry sticks in a heap), heated water, and—since there was no food in the place—with a handful of herbs he made a kind of tisane, of which he gave cupfuls to the sick man and me and drank some himself.

The hermit, who had indeed appeared at the point of death when we arrived, now rallied a little, and said, "My children, you come at a good hour for me . . . Did you indeed see my brother Bertrand?"

We were able to assure him that we had, and repeated the message of fraternal forgiveness. Tears stood in the hermit's eyes as he heard it, and he exclaimed weakly, "But Bertrand does not know—he does not know the blackest sin of all. No, no, I do not deserve his forgiveness! Monster that I am, I have never confessed my mortal sin. But now I think that God must have sent you to listen to the story of what I did."

Aghast, I began to say, "You have no need to tell *us*. It would be far better to confess it all to God—" But Juan hushed me with a finger to his lips.

Raising himself on one elbow, the dying man hurried on: "My brother told you, I suppose, that he and I quarreled fatally over a young girl, and that she killed herself, rather than choose between us?"

We nodded. He cried out lamentably, "But that was not true! She did *not* commit the sin of self-murder! It was I who killed the poor girl—rather than lose her to my brother, I, wild, mad with rage, thrust poor Laura into the ravine. *That* is what he has to forgive! Oh, miserable wretch, murderer, monster that I am."

"Well, my father," said Juan, after a pause—he spoke in a hesitant, thoughtful, troubled tone—"that was a very terrible thing to do; there is no doubt of that; but you have spent many years now repenting your sin, and I daresay God will understand and perhaps forgive you if you ask him very sincerely. I am sure He must have forgiven harder things than that in His time."

"Do you believe so, child?"

"Yes," said Juan more positively. "I suppose you were quite young when it happened, and stupid, and unreasonable—"

"Oh, yes, yes, yes!"

"Well, there! I do not suppose that you would commit such a crime *now*, would you? If—if the lady was to walk in at the door and—and tell you that she loved your brother best—you would not push her off a cliff now, would you?"

"Indeed not!" gasped the poor man. "I would greet her like a blessed angel!"

"There, then! Surely she is waiting to forgive you in Paradise."

The old man burst into a racking flood of sobs, which almost seemed likely to tear him in pieces. Juan tried to soothe him, but I said, "No, let him weep. He is washing away all those years of remorse and guilt." So Juan let him be.

At last the poor thing heaved a shuddering sigh, then another, gulped back his tears, and said, "Child, you have brought me great comfort. God indubitably sent you here. And perhaps He did it for your welfare as well as for mine. Can I assist you in any way, while this feeble husk still holds me together?"

"Yes, my father, you can," said Juan. "Your brother Bertrand said that you would be able to give my friend and me good counsel. We are being dogged by an evil man—or an evil spirit, we do not know which—but wherever we go, he follows our track, and we are very much afraid of him."

In as few words as possible he told Brother Laurent the story of our escape from the Abbey and Father Vespasian's pursuit of us.

Brother Laurent seemed to feel a stir of curiosity or memory at the name Vespasian.

"What was this man's name before he entered? Was it Victor Sihigue?"

"I do not know, my father."

"Strange . . . strange. It sounds the same. And yet . . ." He pondered, seeming almost to nod off into sleep. Juan waited patiently, and presently he roused again.

"Wherever you go, he is able to follow? You have seen him, or his accomplices, at all these different places?"

"Yes, my father. At the grotto, and at St. Jean, at Hasparren and at Licq-Athérey. And then today—we did not *see* him at the fearful gorge, but they said he was there, in the cave."

"Singular. Most singular. No doubt he has more than human powers. But what is there about you that is able to summon him to where you are, like the needle to the lodestone?"

"We cannot guess," said Juan.

"You do not, by any chance, have some article of his in your possession?"

At those words Juan turned completely white.

"*Bon Dieu!* I had forgotten about it. The spyglass! I took his spyglass."

He pulled it out of the saddlebag—a small brass instrument, somewhat tarnished and green with age and damp.

"That article belonged to him?" inquired the hermit. Juan nodded, still paper-white, staring at the glass with huge, terrified eyes.

"Ah, then that explains it all. No wonder he is able to track you down! You could cross the ocean, traverse the polar region, hide yourself underground, and still he would know where you were."

"What can I do, then, Father? Shall I drop the thing into a crevasse?"

"Oh, no, my child; that would solve nothing at all. No, if you took it from him, you must give it back."

"*Give it back to him?*"

Juan's voice was nothing but a cracked, horrified

whisper; and for myself I felt the hairs rise on the nape of my neck. Seek out that dreadful being, deliberately seek his company, in order to give him back the glass? Could we possibly do that?

"Oh, yes," said Brother Laurent, "you must do so; that is the only way. Then, when he has the thing again, when be has no more power over you because of it, then you must endeavor to persuade the unlawful spirit to leave the body of the poor wretch in which it has taken refuge."

"But—how can we do *that*?"

Juan's face was appalled, his voice was no more than a thread. He said, "We are only young, my father, we have no powers of—of that kind. We are not holy."

The hermit moved his head weakly in denial.

"A needle has power in the fingers of a sempstress, a pick in the hands of a miner. Who sent you here to me in my last hour? Never fear, child, when it is needed, the power will be sent you. Now, let me be still in my last minutes, and help me with your thoughts, for I am about to take leave of this world." And he lay back on his pillow of leaves and closed his eyes, though his lips still moved in rapid prayer.

Outside the storm continued to rage; through one tiny high-up window in the massive stone wall, the blue-white glare of lightning could be seen at intervals, followed by a crash of thunder each time, as if rocks were raining down on the roof. I thanked God in my heart for finding us this place of shelter, for saving us yet again; and apologized to Him for my cow-ardice and distrust.

Juan knelt on the rock floor, and when he made a slight gesture to me with his head, I managed to hoist myself onto my knees.

"Oh, Father in heaven," I prayed, "look after this poor man. No doubt he did do a very dreadful thing in pushing that girl off the cliff and spoiling three lives; but, as You can see, he is now truly sorry for what he did, and, as Juan said, a great many years have passed and he is a different person from the wild young character who lost his temper. I think perhaps You should not blame him for the deed of a much younger man. But You do not need me to teach You Your business, I am sure!"

And, clear inside my head, despite the turbulence of the storm outside, came the laughing voice of God. "Let not your heart be troubled, Felix. I will take up this poor piece of human wreckage. He shall be made as new."

Not long after, by an extra brilliant flash of light-ning, we saw that the hermit's prediction about him-self was correct; he had fallen back dead on his pillow of leaves, with open mouth and staring eyes.

With gentle care Juan closed the open eyes and mouth, composed the bony hands so that they lay folded over the rosary on his chest, then said a quick prayer, kneeling by the corpse.

He had just risen to his feet, and was about to ad-dress some remark to me, when the door burst open.

A searing flash of lightning illuminated the figure who stood there. It was Father Vespasian, with a hand on either lintel, leaning forward, as if about to throw himself upon us. Words fail me to describe the horror of the dreadful mask which formed his face—so white, creased, puffed, dead—yet with its eyes fixed on us, burning like coals.

"Now!" he cried out. *"Now, you must tell me—!"*

The mouth in the face did not move as he spoke; the words came out, as from a hole in a mask, spoken by the actor behind. And they came in a roar, like that of the wind.

I could see that Juan, half risen, was wholly petrified by terror. He glanced round, desperate, as if trying to recollect what it was he had to do. I myself was in no better case; I crouched down, like a coney in its burrow, expecting the jaws to open and crush me.

But a strangely long silence followed, and, venturing to look up, I saw that Father Vespasian's eyes were now fixed, not on us, but on the corpse of Brother Laurent. A long, keening, babbling wail came from that open mouth: "Ahhhhh-h-h-h!" like the air from a pricked bladder; then suddenly he turned, vanished from the doorway, and was gone. Could we hear his shriek diminishing in the distance? Or was it merely the voice of the storm?

"You should"—I gulped, after a while finding my voice—"you should have given him the spyglass."

"You think I could remember such a thing at such a time?" But after a moment Juan added despondently. "Yes, you are right. I should have done so. Now it is all to do again . . ."

"Well," I said, "we had better snatch some sleep while we can. I do not think he will come back here," remembering Father Vespasian's hatred of any dead thing.

So we huddled together on the heap of moldy cloth.

"*Gab-boon,* Felix."

"*Gab-boon,* Juan." And I added, remembering his rhyme, "If I die before I wake, You can have the birthday cake!"

"You are not going to die this time, Felix," said Juan. "You are going to get better." And despite the horror of all that had happened, there was something of a smile in his voice.

EXHAUSTED though we were, we could not sleep for long. The storm abated, but then came back, even wilder and louder; daylight of a sort presently lit the hut with pale gray, but the rain did not diminish, the thunder reverberated, and lightning every now and then shattered the gloom.

"This is no place to remain," said Juan at length. "Let us bury that poor man and be on our way."

In the rude lean-to at the side where he had stabled our ponies, we found a few tools: a pick, a spade, and a saw. We fed and saddled the ponies, then carried out the tools and began trying to dig a grave in a grassy patch beyond the track, the only spot in that rocky pass where there seemed a chance that the ground would be soft enough to dig.

My right arm was still too stiff and sore to wield the pick, so I was working with the spade, while Juan hacked away somewhat ineffectually with the pick, when there came the most vivid and blinding flash that we had yet seen, causing us both to cry out, drop our tools, and cover our eyes. That was followed by such a shattering clap of thunder that we involuntarily clung together, still with our eyes closed, expecting imminent extinction.

"Are we still alive, Felix?" faltered Juan doubtfully, after a moment or two.

"I—I believe so." Warily I opened my eyes, wondering if I had been struck blind, then shook my head with astonishment, stared, and stared again. Where the hermit's stone hut had stood, there was now nothing but a battered, blackened, smoking ruin.

"*Ave María!*" I whispered, crossing myself. "I think God has done our business for us, Juan. We have no need to bury Brother Laurent."

Juan opened his eyes, gasped, and crossed himself likewise. Then he suddenly called out in a lamentable voice, "*The Harlequin!* Oh, my poor pony!"

He had already led out el Demonio, with the tools on his back, and tethered him to a pine tree, but the unfortunate Harlequin had remained inside the lean-to, and was now burned to a crisp, along with the body of Brother Laurent.

"Oh, poor, poor Harlequin!" said Juan, and burst

into uncontrollable weeping. "Oh, why, why did he have to die? Why did God have to kill him?"

I had no answer to his question, and could only try to comfort him as best I could.

"At least he suffered nothing, it must have been over in a second. Come, Juan, you have been brave for two of us during the last day; do not give way now! I am surprised to see you show such grief for a mere pony. Be a man! You shall have another as soon as we find a horse fair."

"He was *not* a mere pony!" wept Juan. "He was cowardly and lazy, and I loved him."

What could I say? I remembered how I felt when I had to leave a bad-tempered mule behind in a convent in Santander; and I let Juan have his cry out, while I transferred the contents of his *alforjas* (which, luckily, he had already brought from the shelter) into those of the Demon, rolled up the bags, and tied them to my saddle. My hand was sore, but usable, and the swelling was going down.

While doing these things I chanced to pass close to a seared, blackened hunk of stone which had previously, I recalled, been placed across the lintel of the hermit's doorway. There were Latin words carved upon it: SIT TIBI TERRA LEVIS, from which I guessed that the building had once formed a tomb for some Roman; now, once more, it would be a tomb, for a troubled man and a lazy pony.

Slipping Father Vespasian's brass spyglass into the saddlebag, I wondered what would have ensued if it had been left inside the shelter when the lightning struck; would our demon have ceased to follow us? Or would he, once the glass was destroyed, have followed us forevermore? I did not speak of this to Juan; he was too distressed over the death of his dear *pottoka*.

We were glad to leave that spot and continue onward down the pass. At first Juan wished me to ride and he to walk; but I insisted on our taking turn about.

By degrees the storm moved away southward to expend the last of its fury over Navarra, the clouds rolled back, and now, all of a sudden, we were given a magnificent view of the land rolling downward away from us to the south. What a contrast to the steep green French valleys! Now I knew that I was in my own country again; that, during our miserable night journey, we had crossed at some point from France into Spain. Far, far away the land stretched, with mountains rising in the distance; a bare land this, different from France, parched and dry-looking. Yet close at hand below us were forests; great beech woods wrapped the sides of mountains.

After an hour's traveling we met a boy with a yoke of oxen, and I was confirmed in my certainty, for the fly shield they wore over their eyes was made of sheepskin, whereas those in France habitually wear one of cloth.

"Now, I daresay we shall not be long in finding your uncle," I said to Juan, and he gave me a strange look, as if we had been too long in a world of our own to have confidence in ever again discovering the real one.

Presently the mist came down again, for I suppose the sun was sucking up moisture from the soaked mountain slopes, and we must go carefully and cannily, listening to the drip of the trees and the distant roar of a torrent, now on one side of the track, now on the other. From time to time the mist would lift for a few moments, and we could get a glimpse of great aisles in the woods, and huge trees.

Sometime after noon we reached a village named Ustarroz, where we were able to purchase food, but no mounts were to be had. Go on to Ochagavía, they told us. We, however, by that time were desperately tired, and turned aside from the track to sleep on a pile of hay in a great many-arched barn where the shade was deep and none came to disturb us.

7

We arrive at Pamplona; the message from Uncle León; the forest; what happened in the forest.

We traveled soberly westward from Ustarroz, on a little road that wound along a mountain valley, with great views of peaks to our right and, later, to our left also; we could not achieve a rapid pace, for both of us were still desperately weary and I a touch feverish, still, from my snakebite. So, as evening fell before we had found any place large enough to have ponies or mules for sale, we turned aside and slept under the roots of a great fallen pine. The mountains were much forested here, especially on our right hand; Juan told me this must be the edge of the great Forest of Irati, or Iraty, as the French spell it, where the little friendly *laminak* are reputed to dwell.

"Not so friendly to the Gente, however," I said, laughing. "Whatever in the world, Juan, gave you the notion of letting out that yell in the gorge, when Cocher was about to stop us? But for that shout of yours, I believe that we should be there still. And God Himself only knows what would have happened to us by now."

"What gave me the idea? Why, you did, yourself!" said Juan. "Don't you remember? You said, 'The *laminak* are waiting to help us . . .'"

"*Did* I? I have no recollection of that at all."

"Felix," said Juan. "I have been thinking, as we came along. That day . . . it seems long ago now . . . I was angry with you, when you took me to task for stealing Father Vespasian's spyglass—and the other things; I thought it was arrogant of you, and priggish, too, to make such a to-do about a few unimportant trifles; yet see what trouble it has led to. So you were right, I think, and I was wrong."

"Yet it *was* arrogant of me," said I. "I see now very plainly that I should have said it all in a different way. Also—who knows?—your taking Father Vespasian's spyglass—for all we can tell, that may have been part of the plan?"

"I *wanted* to take it," said Juan obstinately. He drew it out of the saddlebag, handling it as if it might be red-hot, and we both stared at it with a certain dread. Yet it was no more than a tarnished little brass object. Turning it in my hands I observed the letters v.s., very tiny, incised on the rim. The maker's initials, no doubt.

"How I wish I had never laid eyes on it! Yet perhaps," said Juan hopefully, "the Gente and that—that creature will stop following us, now that we are in Spain."

I, secretly, had been entertaining the same thought, which was not, perhaps, a very logical one.

"There is another thing I have had in my mind," Juan went on. "It is no great distance from where we are now to Pamplona, to the house of my uncle. Forty kilometers, perhaps? Not more. Why should you come any farther with me, Felix? I can manage the rest alone, very well. You should be traveling westward, not south."

"What, leave you now?" I said. "Are you mad? Alone, and on foot, and with no certainty that your uncle is there? Put that thought out of your head!"

"Well, at least," he said, "it would be wasteful to buy another pony or mule for that distance. We can walk it, turn about, as we did today."

His tone was wistful. What a singular thing, thought I, as I had often before, that this boy, son of a moneyed family (for, though he had not said as much, everything about him, including his abduction by the Gente, suggested this)—how singular that he should not ever have had a horse or pony of his own! Though I had been unloved in my grandfather's house, and continually rebuked, and held to be of no account, yet it was taken for granted that, from the age of eight or so on, I should have my own riding horse; my grandfather would have considered it a slight on the dignity of the house were I seen riding abroad on some insignificant animal. Yet Juan, though he could ride, and ride well, had never, before the unlucky Harlequin, possessed a pony. No wonder he was so attached to it, and grieved when it was killed.

"Well, I still think that we should purchase another

pony," said I. "Who knows? Perhaps your uncle may have moved elsewhere from Pamplona; perhaps that is why the letter never reached him. Pamplona may not be the end of our journey."

"That is true. I had not considered that." Juan's tone suddenly became more cheerful. "And after all, he can buy it from you, Felix; you will be certain to get your money back."

"Stop troubling your head about my money! There still remains enough to get you to your uncle's house and myself back home."

No demon came to trouble our sleep that night. We slept lightly, having rested during the day, rose before daylight, and made our way onward to Burguete, a large, pleasant village of white-faced houses on a southward-facing slope of mountain; there was no market that day, but from a farmer here we were able to purchase a mule, with its harness; he asked nine shillings but I beat him down to three silver crowns. The mule was a humble, docile beast, well content to follow wherever el Demonio led the way.

"It will do very well," said Juan, sighing. "But I shall never love it as I loved the Harlequin; never."

"You have a faithful heart, Juan!"

"Yes, I have," said he. "Once I give my friendship, it is given for life. Provided the other person does not play me false, like old Anniq."

The road down from Burguete to Pamplona is long and winding, and the hills are steep zigzags, so that el Demonio and the mule (whom Juan christened Rosa) were continually slipping on the rocky track and our saddles almost sliding forward over their shoulders. We rode slowly enough. My heart was cheered to see the round haystacks of Spain, and to hear words of Spanish coming into the language of the greetings we had from wayside folk.

The brooks roared down beside us, full to overflowing after the storm of two nights ago, and we saw many uprooted trees. The pastures here, filled with mouse-colored grazing cattle, were green and lush; not like the high plains of Spain farther on, where never a drop of rain falls from March to October.

Pamplona is a handsome city, situated on a high bluff in a ring of mountains. It has noble walls, and a great viaduct of a hundred arches.

Yet I remember the place with sadness, and would never wish to go back.

As we drew near the city I observed that Juan, too, had fallen silent and had begun to appear more and more downcast. I myself had little to say. My arm still pained me, and the town seemed so grand and prosperous when we approached it, with carriages and cavaliers going in and out, that I began to think what a shabby and ragamuffin appearance Juan and I must present, for our clothes, though purchased not so long ago, had become dusty with travel and stained with drenching. Juan was still sparrow-thin and large-eyed, while I was pale from my recent fever.

Suppose Juan's uncle was some great man of the city?

"Felix," said Juan, as we crossed the bridge over the River Arga and rode in at the city gate. He was paler than ever, and seemed to speak with difficulty. "Felix, I—I believe it will be best if we part here. You should not be held back any longer from your journey to your grandfather. And I remember how to find my uncle's house—I shall do very well by myself from now on."

He sounded hurried, strange; almost ungracious. "I have taken up too much of your time as it is," he went on. "Also you must see that—that so long as the Gente and Father Vespasian are on my trail, I shall only bring danger on you. But, once away from me, you will be safe. Therefore—therefore I wish that we shall say good-bye to each other now—here. I know, I am certain, that my uncle will most p-punctiliously defray all the costs that you have been put to on my behalf. I—I will ask him to send all moneys that are owing to your grandfather at Villaverde. So—so farewell, now, Felix, my good friend. Adieu. Adiós."

He had flushed up somewhat while making this long speech, and now held out his hand, which trembled; I could see that he was holding himself very rigid.

"Come, what is this?" said I. "Are you mad? Part here? Like this? In the street of a strange town? Do you think that I would let you go in such a way, without ensuring that you are among friends? Without entrusting you to some good guardian? When the Gente and that evil demon are still pursuing you—so far as we know to the contrary? And without even being sure that your uncle is here—or able—or willing to receive you?"

I spoke from my heart, and very forcibly. Juan's downcast look lightened somewhat at my tone; yet he continued to argue.

"My uncle lives not a stone's throw from here, in the Calle Santo Domingo. Well—well, if you feel so—"

"I certainly do!"

"Why do you not go to the beast market, then, and sell the mule, while I find my uncle and make sure of his welcome. Then I will return to meet you here."

We were in a small plaza at that moment, I think it was called the Plaza Consistorial. There were arcades, and coffeehouses under them, and people sitting or strolling about.

I bit my lip. I could very plainly see that for some reason Juan felt it of great importance that I did not come into the presence of his uncle. By this I must confess that I was hurt; deeply hurt. It had never occurred to me that I might be thought of such poor birth and breeding as to bring embarrassment or disgrace on Juan by my company. I considered myself of good family, though I knew I was somewhat travel-soiled and worn. But I am not one to kick up a dust about such personal matters, or to discountenance somebody by pressing a request that is clearly unwelcome. So, swallowing a little, I answered, "Very well. So be it. If that is what you wish. But I shall not sell the mule yet, until we know that there is no reason to keep her. I will wait here for you, an hour. So you must promise me faithfully to return, even if it is only to assure me that all is well and your uncle is happy to receive you."

"Yes—yes, of course I will do that. I promise you, Felix," said Juan in a flurried manner, and almost ran away from me along the street.

Somewhat heavily—indeed, my heart felt like a cold, hollow stone inside me—I tethered our two beasts to a pillar, and, as there was a coffeehouse close at hand, made my way there, sat down at a table, and ordered a cup of chocolate. The waiter looked at me oddly enough. I daresay he wondered if I had the money to pay for it. But I snapped at him to hurry up, in a tone taken from my grandfather the Conde, and he answered "Yes, señor," respectfully, and removed himself and his tray.

While waiting, I tried to divert myself by looking about me at the town and townspeople of Pamplona. It seemed most strange to be in a city again, after so many days in the forests and mountains—and before that, so many months in the Abbey of St. Just—but I did find it pleasant and homelike to hear Spanish spoken once more, even if it was a Basque Spanish, not such as we speak in Galicia. That—a very little—cheered my dismal spirits. And indeed, Pamplona—or Irrunia, as it should properly be called, since that is its Basque title—seemed a handsome town: Many of the houses were new and high, with miradors; that is, glassed-in balconies where the ladies may sit and look down to see what is happening in the street without suffering from the cold mountain winds. Under the arcades in the street there were well-stocked stores where a person might buy anything he wanted.

Yet after a while I began to notice a queer contrast to the last English town I had visited, Plymouth; that was a seaport, a cheerful, carefree, noisy place, with everybody going about his business freely and unconcerned; whereas in Pamplona it began to seem to me that the people looked oppressed and anxious; though men talked together at the café tables they did so quietly, glancing sometimes over their shoulders; many alguacils and town officials moved about the streets, and there were officers of the Civil Guard, also, and soldiers from the barracks.

When the French armies left Spain I was quite small, five years of age, only a child, but I can well remember the sullen, harried, muttering silence of a town which has foreign invading troops quartered there; thus—or so I felt—it was in Pamplona, too.

And I remembered Father Antoine at St. Just telling me about King Ferdinand's illiberal rule. His words came back to me: "I have heard that a rebellion, under Colonel Rafael Riego, is spreading and gathering power."

Yet, glancing about me as I started to sip my chocolate, I found the idea of a rebellion hard to believe. Thirty years ago there had been a rebellion in

France; people spoke of it still with horror. Wild mobs and massacres, blood in the streets, the guillotine, and heads falling every minute. No signs of any such rebellion were to be seen in this staid place; quite the reverse, indeed.

After a very short time—much shorter than I had expected—Juan returned, not running, but walking fast, and glancing about him in the same harassed manner as did the men at the coffee tables. I raised my hand, he saw me, and his expression lightened.

He made his way toward me, and said in a low tone, "I have something of an unexpected nature to tell you. But not here. Come."

I noticed that his eye lit very wistfully on my cup of chocolate, so I suggested that he should drink it; he needed little urging to do so. Then we untied our mounts, and he led me to the quarter of the town where the market was held.

This was a crowded, cheerful, and noisy area, with squawking poultry, old dames selling eggs, cheese, oil, oranges, lemons, and grapefruit. Juan took me to a corner where an old lady in a black shawl was evidently waiting for us.

"So *this is* the one that has brought you out of France; *hela,* he looks no more than a day-old chick himself!" She sniffed, giving me a highly satirical glance. She had a sharp-cut face and was thin-lipped with an arched nose and snapping black eyes; her chin was stubbled over with the beginnings of a white beard.

I noticed that whenever her eye chanced to alight on Juan she seemed ready to explode with disapproval and only restrained herself by a great effort.

"This is my uncle's housekeeper, Isabelita Arnaiz," Juan told me quickly. "My uncle has left Pamplona."

Ah! I thought. That was just what I had expected.

"Where has he gone?" I civilly inquired. And to the old dame I said, "Naturally I shall be happy to escort the young Señor Esparza to wherever his uncle is at present residing."

The old lady bestowed upon me an extremely narrow glance, from top to toe, beginning with my face and coming back to rest there. I was able to support this scrutiny easily enough; after the demon glare of Father Vespasian, what other eyes could have power to disturb?

"Well, but, Felix," said Juan, "that is the thing. Señora Arnaiz does not know where, precisely, my uncle has gone."

This did seem singular. His own housekeeper not to know?

"When did he leave?"

"It was more than three months ago."

"So—in fact—he never received the letter your brother sent him about you?"

"No! He did not! I was certain that my uncle would have helped me if he could. The letter lies in his house unopened; Isabelita showed it to me."

"And the Señora has no idea at all where he might be?"

The old lady, her black eyes flicking this way and that before she spoke, said, rapidly, in a low tone, "He was obliged to leave very quickly, you understand. He had been in correspondence with *el coronel,* and that was dangerous. One evening a note, unsigned, was thrown through the window. It said 'Depart while your skin is whole.' So he packed a little bag, saddled a horse, and left immediately. Next day the alguacils were there asking for him . . . he had gone only just in time. There have been many executions, many imprisonments, many people sent into exile—*Ay de mí,* where will it all end?"

I guessed that *el coronel* might be Colonel Riego, leader of the rebellion.

"But my master is a man in his sixties!" lamented the housekeeper. "How can he manage, without me to bring him his fried egg and cup of chocolate and toast sandwiches?"

"And you really have no idea where he could have gone?"

The housekeeper's look suggested to me that, even if she did know, she would not trust us enough to tell. She shook her head.

"But my uncle left a message for me," said Juan. "He told Señora Arnaiz that if I found I could not live happily with my brother Esteban—if any trouble arose—"

The old lady muttered something, evidently Uncle León's uncomplimentary opinion of brother Esteban.

"Well, he was right!" said Juan. "So his message was that if I should ever come to Spain and ask for him, I was to be given this." And, cupped in his hand, he showed me a little ivory snuffbox, no bigger than a gull's egg.

"There is a letter inside?"

"No letter. Only four stones and a leaf."

The housekeeper, now glancing keenly over her shoulder, said, "I see some carabineers approaching. They keep a continual watch over the house, and they follow me, to discover if my master comes back or sends word. I must leave you at once."

And she hobbled off as fast as she could. She was desperately lame, and could only just hoist herself along.

"It seems to me, Juan," said I, "that by far your best course will be to accompany me to Villaverde."

My heart rose as I said the words. I thought how pleasant it would be to have Juan's company on the homeward journey; how greatly I would enjoy showing him my grandfather's house. And *I* would not be ashamed of *his* company! On the contrary!

But Juan, at my suggestion, looked as scared as if I had offered to escort him to the polar regions. He quivered like a nervous horse, shook his head vigorously, and said, "No, Felix. My uncle expected that I would be able to solve his puzzle, so I am sure that it cannot be too difficult."

"Let me see the stones and the leaf."

He opened the snuffbox. The little stones—smaller than dried peas—were strung together on a scrap of silken cord: a tiny ball of ivory, a ruby, a little green stone, a little yellow stone. And under them a slim dry brown leaf, upon which had been written in ink the word TOI. Thou.

"What can it mean?" fretted Juan. "I must be exceedingly stupid not to be able to puzzle it out."

"Well," said I, "such a crowded corner as we are in here is no place to work at puzzles. Somebody might jog your elbow and then your message is lost altogether. Let us buy a little food in the market and leave this city, for it makes me uncomfortable. My shoulder blades prickle every time one of those Civil Guards walks past."

Juan agreed that he felt the same, so we purchased cheese, bread, and oranges and rode out over the humpbacked bridge into the open sierra once more. There, sprawled under an olive tree, we considered the little box and its mysterious contents.

"Why in the world should your uncle give you four little jewels? What a queer gift! Were they, perhaps, your mother's?"

"No, not that I am aware," said Juan. "I have never seen them before."

"What are the colored stones, do you know? The white one is a piece of ivory—"

"The red one is a ruby; the green, I think, agate; and the yellow, topaz."

We were, as usual, speaking French, and he used the French words *ivoire, rubis, agate, topaze.*

"White, red, green, yellow. Do the colors have some special significance?"

"I know of none."

"Is your uncle a jeweler?"

He laughed. "No, a wine merchant! Like my father. That was how they became acquainted."

"The colors are not your family coat of arms."

He smiled. "No, nothing of that nature. My family is not noble, like yours, Felix."

What a puzzle the boy was!

"And the leaf?" I picked it up and sniffed it. It was stiff, shiny, and smelled faintly aromatic. It was from an ilex, or holm oak. They are big handsome trees with small green leaves hanging in great drooping swags; the leaves are not shed in winter but fall at any time of the year; so, under such a tree, you may always shuffle through a scatter of the dried brown leaves. Such trees are to be found in many parts of France and Spain; even in England I have seen them.

"It is a leaf from a *yeuse,*" said Juan, employing the French word. "Some say that they are magical trees. But I do not know whether that is to the purpose."

We sat frowning and cudgeling our brains. It was like hammering at a door that will not open. Juan suddenly let out a long defeated sigh.

"Oh, I am too tired to think!" He added wistfully, "That was a delicious cup of chocolate, Felix! Once, long ago, my mother took me into Bayonne, when I was about four, and we drank chocolate with my Aunt Laura—"

He stopped short, but I said, "Well, I will be glad to take you back into Pamplona and buy you another cup of chocolate. But let us eat now, and perhaps that will sharpen our wits. What do you suppose your uncle means by *Toi*?"

"I suppose, by that, he may mean me."

"White, red, green, yellow, thee."

"Or, yellow, green, red, white, me."

We began to laugh, we could not help ourselves, suddenly feeling light-headed and foolish; we lay laughing helplessly in the dusty grass.

"You should make a poem about it, Juan—'Yellow, green, red, white, Is it time to say good-night?'"

"White, green, red, yellow, Felix, you're a silly fellow!"

So for a while we lay in the shade of the olive tree, laughing weakly and making up childish rhymes in a jumble of languages. For a little while the terrors and weariness of our journey were forgotten; and so was its doubtful outcome; like carefree schoolchildren we amused each other with nonsense. In the midst of which I was moved to say suddenly, "Juan, I have been thinking about what Brother Laurent said."

"About persuading the demon to leave Plumet's body?"

Sometimes the quickness of his thought amazed me. It seemed as if our minds raced on a parallel course, then met.

"Yes! He said that the power would be given to you when it was needed. But perhaps—I was thinking—you already have the power. Perhaps it is by your talent to make poems that the evil spirit will be driven away."

"How could that possibly be?" Juan had gone pale again. He sounded unsure, troubled, afraid.

"If demons hate bells—is it not likely that they also hate verses?"

"Perhaps . . . Oh, let us not think about it anymore just now!"

But our lighthearted mood was broken, and we sat together in a sad, close silence, watching the people on the distant highway passing in and out of the town.

Presently the sight of a troop of Maragatos, or letter carriers, filled me with the wish to write a letter to my grandfather. So, leaving Juan under the tree, I returned to the town, purchased pen, ink, and a quantity of paper, then came back to our encampment, laid my paper upon Juan's book, the book on my knee, and after chewing the quill of my pen for a while, began to write:

To my Honored and much-loved Grandfather,
el Conde don Francisco Acarillo de Santibana y
Escurial de la Sierra y Cabezada, at Villaverde.
This, from Pamplona.
Señor:
I must beg your forgiveness for this long silence and for not having returned home sooner. On the

voyage from Spain my ship was wrecked, and I was knocked on the head, fell sick, and was obliged to pass several months at the Abbey of St. Just, in France, before I came to my senses. From there I agreed to escort a young French boy, Juan Esparza, to his uncle in Spain. Now, regrettably, we find that his uncle has moved away, and we are obliged to search for him. Nevertheless, dear Grandfather, I hope to return home within the next month. If Juan's uncle cannot be found, I greatly wish to bring him to Villaverde. He is—

I paused, nibbling my pen.

What *was* Juan? How could I describe him to my grandfather? He was my dear friend. He had kept me alive by telling me a poem about the wind. He had saved me from the Mala Gente. He had exasperated me by taking part in the *bertsulari* contest. He had nearly won it. He had stolen the Abbot's spyglass. I had saved his life in the seaside thicket. . . .

He was my dear friend.

I wrote: "He is of good family, gentle, brave, and a poet. Your loving grandson, Felix."

Then I wrote to Father Antoine, telling him that we had successfully journeyed into Spain, had not yet found Juan's uncle but hoped to do so, but that we were much troubled about Father Vespasian, who had appeared drowned when we left the Abbey; yet we had seen him subsequently—or what we believed to be the Abbot—and that we should be grateful for Father

Antoine's prayers and anything else that he thought might help us. I sent him some money to pay for the cup, book, and spyglass, and made the whole into a little packet. Then I carried my letters back to the Plaza San José, by the cathedral, where the letter carriers wait. They are very faithful messengers, easily recognizable by their leather jackets, close-cut hair with a few long tufts left, wide zouave trousers, and enormous hats; they take letters all over Spain, traveling in groups at a rapid trot. I felt certain that, before very many days, Grandfather would safely receive my message, and the thought of this hugely lightened my heart.

Having paid the carriers their fee, I returned again to Juan, who had remained outside the ramparts, and found him greatly excited.

"Felix, I think that I have solved the puzzle. I really do believe so!"

"Maravilloso!" I said. "How in the world did you do it?"

"Look, these stones: ivory, ruby, agate, topaz—and the leaf from the *yeuse*. What do their letters spell?"

"I-R-A-T-Y—Iraty?"

"Iraty! The Forest of Iraty!"

"Why, Juan! I do indeed believe that you have hit on it. What a very clever boy you are! But what is *Toi*?"

"Oh, well," he said, going pink, "I suppose that means me—that I—that I should go to the forest, where I think my uncle must be."

"But is not the forest a very large area?"

"Yes, it is, hundreds of kilometers. But now I think about it, I do remember some talk of my uncle owning a little farm there."

"Do you know at all where?"

"No," he said. "But Isabelita mentioned an old coachman, now living in Orbaiceta. He would know, I should think—"

"That is settled then," I said, standing up. "To Orbaiceta we go."

"Oh, Felix." Juan looked troubled again. "Do you really—?"

"Hush! Besides, do you think I would leave you without knowing if that was the solution to the puzzle?"

Accordingly we saddled up and took a track across the sierra, traveling eastward for twenty kilometers or so, until we reached the River Iraty itself, and then followed it northward. The distant snowy peaks of the mountains, now ahead of us, seemed like old friends. The slopes on the Spanish side are not steep and craggy, as on the French, but gentler, intersected with valleys and covered with beech forest. In between were fields of young maize and tobacco, and red-tiled farmhouses. As we climbed higher, the maize gave way to barley, and we saw encampments of charcoal-burners, with their great earth mounds, from which thin spirals of blue smoke emerged. Thrushes were singing, and larks over the cleared patches, and the cuckoos called. The woods were full of wildflowers. Our hearts were peaceful.

We passed the night in a barn, entered the village of Orbaiceta, and inquired for Tomás Aguilar. In the market, we were told, selling his radishes; and there we found him: a red-faced balding fat man with tiny twinkling eyes.

I let Juan do the interrogating, and remained out of earshot, but looking sharply around me.

Juan spoke a couple of words softly in the ear of the fat man, who started, cast him a nervous glance, then nodded and muttered something in an undertone, before exclaiming more loudly, "That is my price, and you won't find better radishes anywhere in the market! Young good-for-nothings, with all the money in the world to spend!" and he turned and spat sideways.

An alguacil approached us and demanded to see our passports.

"Our mother has them," said Juan swiftly. "That stout lady over there with the white lace mantilla." Then, as the man's eyes followed Juan's pointing finger, we both ducked away into the crowd.

"*Venga, venga!*" shouted the man. "Come back, come back!" But we fled round a corner and never stopped running until we reached the point where we had left our horses, on the outskirts of the village.

"Well?" I asked, when we had put a good distance between us and the houses, still following the Iraty stream northward up its course.

"It is a little farm on the Pic d'Occabé, Tomás told

me. Just this side of the frontier. We must continue to follow the river past a lake."

The lake proved to be not too far away. There were marshes around it, which slowed up our progress; the horses slipped and floundered and tossed their heads, bothered by clouds of stinging flies, even this early in the year.

The French frontier, I thought, must now be not very far distant. Juan's Uncle León had evidently chosen his refuge with some care so that, at need, he might be able to slip across the border into France.

Up to our left the slopes of a great mountain thrust out of the woodland. This was the Pic d'Occabé, which, according to Father Antoine's map, lay half in France, half in Spain. Mountains have their own huge kingdoms; they care nothing for human frontiers.

At this point, therefore, we must leave the river and climb; but how could we tell on what part of the mountain Juan's uncle had his hiding place? For hours and hours we had passed not a soul of whom we might ask questions; not a shepherd, not a goatherd, not a charcoal-burner. There were not even many animals or birds in this part of the forest.

"It must be one of the oldest regions of the world!" Juan said wonderingly.

Some of the yews and beeches were so ancient and huge that twenty men, holding hands, could not have encircled their massive trunks. The yew boles were dark red, the color of a withered rose, tall and massive, their dense foliage and mighty branches thick enough to keep off all but the heaviest rain. And the beeches were higher still, towering with silver-gray trunks and layered leaves, pale green at this spring season, which permitted a little sunshine to filter through in pale powdery shafts. Here and there immense fallen trunks (fallen from age, not from any human axe) blocked our path for many yards, and we must laboriously skirt round them, hacking our way through festoons of creepers. Great velvet mosses and gray-green lichens cushioned the dead trunks, and Juan sometimes exclaimed over their beauty and profusion; but, as we slowly penetrated deeper and deeper into the forest, our talk became hushed by degrees and at last we ceased to speak at all. The silence lay on us like a canopy.

Besides the trees in the forest we found huge stones: Here and there upright boulders, twice the height of a man or even higher, stood in circles, sometimes with one extra-large squared rock in the center.

"What are they? Who could have brought them here?" I whispered in awe, and Juan whispered back, "I do not know! I have heard it said that the *laminak* put them here. People speak about these stone circles, but I never understood that they were so huge. How could the *laminak* have brought them? The *laminak* are *little* people."

"But if not the *laminak*, then who?"

For this he had no answer.

It seemed to me that there must be all manner of creations, living in the globe with us, of which we knew less than nothing. Here, in this widespreading dimness and hush, where even the brooks ran softly between banks of moss and beech-mast, it was easy enough to believe in the *laminak,* or in any other fabled being.

Two stone circles we found; then three, four, five, six; then we lost count. Some of the high-standing stones had been thrust aside, in the course of time, by growing trees; sometimes these trees, too, had grown to enormous size, then had died, fallen, and rotted away; which plainly showed that the stones must be more ancient still—discarded, perhaps, from some dark age near the very beginning of belief, when cold winds whistled, and there were no trees, and the earth was all cased in ice.

We found it very hard to keep our sense of direction in the forest, where often the sun was hidden from us. Could we be wandering in circles? Were we covering the same ground, again and again? I thought of marking trees when we passed them, as gypsies do, but felt that it would be an act of discourtesy to the forest, and put back the knife in my belt. God would surely lead us, as He had to the hermit's chapel.

So, at the end of the day, on the side of a hill where some few rays from the setting sun did come filtering sideways, dusty and gold-bright, between the red yew boughs, we came to the final stone circle, set aslant on the sloping ground. The high, upright stones cast great black shadows like dragons' tongue over the forest floor.

And there, waiting for us, were the Gente: a group of men, standing, sitting, and leaning by a couple of the stones in the ring; another man, white-haired, white-faced, motionless, against the biggest stone in the center.

We had been leading our beasts; for the branches hereabouts dangled so low that riding was difficult. I saw Juan beside me stop, draw breath, and stand rigid for a moment; then he carefully attached his mule's reins to a yew bough, groped for a moment in his saddlebag, found something, and walked forward steadily.

Fastening my pony likewise, I was about to follow him, then had a thought. I had found Brother Bertrand's little silver bell by the blackened stones of the burned chapel. Fearing that the sight of it would distress Juan by reminding him of his lost pony, I had tucked it into my knapsack. Now, taking it out, I walked after Juan. Under my sweaty shirt I could feel my heart thundering as if it were about to knock its way out from between my ribs.

From the center of the group I heard the man Cocher call out with a pretense at joviality: "*Hola*, there, my young friends. We come the short way, you follow the long way! But twist as you may, you come back to us in the end."

Utterly ignoring him, Juan walked on toward the center of the circle. But I, glancing warily at the knot of Gente, observed that their numbers appeared to have dwindled very much. The hunchback was gone, and two of the men who had carried muskets. There were no more than five or six left, including Cocher; and all of them looked desperately tired, ragged, and heartsick, as if they had no hope left, as if they had been dragged by demons through terrible paths.

Perhaps they had.

How Juan ever summoned the courage to approach the Thing by the central monolith, I will never understand. No longer had it the least resemblance to the man who had been Plumet; nor to Father Vespasian. It was hardly human at all. The face, dead-white, was seared and scarred, as if the flesh and bone which formed it had been compressed, frozen, buried in quicklime, or subjected to other terrifyingly powerful forces. The mouth began to work, opening and shutting mechanically, but no sound came out; the hands also opened and shut their fingers jerkily like the shuttles of a loom; and the eyes stared, stared at Juan as he approached.

"I have brought back your glass," said he, and held it out. "It was wrong to take it. I know that now. And so I have brought it back."

For a long moment he held it extended, and I thought nothing was going to happen. Let him just drop it, I begged silently. He has brought it, that is enough. Then we can go.

But at last one of the dead arms came up, the peg-like fingers extended, and grasped the brass cylinder.

Juan swiftly snatched back his own hand; only just in time; for with my own eyes I saw the spyglass glow red hot in the lifeless grasp; then the fingers closed, crushing it like soft cheese, and a dribble of molten metal fell to the ground, scorching the mosses, which hissed faintly and turned black. A thread of smoke rose.

"I—summoned—you—back," said a faint voice issuing from the open mouth. It was a high, remote sound, coming, I thought, from a vast distance, of time and place both. The lips did not move; the voice came from them as the sound comes from the mouth of a horn, blown from elsewhere.

"I came of my own wish," said Juan, "to return the glass. Now I am going again."

"You are going nowhere," said the dead voice. "You may not go. I conjure you to remain. And to tell me—"

"I shall tell you nothing."

The light issuing from the eyes began to change. It had been red. Now it brightened, became green and brilliant.

"You will tell me all! Here in this circle you will tell me all!"

"Nothing," said Juan, "I will tell you nothing," and he summoned me with a movement of his eyes to come and stand beside him. I had been a pace or two behind. Taking that pace forward was one of the hardest things I had done in my whole life. I slipped the little silver bell into his left hand. He transferred it to his right, then took mine and held it.

"Tell me," said the unearthly voice.

"No!" And Juan rang Brother Bertrand's bell sharply, once. Then, in the voice that he kept for poetry, he said, with a wonderful quiet authority,

"By the power of Light, I charge you to tell me your name."

The voice issuing from the motionless mouth began to gabble. A stream of mocking inhuman sounds came from it; like the rattle of pebbles being ground together.

"That is no answer!" said Juan. "By the power of Light, I charge you, tell me your name."

His eyes met mine; he slightly moved his head, and in a dry voice that hardly seemed to be mine, I repeated what he had just said.

"By the power of Light, tell me your name."

"By the strength of Rock," said Juan, "tell me your name."

"By the strength of Rock, tell me your name."

"By the goodness of Bread, tell me your name."

"By the goodness of Bread, tell me your name."

"By the purity of Water, tell me your name."

"By the power of Light, tell me your name."

Each time, as soon as he had spoken, I repeated what he had said. And in every pause between our voices, Juan rang the little silver bell.

Time passed by.

The sun sank lower and lower, the shadows grew longer and blacker. Then the shadows all rose upward and vanished, the light went altogether, and the forest turned to a sick gray: the gray of mildew, the gray of corpses. I tried not to think that, but such thoughts would slip in, at the end of each sentence that I repeated. And I thought also, Supposing the unclean spirit does come out of his body, *where will it go?* Suppose it takes refuge in another body? *Whose?*

The alien voice began again on a high screaming note, but intelligibly.

"Your grandmother would not have used me so! You are mine by inheritance! You belong on these mountains! *Here and there! Here and there!* You belong on these mountains!"

"By the power of Light, tell me your name," said Juan, ignoring what the voice said, but speaking a little faster so as to drown the hateful gabble.

"By the power of Light, tell me your name," I repeated after him.

Strange though it seems, as we recited our incantation, ten times, twenty times, a hundred times, perhaps a thousand times, I did not find myself growing weary. Quite otherwise indeed: I was aware of my feet, planted steadily in the moss, as if they were roots and I a tree; my hand clasped in that of Juan, as if he were a rock. The lack of light was no longer of importance, for trees and rocks do not see, they have no need of sight.

But later the moon rose.

"By the goodness of Bread, tell me your name."

"By the purity of Water, tell me your name."

"By the power of Light, tell me your name."

Who knows at what repetition—whether we were in our thousands, or tens of thousands, I had lost track of time entirely—the gaping mouth suddenly opened wide, crazily, unnaturally wide, like that of a serpent which can stretch back almost into a straight line; and a high, monstrous voice shrieked,

"Our name is Legion!"

"By the power of Light, I charge you to leave this man and begone."

Juan raised his hand, as if calling down the rays of the moon to assist him.

"Command us not to go out into the deep!" wailed the voice.

"I have no right to govern your direction," said Juan hoarsely. "But you are forbidden to reenter any human body. That is all. Go where you will."

An even wilder gibbering wail issued from the corpse mouth, rising shriller and shriller until it reached an unendurable crescendo of height and agony; then the body crumpled sideways and slid to the ground, while something—some slight, evanescent something—slipped swiftly away between the stones of the circle. Next moment, not far away, a monumental beech tree, one of the highest in the forest, slowly keeled over and fell with a thundering crash into the darkness.

The body by the rock writhed and whimpered. Juan wiped his forehead with his left hand, gently removing it from mine to do so. Then he knelt by the shuddering body, turning it so that the face became visible in the moonlight. And it was once more the face of Plumet, though aged and white-haired.

I, too, knelt beside him.

After a moment the eyes opened. They looked up at Juan and recognized him. Behind me I heard Cocher whisper, *"Ah, mon Dieu . . ."*

"I tried to hang you," whispered Plumet. "I intended to kill you."

"It is forgotten. I forgive you. Go in peace now."

"Thanks, child," gasped Plumet, and his eyes closed, and he died, faster than the wind can flick away a speck of ash.

Juan turned and tumbled into my arms. At first, with terror, I thought that he was dead, or fainting. Then I realized that he was merely asleep, sound asleep.

"Fetch a blanket," I mumbled to Cocher. Somebody produced our blanket from the saddlebag, and I laid it over Juan, wrapping it round. Next minute I myself was asleep also, huddled beside him.

WHEN I woke, it was late morning in the forest. The remaining Gente, pale and silent, were squatting at a little distance, crumbling bread and sipping goats' milk. The body of Plumet had been removed. I hoped they had buried it.

Juan still slept, deeply, under the blanket. I would not disturb him.

I went over to talk to the Gente.

"You will leave us in peace now?"

"Jesu María, yes," they answered, crossing themselves. "We would not have followed you so far, only—only that terrible Thing which had taken hold of Plumet obliged us to go on."

"Why did you not refuse?"

"*Nombre de Dios,* it made us follow! Do you know what it did to poor little Gueule, on the beach? Tore him apart as if he were paper. And the same with the others, in the gorge—"

"Don't tell me, I don't wish to hear," I said hastily. "But in the first place it was *you* who abducted Juan, before the devil took hold of Plumet—"

"Oh, well, yes, at that time. It is true, the brother hired us to. He said the rich Spanish uncle would pay us ransom. But now the uncle is proscribed—exiled—has no money at all. We were angry when we discovered that. We went back with Plumet—that was after he was devil-ridden—and strung up Esteban and the old woman from his own apple trees. They will never eat soup again."

I shivered at the callousness of these men, who lived so close to death that it meant nothing to them.

"Why do that?"

"To teach men that the Gente are not to be played with."

"But if you knew the uncle had no money—why follow us in the first place?"

"At first we believed that you would lead us to the treasure."

"What treasure?" I said, bewildered. "*I* have no treasure!"

"But you had known a man in Spain who told you about the treasure. The pay that the king of France sent from Paris for the French army—chests of gold coins, and chalices, and silks and jewels and brocades and statues, all the treasure that was in King Joseph's train, and lost when the French army fled home over the mountains. We heard that you knew where it was lost."

"You fools! That man never told me anything at all! I never had any knowledge of such a treasure. Do you not believe me? You had better, for it is the truth!"

They looked at each other glumly. They were a wretched, ragged crew, bloodshot-eyed, skinny, bruised, and trembling; in far worse case than Juan and myself. I felt sorry for them, wicked though they undoubtedly were.

"Yes, my young señor, we do believe you," said the one-eyed man called Cocher. "No one who—who did what you were doing last night—would tell us a lie. I am certain of that. But, to tell truth, by the end, we had given up hope of the treasure, we had given up all hope. We were just driven on, from rock to hill to tree, by that one." He nodded toward a distant pile of earth. Beyond it lay a huge fallen beech tree.

"Let us hope he sleeps sound," I said, crossing myself. They all did likewise.

An hour later they gave me what food they had and departed, melting away into the forest, while I sat on beside the sleeping Juan. Before they went, they told me where to find Juan's uncle, Señor León de

Echepara. He had a holding, they said, very close to the French border: a farmhouse, an acre or so of land, a few goats, a hive of bees, in a sheltered, hidden valley.

"What do you know of him? Is he a good person? Reliable?"

It seemed strange to be canvassing the opinions of this group of rogues, but after what had passed between us, I felt sure that they would give an honest judgment.

"Oh, yes," they assured me. "In the town of Pamplona Señor de Echepara had a very high reputation. He was well liked. *'Notoriamente hidalgo.'* A fine gentleman. He always kept his word and was of liberal principles. That is why he was obliged to flee."

And then they left me.

Juan's request to me; his Uncle León; I go to Vitoria, and en-
counter two English ladies; I return to Villaverde; I hear news
from my grandfather; and form a new resolve.

Toward sunset Juan woke up. At first he looked round him in terror and confusion. His right hand, I had noticed, was quite badly burned. A white scar crossed the insides of the fingers. While he was still drowsy I bandaged it as carefully as I could.

After a while he muttered, "I thought we found all those wicked men here. The light . . . the shadows . . ."

I made haste to reassure him.

"Set your mind at rest. They are all gone."

"The bad spirit, too?"

"Can you not remember? You rang your bell, and spoke those words, and sent him away."

"Ah. Yes. So we did," he said slowly. "And then Plumet came back. And then Plumet died." He shivered—a deep, long shiver—and presently said, "Do not let us talk about it anymore."

"No. It is done with. They won't trouble us, ever again."

I wondered whether to tell him that, before leaving France, the Gente had killed his brother and the old nurse; decided not to. He would learn that soon enough from some other source. I did tell him, though, that I now knew his uncle's farm was no farther away than over a couple of ridges, in a secret valley.

Juan said, "Very good. I am glad to hear that we can find Uncle León without too much trouble. But"—he suddenly sounded wistful, pleading—"Let us not do so tonight, Felix. Let us have one more night in the forest."

"With all my heart," I said.

I had kindled a fire while he was still sleeping, and caught fish in a brook that ran nearby. So, with the bread the Gente had left us, we had not too bad a supper. And afterward, as so often on our journey, Juan tried to teach me some of the Basque grammar, and I taught him various verses of English poetry. *"Where the bee sucks, there suck I,"* he learned, and then broke off to ask me in a doubtful, troubled manner, "Shall I like living with my uncle, do you think, in the forest?"

"Of course you will!" I assured him. "Think of all the things to see—eagles, deer, the wildflowers that you love. You and your uncle can climb the Lost Mountain, you can hunt izard and wild boar—"

"But I had made a—a kind of promise to God, concerning my life—"

"Oh, well," I said, not quite understanding him. "If you had made a promise, then of course you must keep it. I am sure your uncle would not stand in your way. *'Notoriamente hidalgo.'* But if, by any chance, the life does not suit you—or if your uncle should be obliged to move once more—why, then, write to me, and you can come and live at Villaverde. Here, I will give you the direction"—and I wrote it on a scrap of paper. "For—after all—we have been good comrades, have we not? After I had stopped being arrogant, and you had stopped being willful!"

He did not smile. He said, "But a journey like this can never be repeated. Never, ever again. Once we are parted, Felix—even if by some chance we *should* meet again in the future—it could not possibly be the same." And he repeated, "Never, ever again."

His words tolled in my heart like a bell. But I said stoutly, "Perhaps not. But things may be different. They may be better, even. It is no use to refuse the future, which is bound to come. And it may bring even greater good than what we have now."

"I wonder," said Juan.

"I shall hope to see you again, Juan."

"Do not depend on it," said he. "For I do not think you will."

But then he shook himself and seemed to throw off this foreboding mood, and we passed the rest of the evening cheerfully enough. I sang him a ballad that used to be a favorite of my shipmate Sam: "Sweet Polly Oliver," about a young girl who, to follow her sweetheart, dressed up in her dead brother's uniform and went for a soldier.

"But all she did, after all, was to nurse him when he was sick," remarked Juan, when the ballad was finished. "Suppose there had been a real battle, how would she have done?"

"I have sometimes wondered that, too. But still, women can be as brave as men, they say. And they have fought in battles. Think of the Amazons. Or Jeanne d'Arc."

"Yes, that is true," agreed Juan.

Then I made him say again his little verse about the sailor's pie, and I learned it by heart, for it had greatly taken my fancy. "'First you must take a teacupful of sky.' What do you mean by that, Juan?"

"Oh, you must never ask the meaning of poems," he said, laughing. "That is like asking for the meaning of a rose, or a fish. The poem is itself, or should be; that is all." So I carefully wrote it down.

At length we fell asleep, under a huge, seamed, craggy, knotty yew tree that brooded over our heads like a great-grandfather. I was inexpressibly weary, for my sleep the night before had been but scanty, and much broken by lurid dreams. I fell into slumber as into a well, and slept, I believe, for twelve hours, or thereabouts.

WHEN I woke, all was silent. I raised myself up, yawning, and looked about me. Juan was not to be seen, so I thought he was probably performing his ablutions in the brook, as was his habit.

"Oh, Juan! I am going to broil the fish!" I called quietly; the forest made one wish to lower one's voice at all times. "So don't take too long with your washing."

I discovered that the fire was already lit, and smoldering redly; Juan must have been awake for some time. And near the fish, pinned in a split prong of yew, lay a folded paper, a sheet left from the packet I had bought to write letters to Grandfather and Father Antoine.

Before I had so much as seen the writing, I think I had guessed the contents. My heart stopped still.

My dear Felix, [Juan had written]

I have risen early to write this while you are asleep. I am going to ask you to do me a great kindness. The last of many! At the very first, you saved me from hanging. Do not think that I forget that. And you saved me again after that, more times than I can count—on the causeway, and on the cliff above the grotto, and at the masquerade; and if you had not been at my side when facing that terror, I should certainly have given in to it, and that would have been the end of me. And you bought me my clothes, and my dear Harlequin horse. There is no doubt that God meant you to be my companion into Spain, and help me find my Uncle León. And I shall never, never forget you, or how patiently you dealt with my follies and cowardice. Nor shall I ever forget the happy times we had together. I do not think I shall ever have such a companion again. It has been different from anything that happened to me before, or ever will, and I shall remember you every night in my prayers, to the very end of my life. And I hope that your life will be a long and happy one.

Now, Felix, the kindness I ask of you is this. *Do not follow me to my uncle's house.* Do not come to see me there. Before I began to write this, I walked through the forest and saw him working in his garden patch. So I know he is there, and will take me in. He is a kind, sincere man. So do not be anxious for me, Felix. You have put forth enough time and trouble for me already—you were beaten by the monks, and bitten by the snake, and fatigued and frightened on my behalf. So no more now. Don't think me ungracious. Let our dealings end here. But, if you do think of me, let it be with kindness.

Your friend, Juan.

And under that he had written, "I have left you a gift, as I won our bet and learned more English than you did Euskara!"

Wrapped in the paper he had left the snuffbox with the four little stones and the leaf that said TOI.

AFTER I had finished reading this letter I sat, for perhaps an hour, motionless, staring at the red roots of the yew tree. I can summon their shapes still, if I shut my eyes.

I felt as if, by some violent blow, my vital organs had been dragged from me, and I left just a shell—numb, hollow, and stunned. Then at length I began to feel pain, and the pain was so strange, so unaccustomed, so severe, that, despite what Juan had asked, and my own sense of honor, I packed up my things, stamped out the fire, leaving the fish uneaten, and led el Demonio through the forest, over two ridges, until I came to the head of a little valley, where the trees parted to reveal a brook running through a tiny meadow. There, far below, I saw a small stone farmhouse, a tethered goat, and a few beds of vegetables. A wisp of blue smoke wavered from the chimney. As I watched, hidden in the trees, from half a mile away up the valley, I saw a figure, an elderly white-haired man, come limping from the house to sit on a bench under what looked like a walnut tree. Presently a smaller figure followed, carrying a basket, and curled up on the grass beside the other.

If I had Father Vespasian's spyglass, I thought, visited by a sudden mad notion—if I had the spyglass, I could remain here for days, watching them whenever they came out of doors. If I had the spyglass—

And suddenly grief fell on me like a drenching storm. I could have sat there on the ground and howled like a dog. I could have wept enough tears to wash down the bed of the brook in a torrent, and flood the little pasture, and wash away the house.

But I did not.

Instead I turned, and with a heart of lead, walked away upward through the forest, over the shoulder of the Pic d'Occabé, and away from that peaceful place. If I could have done so, I would have mounted the pony and ridden at a gallop. I longed to put as much distance as possible, as speedily as I could, between me and that hidden spot.

It cannot be more than a kilometer yet, I kept thinking; perhaps two kilometers by this time. Now, perhaps three. My slow footsteps were like a heavy chain, pulling me back.

At last, after a long, dreary march, I came to the Lake of Iraty, traversed the marsh, mounted, and so followed the river down as far as Orbaiceta. Every place where I had been with Juan seemed miserable, filled too full with memories. I did not, therefore, waste any time at Orbaiceta, but purchased a little food and struck off across country to Burguete. For this reason, too, I resolved not to return to Pamplona, but continued westward, coming out of mountains into sierra, then back into mountains again, sleeping at night wherever darkness chanced to find me, until I came to the town of Vitoria. This is a large and grand city, larger than Pamplona, set on a green plateau and ringed by green mountain slopes. There are eight streets in circles around a lofty cathedral, and high houses so lined with miradors that they glitter in the sunrise as though all built of glass from roof to street. My poor Demon had fallen lame, so here I planned to sell him and find myself a mule or horse to continue on my way to Galicia.

I was looking at mules in the marketplace when I heard a voice upraised in a familiar tongue, asking if anybody there spoke English. I discovered two elderly ladies asking for help with their bargaining: They were trying to buy two Seville shawls, at a ruinous price, from a marketwoman. I offered my services, which were gladly accepted, and for a couple of hours I was able to distract my sad mind by helping the pair with their various commissions. The end of it was that I learned they were making a journey to Santiago de Compostela, and hearing that I was bound in that direction myself, they invited me to accompany them and be their courier.

At another time I would have said no. What! Travel in a coach with a pair of elderly ladies when I might have rambled along at my own pace, seen what sights I chose, and enjoyed my own adventures? Never in this world! But just at that time I had had enough of adventures. I was heartsore and weary, and wished for nothing so much as to be back at Villaverde. The wealthy English ladies had the best of horses and postilions; they proposed to travel to Burgos, to Valladolid, to León, at a spanking pace. So I accompanied them, having first sold el Demonio, for much less than he was worth, to a kind-faced baker's wife, who promised to treat him as if he were a member of the family.

I remember little of that journey. I talked to the

ladies, told them many things about Spain, and left them at León with good wishes from me and fervent thanks from them. If I ever came to Norwich, in England, they said, I should be kindly welcome at their house.

From León I struck off across country once more, riding a mule purchased in the market there, and so, at long last, in late afternoon, came within view of Villaverde, gray walls and golden roofs, perched up on top of a high sweep of hill, like the crest of a breaking wave. How that sight warmed my sad heart!

When I rode up to the gate, half a dozen dogs came racing out to greet me. I had been away from home for over half a year; however, it seemed they had not forgotten me. And behind them came my friend Pedro, great-nephew of our old cook, who had died.

"*Madre de Dios!* Is it really you, Felix?" says he, big-eyed, gasping and yawning at the same time; plainly he had been taking his siesta on some heap of straw in the stackyard.

"Well, it's not my ghost, at all events," said I. "Quick! Tell me! How are they all? My grandfather? Is he well?"

"Ay, ay—the same as ever he was, sharp as an old eagle, with his eye into everything. Who has done this, who has done that, why is the Andalusian mare lame, who has been riding her—suppose el señor Felix came home and wished to ride her? Better a lame mare than *that* bag of bones, anyway," he added, giving my mule a disparaging look.

"And who *had* been riding the mare? You, I suppose," I said, grinning at him as he led my mule off toward the stables. The dogs boiled round me in a sea of fur, and I hugged them and pummeled them and threw them off me in armfuls, making my way toward the arched stone doorway that led to the main house, which is built all around a colonnaded courtyard.

News of my arrival had already flashed ahead, and there, in the arcade that surrounded the court, was my grandfather coming; not on his feet, alas, but propelling himself in his wheelchair.

No surprise ever caught my grandfather unprepared. If *he* had been taking a siesta, he showed no signs of it; not a wrinkle creased his gray satin jacket, not a pin, not a ruffle, was out of place in his snowy cravat. In all respects he looked exactly as I had seen him last—except that his hair, which had been iron-gray then, was now cloud-white. But his eyes were just the same—black, and full of fire.

"Ah! My dear grandson! There you are," he said, and held out his hand to me. Then he did a thing that was unprecedented for him: drew me to him and kissed my brow, before making the sign of the cross over me.

"*Buenas tardes,* Grandfather," I said. "I am very happy to be home again at Villaverde."

And so saying, I found my words to be true. Some of the weight of pain and incomprehension and loneliness that had oppressed me since the sudden parting from Juan had now lifted; I was able to raise my head and look about me and sniff the familiar high upland air of Villaverde—and the smell of the house, lavender and polished wood and beeswax—with sharp recognition and delight.

"You will wish, no doubt, to bathe yourself and put on some more presentable garments," said my grandfather, observing with raised eyebrows my tattered dirty sheepskin jacket and disreputable breeches. "And then to greet your grandmother and great-aunts, who are waiting with immense impatience to see the returned prodigal."

His fine keen mouth twitched, very slightly, as he said this. In the past my great-aunts had always been my chief tormentors—rushing with a cackle like angry old geese to report any misdemeanors of mine, and to exact the utmost degree of punishment for them. In those days I had believed that they and my grandfather were all of one mind. Now I realized that it was wholly otherwise. Deep in the Conde's eye there was to be detected a spark as he looked at me. Oh! I thought, if only I can have jokes with my grandfather as I do sometimes with God! How very different life will be at Villaverde!

I said sedately, "Well, I will go and wash off the dust at once, señor, and then return to you. I am glad to see you looking so well."

"And I may say the same to you, my boy. You have even, I think, grown—just a very little!"

"I have no great hopes of more!" I said, laughing. "My English grandfather is no taller than I am. And he is past seventy."

"Well, we will not entirely give up hope. Perhaps in another fifty-seven years . . . I shall greatly look forward to hearing about your English grandfather. And about everything that has befallen you."

"Oh, I have so *much* to tell you, Grandfather!"

AFTER dinner—which was a tremendous, stately meal, with my grandmother and all my great-aunts in their best mantillas and jet combs, as many neighbors as could be gathered, and all the servants in the background, lurking about the grand dining room with its marble side-tables and mahogany, and massive leather-armed chairs, and gold-framed portraits of ancestors, and Toledo sabers on the walls—after dinner was over, which was not until well past midnight, my grandfather beckoned me to his study.

"You will not be tired yet, Felix; the young need little rest. And the old, such as I, do nothing but rest, and so require little sleep. I have a letter to show you which arrived yesterday, because of which I knew that we must soon have the happiness of seeing you here. It is from Señor León de Echepara." He added, as he ruffled among the papers on his beautifully inlaid desk, "Of course the name of Señor de Echepara is well known to me. We share identical political beliefs. But he has, at times, been active, as I, alas, am no longer able to be. And now he, I understand owing to those same beliefs, has been obliged to leave his home."

"Yes, Grandfather. That is so."

"Señor de Echepara is a very upright and honorable man, for whose opinions I have a great respect," said my grandfather, and handed me the letter.

To the Conde de Cabezada, etc., etc.
Esteemed Señor:

Permit me to express my deep sense of obligation to you for the kindness, courage, and honorable conduct of your grandson, Sñr Felix Brooque, who during the past weeks, has often, I understand, at considerable risk and hardship to himself, escorted my niece, Señorita Juana Esparza, from France to my present domicile in the forest.

I understand from my niece that nothing could have excelled the delicacy, intelligence, good breeding, and resourcefulness of your grandson on this journey. I bitterly regret that, owing to political difficulties, I am unable to call on you myself in person to express my sense of gratitude for my niece's safety. I hope that, some day, matters may be otherwise. Meanwhile Juana and I must live secluded, pursuing a course of studies in science and natural philosophy. She has all her life expressed a wish to enter a religious order, in order to expiate the tragic and untimely death of her aunt Laura, my youngest sister. (This intention Juana's execrable half-brother had proposed to set aside by marrying her to an elderly neighbor of his.) But Juana will, for the present, remain with me and order my household, until the future lies more plainly before us. It may be that we shall be obliged to travel into France to arrange the estate of my brother-in-law, which, since the death of her half-brother, my niece has inherited.

Meanwhile I remain, señor, your most obliged servant, and I would ask you, also, to express my gratitude to your grandson.

I am instructing the bankers of my deceased brother-in-law, Auteuil Frères, at Bayonne, to forward you moneys to defray the expenses which your grandson was obliged to undertake on behalf of my niece.

      I remain,
      Enrique François Urbain León de Echepara.

Well! What a thing!

I read the letter; read it again; reread it yet a third time.

Twenty—thirty—a hundred details fell into place.

How could I have been so unseeing, so stupid, so crass? I felt like scourging myself for a blind idiot. Juan's distress at being dragged away from the *bertsulari* contest—for, of course, women are not allowed to compete in these; and the masquerade; his actions over the cat, in St. Jean, and his love for the pony;

chance remarks that he had let fall about his brother; the haste of Father Pierre and Father Antoine to get him out of the Abbey—wise old men, they had known, of course they must have known! His views on the usage of girls, so often expressed; innumerable remarks, intonations, implications, came back to me. What a thick-skinned numbskull I had been! How Juan (I could not think of him yet as Juana), how he must have been laughing at me up his sleeve!

But no, I thought; no, he had not been laughing at me. We were happy together. Perhaps as happy as it is possible to be. God, I suppose, had not intended me to see through his disguise. And the reward I reaped for that was the friendship we had had—different from any other, better than any other. Deeper than any other.

Now I understood his parting. No wonder he had said, "If we should meet in the future, it would not be the same. Never, ever again."

For that was true. The pair who had lit fires in the forest, and cooked fish, and quarreled, and made up again, were gone forever. Nothing could bring them back.

Yet I had said, "The future may be different. It may bring greater good."

Which of us was right?

At all events, one thing I knew for certain. Somehow, whether in France or Spain (looking again at Señor de Echepara's letter, I observed that it had been sent from France), somehow, by some means, I must see Juana again. To say—what? That I understood. That I honored her. That I would always have an especial feeling toward her. That I would always remember our journey.

Suddenly I found that my eyes were dimmed by a mist of tears. I took a deep, deep breath, blinked the tears away, and looked up at my grandfather, who was regarding me, I noticed, with extreme shrewdness.

I said: "I never knew. I thought, the whole time, that she was a boy!"

"She must be quite a doughty young lady, this Juana," said my grandfather.

"Oh, Grandfather! If you knew the things she had done—the things she dared. There is nobody like her!" Surely, I thought, she is not intended to be a religious? Expiation for the tragic death of her Aunt Laura? And then another blinding flash of revelation came to me. Her Aunt Laura—

"Is she a handsome young lady?" my grandfather was inquiring suavely.

"You could hardly say so. Oh, I don't know—I have only seen her thin and scrawny and half starved, with her hair cut off—"

And her lies and her thefts, I thought; her deceits and her poetry and her nonsense and her kindness. No, there is nobody like her. I have to see her again.

"Well, you must tell me all about her," said the Conde. He added, half to himself, "Very old, honorable race, the Euskara. *Notoriamente hidalgos.*' Hmm.

Also about the Abbot of St. Just. I have had a most singular letter from a worthy man who signs himself Fr. Antoine at that establishment. He tells a strange rigmarole. But that, I think, must wait until tomorrow, perhaps, for you are beginning to look somewhat weary."

Could I ever tell that tale to Grandfather? I wondered. It seemed, here, like news from another world.

"I suppose that as soon as you are rested you will be wanting to gallop off and visit all those other disreputable friends that you seem to have made on your travels."

"Oh, yes, Grandfather, I shall! Sam and Don Enrique—the good sisters who are looking after my mule in the convent at Santander—and Don José Lopez and Nieves—I hope that some of them may come and visit me here."

"Well, well," he said indulgently, "we can do with the sound of young voices about the place. It has been quiet for too long. Run along, now, however, to your bed. It is a great happiness to me to have you back with us, Felix."

But after I had kissed him good-night and left his presence, I did not go directly to bed. I was too restless for that. I went out into the courtyard and looked up at the stars—the huge, cold, blazing stars of north Spain.

Those same stars, I thought, were blazing down on Juana in the Forest of Iraty—or wherever she was now.

I remembered her poem:

> "A strand of hemp, a silent star
> And the wind's lullaby . . .
> A taste of salt, a touch of tar
> And a sorrowful good-bye . . ."

I had left out a couple of lines, the poem was not quite fast in my head yet, but I would scan them when I went in. I felt the paper crackle in my jacket pocket.

Repeating those four lines again, I wandered on into the stableyard. And there a purring shadow detached itself from a pile of sacks and came to rub its head against my leg.

My old cat Gato, waiting for me. I picked him up, buried my nose in his hay-scented fur, and made much of him, thinking of all that awaited me in the coming days: There were friends to see, visits to pay, old tasks and occupations to resume.

And now, as well, I had another journey to make.

JOAN AIKEN (1924–2004) was the author of many books for adults and children, including *Black Hearts in Battersea* and *The Wolves of Willoughby Chase,* which won the Lewis Carroll Shelf Award. Her 1968 novel, *The Whispering Mountain,* was a Carnegie Medal Honor Book and winner of the Guardian Award. She was named a Member of the Order of the British Empire for her services to children's literature.

Don't miss Felix's other adventures!

In the first book of the trilogy, twelve-year-old orphan Felix Brooke is given a letter that contains a clue to the whereabouts of his father's family. So he gladly leaves his unhappy home in Spain to follow the trail. But it's a long way to England, and many dangers stand between Felix and his destination.

In the thrilling conclusion to the trilogy, eighteen-year-old Felix is summoned to rescue three children kidnapped by their father, an escaped inmate who is allegedly mad. Felix leaves his studies at college and accepts the dangerous mission in hopes he'll be reunited with his true love along the way. But when it seems the rescue party is being followed, Felix fears they are being led into a trap.

Praise for this trilogy:

"Each leaves the reader eager for more."
—*VOYA* (5Q—highest rating)

"I can't recommend these too highly."
—novelist and reviewer Amanda Craig in
The Independent on Sunday

"These books get better with each reading."
—*School Library Journal*